MW00715120

To Tiffany,
Thank you so much for your support! I hope you enjoy.

Seascape

Shannon Raelynn

This book is a work of fiction. All names, characters, locations, and incidents are products of the author's imagination, or have been used fictitiously. Any resemblance to actual persons living or dead, locales, or events is entirely coincidental.

www.shannonraelynn.com
Edited by Marlene@FirstEditing.com
Cover design and publishing by Book Baby

For Denis and Suzanne,
because I couldn't decide who deserved it more.

Chapter 1

Lexie thinks she is making me an offer I can't refuse. With an excited squeal, she reaches forward to grasp my hands. The last thing my bossy older sister expects is for me to tug free of her clasp and turn her down flat.

I leave her standing alone on the sliver of linoleum at the entryway to my apartment. Without bothering to kick off her black stiletto boots, she advances, following me into my tiny kitchen. I take a step back, defensively giving myself a little extra room. Lexie is a wayward freight train. She shows up when you least expect her and she leaves miles of permanent track behind. She doesn't like my answer. I watch her build up steam and gather her momentum for a trip straight through my boundaries.

"Eleuthera is the most beautiful island in the Bahamas, Skylar. This isn't a crappy resort packed with over-lubricated morons. Before you turn your nose up at my offer, have enough sense to get the details."

"I haven't heard from you in almost two months. When I do, you show up here unannounced, demanding I hop on a plane with you in two days. Get real," I say.

She tosses her purse on the counter and pulls a clean coffee cup from the stack which has been drying for the past two days on the dish rack. I watch day-old coffee fill her cup. She sips and wrinkles her nose in distaste. Opening my fridge, she grabs a carton of milk, adds a splash to the cup, and sticks the concoction into the microwave. Lexie is a doctor. An internship, followed by a residency, killed her pickiness over coffee, years ago.

"Look, sorry, it's been crazy. With staff shortages I've been working crazy hours and then I went to Fort Lauderdale last month for a medical seminar. That's how I found this place. Sheer boredom drove me into hooking up with another doctor. I know better but he was hot. Anyway, he rented a cottage on the island of Eleuthera and asked me to join him. I fell in love - with the island- not him. He was a horrible lay. I jotted down the number on the little 'For Sale' sign out front. My lawyer did some research and helped me put in an offer. I got a phone call yesterday. I own a beach house in the Bahamas." The microwave pings.

"That's great. I am happy your fling wasn't an entire loss."

"I am happy for me too. This place beats any other tropical place I've seen. My house sits on a small bluff overlooking the Atlantic Ocean. It's so close to the water I hear the waves at night. Can you imagine?" She does not pause for me to answer. "There are fruit and palm trees everywhere. My cottage has three bedrooms, a swimming pool, and was recently renovated." She sips from her cup before asking, "So? Are you up for a little trip down south?"

I shake my head. "I'd love to see your cottage but you want me there in two days. Not gonna happen. E-mail me some pictures. I've got to be up in six hours for a double shift. Don't let the door hit your ass on the way out."

Lexie refuses to take my hint. "C'mon. When was the last time you did something spontaneous?"

"Almost fourteen years ago and I got pregnant. My ability to indulge in spontaneity disappeared with motherhood. I have responsibilities."

"And I don't? These hands save lives." Lexie's fingers swish the air. "I'm a workaholic. I still take vacations."

"I've got too many weekends booked to work at the group home and the school won't let me go during the school year because I get summers off."

"Play hooky. I'll write you a doctor's note explaining you need a week off due to mental fatigue."

She'd do it in an instant. My warning scowl makes her laugh.

"Okay little Ms. Responsible. Forgive me for trying to throw a little spice into your life. In two months school is out. You have the summer off. Come then."

I release a sigh that is half exasperation and half frustration. Responsibilities aside, I can't afford a trip. Even with child support and an income from two jobs, I live little better than from paycheck to paycheck. Any money left over is tucked into a high-interest savings account so someday I can buy a house. I want out of this tiny, two-bedroom apartment. Lexie already owns a home; I guess now she owns two. She makes tons of money, and often forgets we have different financial situations. Other than pointing this out to her, I see no other way of refusing.

"I can't afford to take a trip."

"All you need is a passport." With a flash of perfectly whitened teeth, her mouth curves into a generous smile. "I'll pay for Rachel too. Actually, bad idea. Come this summer when she is with the jerk you picked to be her father. That'll make it a real vacation. No work and no kid." Leaning back with her curvy butt pressed into the ledge of my counter, one side of her bold, red mouth lifts into a cocky little grin. She believes my arguments have all been defeated.

I have plenty of reasons to stay right where I am. Rachel, my daughter, has one absent parent, she does not need another. My ex thinks a day and half of parenting twice a month is enough of a contribution. It's not. In addition to doing the job of two parents, I am stretched even thinner by my two very stressful jobs. Monday to Friday, I am a school counselor at an inner-city high school. Every second weekend, when Rachel is with her father, I also work the graveyard shift at a group home for teenagers. In both positions, I work with children whose parents don't put them first. I know the results; I see them every day. That is why my daughter comes first.

Most people would be proud of my focus; not Lexie. My responsibilities have no business getting in the way of her fun. She has a hard time understanding her authority doesn't extend outside of the emergency room because, even when she isn't in scrubs, shouting orders with expert confidence and control, people fall over themselves to please her. Men are drawn to her blatant sexuality. Almost everyone is distracted by her beauty. This morning, her voluptuous assets are accentuated by tight fitting blue jeans and a red, plunging, V-neck sweater. Her short, black hair has been tousled into a sexy, fresh-from-a-bed, halo of curls. It's no wonder Lexie refuses to accept being turned down; it rarely happens.

I decide to stop volleying my reasons at her because she is like an expert tennis player, lobbing solutions back at me. It's time for an iron clad refusal.

"No. I can't go."

"It'll be an early birthday gift. You can thank me by enjoying yourself without bitching," she bargains.

"It is too expensive. Besides, I need to work the summers. The extra money comes in handy all year long."

"I'll replace what you would make. Don't let money be the blocker. Sky, c'mon. We'll have so much fun!" Like a starving dog with a bone, she isn't going to let it drop.

"Being away from Rachel is never fun. I guess I am a homebody."

"No, you are a damn recluse avoiding life, a freaking hermit who doesn't want to go anywhere or do anything."

"That's not true. I am always out at Rachel's sporting events."

"What do you do for yourself?"

"I still paint."

"Regularly?"

"Often enough," I lie. I haven't picked up a paint brush in months.

"One hobby does not make a life."

I resist the urge to laugh in her face. Lexie's only pastime is chasing men. I can't resist pointing out the irony of her accusation.

"I'm single. I should be chasing men. And so should you. It's been what, four years since Rand walked out? You haven't been on a single date that I know of; so unless you pay for it, it's been at least that long since you've been laid."

"I knew this conversation would wind its way to your favorite topic. Sex makes your world go 'round, not mine. Rachel went through enough with the divorce. The last thing she needs is more disappearing men in her life. Besides, any day now she is going to want to start dating. I can't expect her to abstain if I won't."

"My God! You are so sanctimonious. Do you listen to yourself?"

"I am trying to set an example. The moment I became a mother, I lost any right to be selfish. I'm required to place my child's needs before my own. And guess what? I'm okay. I'm surviving. I'm perfectly content."

"Bull! I just have to look at you to know you are not happy or fulfilled. You look like shit. You could pass for my older sister." She pulls my braid from behind my back and gives it a tug. "Nobody wears their hair in a French braid anymore."

I knock her hand away, stinging from her unfair comparison. If I look older, it is because I don't expend the same time, energy and money she does on appearance. We've never looked like sisters. She takes after our tall, fair-skinned, dark-haired father. I favor our average sized, auburn-haired mother. We've always shared the same silver eyes and curvy figures, though.

"I'm not trying to impress anyone."

"You're succeeding."

"Good. It's not my goal in life to find and discard men like used tissues. I may not live a riveting lifestyle-"

"So you realize you're boring? I was worried you had your head too far up your ass to notice. Years are passing by, Sky. You won't get them back. Every time I stop by, it's the same old story. I ask what's new and you say, 'Not much. Same old stuff.'" Her impersonation sucks; the content is bang on. My sister's mimicry sparks an old itch to lash back. I know her buttons as well as she knows mine.

"You are not going to make me feel bad about being a good mother or about working hard to provide for Rachel. If you'd ever been a mother, you'd know the futility-"

"Skylar." My name becomes a warning.

"Lexie, let me finish," I demand, surprised when she listens. I take a deep breath and stand a little taller. She might not want to accept my refusal but she is listening. We have both crossed lines today. I know all about diffusing escalating situations. My level-headed counselor persona takes over. Removing the coffee cup out of her fingers, I place it on the counter. I punctuate a gentle squeeze to her hands with a warm smile.

"This is getting pretty personal. We need to cool off. I did not mean to hurt your feelings by that last comment or by turning down the offer to see your new home. Of course I would love to visit the Bahamas with you but right now, I need you to appreciate my priorities conflict with your request. "

Now she is the one to tug her hands free. "Don't use your conflict resolution skills on me, Sister. I will not be psychologized." She continues speaking, voice dripping with sweetness. "I'm sorry I have more money than you. I'm sorry I can afford a beach house in the Bahamas and you can't. I am not trying to throw charity your way or rub your nose in my success. Something wonderful has happened to me and you are refusing to share it. Are you a little jealous?"

"This conversation is done!"

Anger makes me forget we are adults and have long outgrown physical altercations. I grab her purse off the counter, open my door, pull her to the doorway and shove her into the apartment hallway. Lexie might be taller and stronger than me but taken by surprise in her stiletto boots, she is easily maneuvered. I throw her purse at her before slamming and locking the door in her face.

"Fine! I'll leave but this is not over." Her yell is muffled by the closed door. I consider opening the door to have the satisfaction of slamming it in her face again.

I resent any insinuation that I don't want the best for my sister. My daughter comes first but there is no one else on this Earth I love as much as Lexie. As a child, I worshipped her. I may no longer have her up on some distorted, big-sister pedestal, but I remain terribly proud of her. My sister has never shied away from hard work or sacrifice. If there is one thing I know, one thing I truly believe, it is that she has earned, and will continue to earn, every wonderful thing in her life.

I stomp around my apartment infuriated until I realize Lexie doesn't really believe I'm jealous. She is hurt by my refusal. More importantly, she is determined to get her way. There isn't an older sister alive who does not know how to get under the skin of a younger sibling and Lexie has always excelled at prodding me for a reaction. She is also ruthless in her pursuit of an objective. I'll be better prepared next time. The subject is not closed. I'll be hearing from my sister again.

Chapter 2

After a few hours of sleep and a sixteen hour shift, my fight with Lexie is forgotten. Yawning through sips of coffee, I am filling out paperwork when my replacement arrives at the group home the next morning. After a quick exchange, I leave to pick up my daughter in Red Deer, a city midway between my home in Edmonton and my ex-husband's home in Calgary.

Edmonton used to be a small town city; now it takes forever to reach the outskirts. As soon as it became financially feasible to separate oil from the sandy ground, Alberta became the place to find work, build a house or open a new business and the days of crossing the city in thirty minutes all but disappeared. Edmonton's boundaries continue to expand with new housing developments and the streets remain congested. The open highway is a relief.

With only the radio for company, I can't stop myself from thinking about Lexie's offer. After working two jobs for four years, I could use a break. Eleuthera sounds wonderful. Unfortunately, I can't afford to go and I will not let Lexie pay for it. The thought of owing my sister anything makes me shudder. She is pushy without leverage. Owe her and she becomes intolerable.

Lexie can't help herself, especially where I am concerned. She has always been more of a parent than an older sister since our mom died in a car accident when we were children. Our father was driving. Afterward he buried himself in alcohol and guilt, leaving ten-year-old Lexie in charge. We don't have anything to do with Dad; not because of the accident, but because he started drinking afterwards and never stopped.

As soon as she graduated high school, Lexie moved us both out. She refused to leave me behind with our father, who was changing from a depressive drunk to a belligerent one. My sister bullied, browbeat and pushed me into adulthood, making sure I graduated high school and entered university. She ran my life up until the moment I got pregnant and married Rand. I never want to be under her thumb again.

I arrive in the city of Red Deer no closer to finding a way to turn my sister down without broadening the gap between us. I park behind a gas station, the regular exchange spot, where I meet Rachel and my ex-husband. I recline my seat. Work has left me drained. Maybe on Rachel's next weekend with Rand, I won't work at the group home. I'll lose myself in paints and a canvas. I don't get to paint very often, but when I do, living is a little easier. I close my eyes and visualize a blank canvas, my brush in one hand, and a palette in the other. I fall into a heavy doze until Rachel opens the car door and drops her suitcase in the backseat. Startled awake, my eyes fly open. My hands reach to grip the steering wheel.

"Rise and shine, sunshine!" She plops into the front seat. Her long, straight, brown hair is pulled back into a ponytail. My thirteen-year-old daughter is an exact replica of me, only fresher, prettier and younger. All her features are mine from her full lips to her pale grey eyes. We share sharply arching eyebrows and high cheekbones. A small upturned nose is the only feature she shares with Rand.

"Is your dad gone already?"

"Yeah, Sherry is not feeling good. She puked all weekend. Were you that sick when you were pregnant with me?"

Sherry is Rand's wife, the woman he left me for. Hearing her name is still enough to make me want to grow my nails and use the home wrecker as a scratching post.

"You never gave me a moment's grief until it came time to push you out. Then you were hell," I tease. "Did you get your homework done?"

She nods. "How was work? You must be pretty tired?"

"I'm fine after my little nap. I'll use the washroom before we head home."

Once we are underway, I share Lexie's news.

"Why'd she buy a new place? What's wrong with her condo?" Rachel asks as she fiddles with the radio.

"Pick a station and leave it, please. She still has her condo. What she bought is a vacation home."

The bright midmorning sun has me sliding my sunglasses off the visor and slipping them on. It is not exactly Bahamian weather, but it's warm for early May in Alberta. The snow is only three weeks off the ground but already the first shoots of jade grass are poking up and the trees are sprouting green buds.

"Can you imagine going in the winter? Maybe like January, and when everyone is freezing up here, we'd be roasting down there."

"She asked me to go with her..."

"Oh, you should!"

"Maybe in a few years; it's something to think about."

I change the subject. We spend the rest of our drive chatting about our separate weekends. Back in Edmonton, we stop at our local mall for a couple of hours and then load up a week's worth of food from the local grocery store. At home, Rachel helps sort the week's laundry before I allow Amanda, her best friend and our neighbor across the hall, to hang out with us and have supper. By the time I sit down to eat with the girls, lack of sleep catches up with me. My body and eyelids are weighted.

"I need rest more than food," I announce, shuffling off to my bedroom.

* * *

The only thing worse than being late to work on a Monday morning is getting caught by the boss as you walk in the door. I feel more like a tardy student than a school counselor when I see the principal waiting by my office door.

Tall and reed thin, Bill Krakow is fully armored in one of his severely tailored, funeral-black suits. His receding hair is no loss, its color being dishwater brown. Radiating arrogant displeasure, his eyes are also slightly triumphant. He is the worst kind of boss, noticing everything I do wrong and nothing I do right.

"Good morning, Skylar. You're running late." He motions to the clock on the reception area wall. "I hope your time sheet will reflect your tardy start this morning."

I paste on a facsimile of a smile until he turns. I mentally kick his nonexistent ass as he walks away.

It's a bad start to a bad day. Each passing hour is more dismal than the next. My first session is with my least favorite client, a sullen young man who spends most of our time together staring at his feet. I get chewed out by a teacher and then remember my lunch hour is to be spent with the Peer Support Group. Instead of planning our end-of-the-year celebration, I end up disbanding everyone when arguments erupt.

After lunch, Krakow calls me to his office to inform me I will be required to present two, hour-long presentations on the topic of bullying for the staff and students the following week. He announces his will and I am to make it happen. With no time available during the day, I'll have to put something together on my own time at home. I leave his office incensed. The afternoon drags on but eventually the school bell rings, dismissing the students.

I am writing up notes from the day's sessions when the mother of a client knocks on my office door, forty minutes late for our appointment. With her big hair, pounds of makeup and sexy clothes, Heather Morgan captures plenty of attention when she pops into the school to pick up her daughter. Inevitably she ends up chatting with at least one male staff member, even though Lisa's teachers are all female.

We exchange small talk before I get to my reason for requesting the meeting.

"Heather, occasionally I am required to refer clients elsewhere. I think we have reached the point where you and Lisa should consider seeing someone else."

From a relaxed slouch in the chair, she sits forward. "You told me the cutting was no big deal."

"Self-mutilation is always a big deal. What I actually said is that it is not uncommon to see cutting within a group, as was the case with Lisa and her friends. Such breakouts usually resolve quickly. The other two girls stopped but Lisa has fresh cuts on her arms every day. I'm not helping. If I may, I would recommend Dr. Conner." I hold out a card. "He is a clinical psychologist who specializes in family work."

"Why do I need to see a therapist?" She glares at me with mascara-encrusted eyes.

"I don't know that you do. The only thing I have been able to get out of Lisa is she doesn't like your new boyfriend. She has disclosed no other possible source of pain so it's all I have to go on. When a divorced or single parent starts a new relationship, it is seldom at a time, or with a person, of the child's choosing. It is an adjustment that needs negotiating, and I don't do intensive family counseling."

Heather's head inclines affirmatively but her blonde, salon-styled hair refuses to move with the motion. "We've had battles about my dating. She doesn't want to share me. Lisa is going to have to accept the fact I'm done living like a nun."

I shift in my chair. I have to be careful my views don't spill over into this conversation. I pride myself on being an empathetic listener, capable of seeing almost any perspective but when it comes to single parents dating, I am a tad biased. Rachel was torn apart when Rand began his second marriage before she had time to adjust to our divorce. I know how hard a parent's new relationship is on their children so I will not even think of dating until she is grown. It hasn't been an easy decision to stick to but it beats ending up in Heather Morgan's position. At least I've never ended up in some school counselor's office, talking about why my daughter is cutting her arms.

"Negotiating this new change in your family is something Dr. Conner can help with. Your daughter is going through something we don't have the skills to deal with. Heather, Lisa needs more help than I can provide."

Heather's arms cross defensively. Her cheek twitches as her jaw clenches.

"I'm also a single parent to a teenager. It is a hard job. Sometimes we need help. But you are not obligated to see the person I recommend. Feel free to choose your own psychologist, if you know one. Your family doctor could suggest someone as well."

"I'll see the person you recommend." She takes the card and stands, surprising me with her quick compliance. "Will you continue to see Lisa?"

"I have to close her file now that a referral has been made but don't hesitate to come back and see me if you need anything else at all."

Heather thanks me before leaving. I jot down a few notes in Lisa's file and pack up. It's been a crappy day but it is ending on a good note. I've closed a file and I can go home.

Rachel is waiting at the baseball diamond, the last of her team to be picked up. She jumps in my car, waves goodbye to her coach, and slams the door. "It's about time."

"I had a parent meeting. It went longer than I expected. Why didn't you catch a ride home with Amanda?"

"You said you'd be here. You missed the whole game."

I grit my teeth. "I know. I'm sorry. It's my job, it pays the bills," I defend myself before trying a change of subject. "On the bright side, I figured we can pick up something for supper?" I dangle an offer of takeout food as I start the drive home.

"I want pizza." Her demand is made to the car window.

She ignores me for the rest of the drive. Supper and dishes pass in silence. After our meal, I grab my satchel and begin stacking its contents on the table.

"Why don't you get your homework and I'll work on mine?"

She ignores me.

"Rachel, I'm sorry. I know you hoped I'd make it to your game."

"Whatever."

I'm not sure if it is the dismissive wave of her hand or the accompanying sneer but I lose my temper. "Who do you think you are speaking to? I'm not one of your friends."

"That's for sure."

"I'm doing the best I can. What do you want from me? If I don't work, you can't play baseball." Every day I try to be the best damn mother I know how to be, but on days like today I feel like it isn't good enough.

"I'm going to Amanda's." She thrusts her chin up and out at me in a challenge.

"Fine," I say, giving in.

I'm packing a day's worth of accumulated anger, most of which shouldn't be vented at her. The apartment door closes as I phone Amanda's mother, Karen. My neighbor answers her phone with typical cheer.

"Karen? Rachel is on her way over in a snit."

"She's here. Oh yes. I can see this has the makings of a full blown pout. She still angry you didn't make it to the game?"

"I let her down. She should be upset."

"She should understand how hard you work. A kick in the butt and some work on developing some empathy is what she needs. I know she compares us. It's not fair. I don't work. Don't feel bad. Take care of yourself."

"I just wanted to make sure she got there. She doesn't have homework so she can stay for an hour." I hang up before she hears my defensive tears. I'm so used to hearing what a great kid Rachel is, it stings to hear something negative.

Before I can recover, the phone rings.

"Are you ready for round two?" Lexie asks.

"I-I'm not fighting with you," I stutter. I clear my throat and swipe at my tears with the back of my hand.

"Whoa! What's wrong?"

I try to quell my tears. "It seems like I have been fighting with everyone today. Did I miss the memo? Is it 'Shit on Skylar Day'? Work was horrible then Rachel and I got into it. Now I am stewing because Karen said Rachel needs to develop empathy."

"I love my niece but she has your number. You're so worried about her feelings, you miss her abusing yours."

"She's not the only person who tries to walk over me."

"I was pushy yesterday. I am sorry. I'm just worried. You sound exhausted. I think you are starting to burn out. You need to take care of yourself."

Twice in ten minutes I have been told the same thing. The accusation makes my jaw clench. I don't say anything. My throat is thick with emotion. I sit and breathe into the phone. Lexie, long used to my silences, waits. My sudden rush of anger fades.

"It's hard to get up in the morning, harder to get through each day," I admit.

"I know. I've been watching you struggle, trying to figure out some way to help, to share the load. I'm not trying to take over your life, or make you feel incompetent. You're too capable. I know you can and you will keep going. But every now and then, you have to stop. I want you to pack a suitcase and come away with me. Let me help."

Sometimes we need help, I had chided Heather Morgan. My words return to bite me in the ass. I'm being as proud and defensive as she was towards an honest offer of help.

"It won't cost much. If Eleuthera can recharge my batteries, it can do the same for you. When you come back, you'll be the best mom in the world to Rachel. You'll be able to take on all the problems of the city."

I've stopped arguing. My sister knows I am weakening. She tells me again about the beaches and gorgeous skies. She dangles endless days with nothing but sunshine to fill them. She spins a fantasy for me I haven't even dreamed of for myself. It is an unbelievable opportunity but my pride is hard to put aside. I tell her it feels like charity.

"You are my poor sister. You have no money. But I am doing this because I want to share Eleuthera. Do you have any idea how lonely it is to buy a place this friggin' beautiful and not have a soul to share it with?"

"I'm sure you could find someone on a moment's notice," I tease.

"They won't see what this place means to me. We are family. My home is your home. Your home is my home. Come and see our new home, Skylar." She pulls out the family trump card. I melt.

"Thank you, Lexie. If you are willing to wait the two months until school is out, I will come."

"Without Rachel and you'll let me pay?"

"Yes."

"Great! I've got to go. We'll get together soon and plan the trip. Get your passport and shots up to date; Rachel's too. She can come later in the summer. You will love it, Sky. Try to make it through the next few weeks as best you can."

"That won't be a problem. Thanks, Lexie." I hang up the phone. And squeal.

I'm going to the Bahamas!

Chapter 3

I can't believe he is doing this to me!

Ex-husbands never stop being a problem. With two days to go before our trip, what seemed to be a sure thing is dissolving like a teaspoon of salt in a cup of hot water. My hand tightens on the phone. I swallow a wave of nauseous rage.

"Rand, I leave in two days. Lexie and I have spent weeks planning this trip. She spent a fortune on it."

"Like she can't afford it. Look, I'm sorry. Even if I left now, I can't guarantee I'd be back in time to be of any help. When we came out here to Sherry's family reunion, the plan was to be back today. She wants to stay a day longer and catch up with her family."

"Then you should have come back without her. This is the first time in years that I have something important going on in my life. You can't do this to me!"

"Everything is not always about you, Skylar. Besides, it's only a few days delay. I'll pick Rachel up Thursday."

My voice and body are vibrating with rage. "I have never been so much as a half an hour late dropping her off or picking her up. Something is always coming up with you. Everything is more important than your daughter. Tomorrow is the first day of your scheduled visitation. What am I supposed to tell Rachel? Did you even think about her?"

"Don't try to make me out to be a terrible father when your trip is what you are really concerned about."

"You better figure out a way to come and get her or-"

"Or what, Skylar? Just what are you going to do? If you keep her from me, I'll have your ass back in court so fast it will make your head spin. And the next time we go in front of a judge, Sherry will be a stay-at-home mom with nothing but time to devote to Rachel. Rachel's old enough to pick where she wants to live. I can make living with us damned attractive. Then you'll be paying me child support."

"Up yours, Rand!"

"See you on the fifth. Same place as usual?" I hear the smug satisfaction in his voice as I slam the phone down.

I want to scream. I want to cry. I want to take my hand-held, cordless phone, pretend it is my ex-husband's face and stomp it into tiny little pieces. But Rachel is in her bedroom, and any of those options will only drag her in.

I should have seen it coming. Things had been going too smoothly.

Rachel and I have been getting along wonderfully. As soon as she heard she might spend some time on the island this summer with Lexie, our fight was forgotten. Since then she has been on her best, most helpful behavior.

I've been unflappable, sailing through the year-end chaos of stressed students, irritable teachers, spring fever, graduation and final exams. Infused with energy, I even picked up extra shifts at the group home to earn extra money for the trip. I'm supposed to be on my way to meet Lexie at West Edmonton Mall. The plan is to get our hair done and buy new beach wear before returning to my place to pack.

Somehow I stuff my anger and frustration aside, gather Rachel, and leave. Waiting in the mall food court for my sister, I can only manage a brittle smile. I only realize how unconvincing my act is when Rachel sighs in relief as Lexie finally materializes.

My sister strolls through the crowd oblivious to turning heads and staring eyes. I have more cloth in my t-shirt than she has in her entire outfit. Her halter top isn't much bigger than a handkerchief and if her denim cutoff shorts were frayed any further, they'd be obscene. On her feet are ridiculously high, wedge sandals. Though she is dressed like a stripper, Lexie carries herself with an I-don't-give-a-crap attitude.

Her body is showcased in such a way as to make every straight male sit up and take notice, and every woman throw visual daggers. Not only does she have full, beautiful curves and smooth skin, she also has the courage to put it all out there. Diamond studs glimmer in her ears and belly button. Four inches of solid gold bracelets cover her left wrist and part of her forearm. Lexie bought each one in a different country and she is never without them, except when she is at work. Over the years, they have become an inseparable part of her. To deduce Lexie's mood, I simply listen to whether her bracelets are lightly tinkling, frantically jangling, or lying quiet.

"Skank alert," I say loudly to Rachel.

Lexie grins and gives me the finger. "What? It's supposed to hit plus twenty-seven today."

"And if it doesn't?"

"I prefer to dress for the possibilities. I'm buying Rachel the exact same outfit," she jokes before hugging me and Rachel.

"Really?" My daughter's eyes widen.

"You buy my kid anything this slutty and I guarantee it will see the garbage can before it sees her skin."

My irritation widens her smile. "Then you'll just have to watch close and make sure I don't tart her all up."

"Ugh, Aunt Lexie. She's not going to let you buy me anything cool." Rachel pouts as Lexie gives me veto power over the shopping trip.

Lexie shrugs. "Sucks to be you, kid. So, are you gals ready to shop until we drop?"

"Actually, I want to grab a coffee first. Rachel, why don't you check out the pet store?"

"You need to talk. I get the picture. Just don't take too long."

"And let me know if there are any really cute puppies."

"Don't either of you even think about it. We'll meet you there in a bit." Once Rachel is out of ear shot, I park myself back on a chair and wait for Lexie to sit.

"Up, up, and away! In a few days, you'll be sitting on a beach, beer in hand, and toes in the water."

My chin quivers. She doesn't miss the tell.

"Let me guess… Ah, crap. Rand's not taking Rachel for the summer?"

"Not quite. He isn't able to pick up Rachel until later in the week."

"That's bullshit."

"When is this ever going to end? When is he going to stop having the power to screw with my life? I could scream! Is there any way I can change my ticket?"

"Probably but that's not the point. I can't believe he can do this to you."

With my elbows propped on the table in front of me, I cover my face with my hands. "As much as I want to dump his body down a dirt road, I want this trip more. And I want him to be a good dad. I haven't told Rachel a thing. I don't know how to explain this. I'm not sure I can without showing how positively livid I am."

"Hey, wait a minute. Why don't we just bring Rachel with us?"

"He isn't refusing the visit; he is just delaying it until Thursday. If I refuse his visitation and took Rachel to another country without his permission, I'd be screwed."

"We should call his bluff. Let me bank roll your lawyer. We'll bury him!" Her malicious smile is punctuated by a flick of her wrist. Her bracelets flash.

"When it comes to custody of Rachel, I am not willing to take any chances. I'm sorry, Lex. You go on ahead of me. I'll stay behind and drive Rachel when he's ready for her. If I can change my ticket, I'll fly down and meet you."

"Not in this lifetime. I'll stay behind."

"You've done too much as it is." Horrified at the suggestion, I dismiss the idea.

"I own the house, Skylar. I have the rest of my life to spend there. This way, you'll get a few days to yourself to recharge your batteries before I show you how to properly drain them. I don't want you shortchanged by even a second of this trip. Once Rand knows he's dealing with me, he won't be stupid. I'm not letting you out of this trip for any reason." She slaps the table with finality. I would not put it past Rand to dream up some further delay so what she is proposing makes sense.

"It is times like these I know why I love you, even though you are the bossiest older sister in existence."

"You can bow, pucker up, and kiss my ass in gratitude," she suggests, slapping her hip.

"Bend over, Sis. I'm so relieved, I'd be happy to!"

"I'll take a rain check. Let me spoil your daughter instead. She told me her report card was super. I promised her a few new outfits and a new bathing suit as a reward." I groan because what Lexie really means is Rachel is about to get a whole new wardrobe. Lexie can't say no; she doesn't even try. "Didn't she do well?"

"Yes, her report card was awesome. She passed with honors." I'm in such a good mood I don't even bother to argue. "That's sweet of you, Lexie. Just a couple of things..."

She stands up and pulls me to my feet. "I'm going to spoil the two of you so rotten; my poor bank account isn't going to know what hit it." She entwines her arm with mine.

"Lexie..."

"Shut up. It's all part of the trip experience. I'm not going anywhere with you looking like you do."

Lexie is unstoppable. I end up with enough clothing for two trips, a new hairstyle, gel nails on my fingers, a pedicure, and my first bikini wax. I'm still buzzing from the shopping high when we get back to my apartment. We spend the evening polishing off a pizza, sipping wine and packing my new clothes into my new suitcases. Rachel and Amanda are trying on Rachel's new clothes in her bedroom.

"I can't believe what you spent today, crazy woman. I have some money. I've been working extra shifts. Take some of this." I reach in my purse and pull cash out of my wallet.

She waves the money away. "This money thing, well, I know it bothers you. Don't feel a minute's guilt about what I have spent. I can afford it." Sitting cross-legged on my bed, she is cutting price tags off my new clothes. "I know it is important for you to be self-sufficient. Neither one of us wants to go back to the days of food banks and donated clothing. We came from shit, Skylar, yet you live your life as if you had the best of foundations… except for the whole getting pregnant out of wedlock thing." We both chuckle. "Not even when you had the huge bill from the divorce lawyer did you ever ask me for anything. All you have is me, and I haven't done enough. So, put it out of your head. You deserve it."

She accepts the tight hug I wrap her up in.

"Thank you, Lexie. This trip, well, you were right. I do need it. I need to make some changes. I can't go on like this. Maybe a trip is just what I need to shake myself up. I wouldn't know, though, I've never been anywhere before."

"Yeah, you're so pathetic. But seriously, you know I could help you more. If you need money to quit working and look for something else…"

I stop her in mid-sentence with a glare. "Thank you for the offer, but no." I soften my refusal with an explanation. "I need goals, Lexie. In the grand scheme of things, a shopping trip and vacation are not life changing. Giving me money to live on, well, it would change us. As long as I pay my own way and have my own space, I can tell you to jump off a bridge if I disagree with you. I lose the ability if you pay my way. So thanks but no thanks. I'll stick to trips to the Caribbean, and a once-in-a-lifetime shopping trip. And for the record, I'll still find a way to pay you back."

"If you really want to pay me back, you can go to the island, relax and be ready to have a blast when I get down there with you." She lifts her glass of wine.

I clink my glass against hers in agreement. We exchange grins and empty our half-full glasses in one gulp.

Chapter 4

It isn't easy saying goodbye to my child for a month, no matter the circumstances. My sister and daughter ignore my weepiness and threaten to lock me in my car and push my vehicle until I start driving. They are anxious to get at their own plans. Assured by my sister that these plans will not include piercing, funky hair colors, or tattoos, I am finally able to say goodbye.

Rand is fine with Lexie doing the exchange. Our last phone call went great once he realized we could both get what we wanted. In fact, once he heard my flight to Nassau was leaving from Calgary, he suggested I drive and park my car at his place. I only hope Rand spends some time with Rachel. With his new baby on the way, she feels a little disposable and is in need of a good visit with her dad. I park my car at his house, call for a taxi, and leave the keys with Rand's neighbor.

It is not until the plane lifts off that I relax and let myself feel excitement. At this point, I'm safe from any further impediments. Throughout the seven hour flight, I check the little television map and celebrate every incremental move closer to Nassau. When I land, I have a little over an hour until my connecting flight to Governor's Harbor, Eleuthera. There is barely enough time to claim my luggage and get my boarding pass before checking my bags for the final flight. Six passengers, including myself, follow the flight attendant out of the airport on to the tarmac. A 19-seater plane waits.

As I leave Nassau behind, with my nose pressed against the window, I can see waves and clouds and then, as we pass over islands, blobs of green in a sea of blue. After what seems like only a few minutes we begin our descent and I strain to catch a glimpse of the island. Eleuthera is a long sliver of green rising up to meet us. Beaches, roads, and houses pass below. Just before we touch down, I see the tops of palm trees.

The landing is smooth; the runway short. In seconds, the plane is turned and parked. The minute the propellers stop, the door is opened and we are allowed to disembark. Heat and humidity greet me as I leave the plane, exiting right on to the airstrip. My fellow passengers and I follow the flight crew to a small, yellow concrete building with a deep red roof. Inside the terminal, serious looking Customs agents greet us. I have the biggest, goofiest, friendliest grin on my face. They ignore my excitement, check my passport and ask about the contents of my luggage. Then I am dragging my suitcases outside.

A short, stocky, middle-aged Bahamian man is leaning against a taxi, smoking a cigarette. I'm not sure where I get the impression of his age because not a wrinkle mars his skin, nor is a white hair visible in the tight black curls on his head, but something tells me he is older than me. He tosses the cigarette and lifts his hand in a beckoning wave.

"Are you Lexie's sister? I'm George. My wife Nancy works for Lexie."

"Yes. I'm Skylar. It's nice to meet you."

"Lexie called to say she'll be flying down on Friday? Is this everything?" he asks, loading my luggage into the trunk of his car.

"Yep," I answer before sliding into the front passenger seat. "Thank you."

He gets in beside me, starts the car, and pulls away from the curb. As we drive, George tells me we are on Queen's Highway. The concrete road winds over hills and around curves and all along the way, George points and talks. I catch glimpses of water, rock and sand but they pass before I can soak them in. I'm distracted. It takes concentration to understand George. English is widely spoken in the Bahamas but George's accent is thick enough to resemble a different language. Perversely he has no problems understanding me.

The sign for the town of Governor's Harbor comes into sight, prompting me to interrupt. "I need to make a few stops."

"No problem. I'll take you wherever you need to go."

As per my sister's instructions, I grab a bottle of rum and a case of Kalik beer from the liquor store. The grocery store is a longer stop. The old building is crammed with deep freezers, narrow aisles, and a steady stream of people; all of whom know George. When we finally get my purchases to the car, the sun is setting quickly. At home in the summer months, daylight lasts well until eleven o'clock in the evening, but I am near the equator. George takes me for a quick bite to eat before we are back on Queen's Highway. The supper hour has long passed and with only the headlights for lighting, there is little to see beyond the winding road. He continues driving for several more minutes before stopping to ensure I notice the proper turn off. There are no road signs.

We follow a rough, rocky road for a couple of miles before George slows and turns off. The drive winds its way into the darkness. After a few hundred feet, we round a bend. The white cottage is lit up by the headlights. Behind it is only inky blackness but I know the darkness hides the ocean. A spike of excitement slashes through me. I barely register the thick palms and native plants bordering the small yard. My eyes are focused on the white cottage perched high atop a sand bluff.

"You have the keys?" George asks, bringing the vehicle to a stop. I dig into my purse and pass them on.

I open the car door to the sound of crashing waves. A warm breeze whips across my skin. I can't believe I am here. I'm so excited I want to race into the cottage; I want to keep smelling the warm wind and touch the nearest palm tree to confirm the reality of this moment. Instead I help haul in my luggage and groceries. I find my wallet and pass George some money.

"Our phone number is on the counter. Call if you need anything or have any questions. Nancy wanted me to ask if you want daily cooking and cleaning service."

"No, but she'll have to check with Lexie for anything past Friday."

"Good. The other man she works for has her pretty busy. Mack's a good guy. He's in the house down that way." George points out the living room window. "Not far. I'll leave you his name and number, in case of an emergency." He writes a number next to his on the note pad. "Nancy will be by later this week."

"Lexie said she has a jeep in the garage and some maps but before I can drive anywhere, I need to know my directions. I'm a little turned around."

"East," he points out the kitchen window. "The driveway travels west. If you turn right you are headed north. Turn left and you are headed south. This area is Double Bay."

"Thanks." I shake his hand. "Is there anything else I should know?"

"I'll take the cover off the pool. Unless you are a good swimmer, I wouldn't swim here. Try Ten Bay beach. It's a couple of miles from here, on the Caribbean side of the island. Take your first right after turning south on the Queen's Highway. It's a rough road. Follow it and you'll come to a nice calm beach with no coral. Remember to drive on the left." He delivers his instructions seriously, like a protective dad.

"I'll stick to the pool until Lexie gets here." I walk him to the door.

The cottage is warm and has a musty, closed up smell so I open the windows, welcoming the fresh breeze. There are several air conditioners but I'm not interested in mechanically-cooled air. I can't wait to see the views, to see the inside of the house lit up from the floor to high-vaulted ceiling with an abundance of natural light. New wicker and wood furniture pieces are arranged throughout the rooms. The floors are covered in newly-laid red tiles. The walls are one white expanse after another. To me, they are crisp canvases waiting for color and my hands itch to paint something on their stark blankness. I smile. A mural would be a great thank you gift for Lexie. As soon as I settle on an image, I will get painting. *Right over the couch*, I decide.

Lexie paid extra for me to bring a second large suitcase. It contains six, pre-stretched canvases, my palette, assorted brushes, and a lightweight collapsible wooden easel. I don't think I have ever received a better present.

I find the smaller of the two bedrooms and drop off one suitcase after extracting a few CDs to listen to while I put away groceries. Jewel, my favorite singer, serenades me as I open a beer and unpack. Once I am settled, my supply of travel excitement wears off. I call Lexie to let her know I have arrived, change into a nightshirt, and crawl into bed.

* * *

After waking the next morning, I check my watch, unable to remember the last time I was willingly up at six-thirty. I allow myself one long luxurious stretch before looking out the window, slightly disappointed to be greeted by a grey sky. Slipping on sandals and a housecoat, I enter the kitchen. What I thought was a cloudy rainy sky is, in fact, the first stirrings of morning light. Already the brilliant orb is lifting and coloring the clouds with pink and purple. The palm trees past the deck sway in a strong breeze. I open the patio doors, shocked to find warmth and softness in the blowing strength of the wind. An Alberta wind this strong would be cold. But this isn't Alberta; it is Eleuthera, a paradise.

The first time I saw the mountains, I felt insignificant. Looking out on the endless moving body before me, I'm again reminded of my smallness. The ocean is beautiful, powerful, and it fills me with awe. The sun continues to rise as I watch, changing the sky and water swiftly from silver to a deep blue and the sand from beige to pink. I want to stick my toes into the ocean, connect myself to its energy, so I go down the stairs leading off the deck to the beach.

The ocean in front of Lexie's beach house is not calm. Where the water is forced against coral, a white frothy spray shoots up into the air. There are powerful, rolling waves and shoreline lapping waves. The sand is soft and powdery until I reach the waterline, where it has been wetly packed into firmness. Anxious to feel the water, I lift my housecoat and step into the ocean. Little waves lick at my toes, my ankles and then my calves. The water, like the air, is warmer than I expect and it tingles effervescently against my skin. The undertow tugs the sand from under my feet. I want to stay and play longer in the water, to look for sea-life and to examine the various items that have washed up on the beach but, though I am not done exploring, I climb back up the stairs to the cottage. I'm hungry and I want to finish getting acquainted with my new location.

Off to the side of the deck, steps lead to a wide expanse of stone patio containing the pool and a barbecue. There is also an immense picnic-style table with benches. Crafted from treated lumber and stone, the furniture is meant to remain outside year round. As promised, George had removed the pool cover. Clear blue water sparkles. The lawn bordering the patio is a solid green carpet, perfect for bare feet, and beyond the lawn is jungle-thick vegetation. The only other building in the yard is a small garage.

My God! My sister is so lucky. This place is incredible.

I change into denim cutoff shorts, a white tank top and comfortable walking sandals. I enjoy a simple breakfast of toast and coffee on the deck and analyze the view, my mind working on ideas for a mural. A few ideas roll around in my head but I want to return to the beach for proper inspiration. Walking in the sand and sometimes in the water, I meet no one. I can't believe that miles of beaches lay before me empty, deserted. The bluffs are lined with a few houses, but maybe they are all empty. For hours I explore. No one joins me on the beach.

After a quick lunch, I return to the beach. I remain intoxicated by the exotic; and wallow in the freedom to enjoy the beauty without interruption. Torn between exploring the sand and the water, I feel certain I could spend every moment of this trip on this beach, until I realize the beach is shrinking. The tide, swallowing a little more of the beach with each wave, is something a landlocked woman like me has only read about. In a couple of hours the sun will be setting, and I'm starving again. I shower and change into flowing dress and sparkly sandals. After plucking a book from the bookshelf and taking a map and a few island brochures from a kitchen drawer, I grab the keys to Lexie's jeep. Driving on the opposite side of the road takes concentration. Thirty minutes of nerve-racking attentiveness gets me to a highly recommended restaurant a few minutes' drive out of Governor's Harbor.

The view is spectacular from my outside table overlooking the ocean. I don't open a page of the book I brought with me to read. The dancing waves are all the company I need as I work my way through the best lobster I have ever tasted. The flesh is tender and sweet; salty melted butter accompanies each bite. The salad and spicy rice are excellent but I don't finish them. I save what room is left in my stomach for a slice of thick, gooey, creamy chocolate and caramel cheesecake. My tongue works each forkful into oblivion.

Later, back at the cottage, beer in hand, I sit by the pool as Jewel gives repeat performances from the stereo. Today was the best day I have had in years. My stomach is full. I am warm and fuzzy from the beer. Better still, I know what I am going to paint on my sister's living room wall.

Chapter 5

For years I have struggled to find even an hour to paint. On Eleuthera, I spend full days with a brush in hand. I've started two separate projects; a mural on Lexie's living room wall and a seascape of the beach in front of the cottage. The mural is nearly complete. The small seascape I am painting out on the deck is taking shape but it will have to be put aside. The pockets of sunshine and blue sky are disappearing as clouds are being blown in by a light wind. I am moving my easel inside when there is a knock on the front door.

"Your sister asked me to drop in and take care of a few things," a woman explains by way of introduction. Her smile is brisk; her eyes dart around with business-like intensity. Her hair has been smoothed back into a stub of a ponytail. On her thick frame is a loose t-shirt and snug denim jeans. Hands braced on her waist, she looks me up and then down.

"You must be Nancy."

She nods. I lead her into the cottage.

"You don't look like sisters but you keep house the same." In a last push to get the mural done before Lexie arrives, I have let a few dishes stack up.

"Please don't worry about the dishes. I'll take care of them."

"Your sister knows you are coloring up her walls?" Nancy points to the mural.

"It's a surprise. If she doesn't like it, she can cover it over with white paint."

With bold bright colors, I've captured a simple representation of a naked Lexie sitting on the beach, back to us, looking out over a sunrise. She has just emerged from the water; her black hair clings wetly to her head and her delicate neck. Water droplets cling to her otherwise smooth back. A towel hugs her hips. On her arms are the ever-present gold bangle bracelets.

"That'd be a shame. You paint like a comic book artist. Even though I can't see her face, there is no mistaking her."

I beam. "Thank you. Would you like a cup of tea or coffee before you get started? I've been alone without a soul to talk to for days and I'd love a chance to chat. I'll give you a hand with whatever you need to do."

She shakes her head, refusing both my offers. Her fuchsia nail tips wave me away. "Your sister don't pay me to visit or you to work." I know Nancy has other houses to attend to so I am not put off by her single-minded focus on getting to work. I follow her to the bedroom where she strips my bed of the sheets and blanket.

"I'll do the dishes. After that… well, it looks like rain so I'll have to quit painting outside. I'm not sure what to do with my day."

"Snorkeling, diving, fishing, and lying on the beach are what most do. But maybe you'd be interested in the gallery on the south end of the island, in Tarpum Bay? It's open 'til three in the afternoon."

"Wonderful! I have my plan for the day. Thank you."

I tidy up my painting mess from the deck and do up the dishes. When I leave, Nancy is sweeping floors and bustling efficiently around the little cottage.

Accompanied southward by thick clouds which threaten but shed no rain, I reach Tarpum Bay before noon. The gallery sits on the outskirts of the town. The older weathered homes in this area are set back a distance from a shoreline of rocky coral. I park the jeep. A small wooden sign hanging in the door's window instructs visitors to walk in during the posted hours of business. A bell chimes as I enter.

"I'll be right with you. Feel free to wander the house. All the rooms, both up stairs and down, have art and are open to the public," a man calls out from another room. A brogue-filled accent leaves me in no doubt of his Scottish ancestry.

Kicking off my sandals, I step forward and examine the first work of art I see, a small oil seascape in the entryway. It is a simple painting of the sea. There is no land, no rocks, and no beach, just waves and sky. Only a few colors have been used, mostly blues and grays. Bold brushes of white and black help delineate the shape and depth of the waves. As I move closer, the waves appear to shift. I peer closer, examining the brushstrokes to find out how the effect is achieved. I note the price. It is a tempting purchase. I would love to study it closer.

Off the entryway is a living room with a stone fireplace, wooden floors and big comfortable wooden furniture. Artwork is everywhere. Sculptures cover the coffee table, the mantle, and fill the four corners of the room and paintings cover the walls. My eyes are drawn to a life-size oil portrait of a nude woman reclining. It dominates the full wall. Hooded and haughty, her eyes are heavy lidded. She rests on a background of burgundy fabric. I swear if I reach out, I will feel skin, not paint.

"Is she not the loveliest thing?" A silver-haired man, wearing paint-splattered denim, joins me. His eyes skim the painting with a quick familiarity. Etched-in laugh lines surround his blue eyes.

"Yes. She is quite beautiful. Who is she?" I ask.

"She'd be my missus."

"You painted her." It's a statement, not a question. My eyes return to the painting.

"Portraits are my specialty but I shine when I paint her." He bows to the portrait.

"Your work is exquisite," I agree.

"She's an artist as well, and this is our gallery. We have art from the islands and all over the States. What brings you by? Shopping, boredom, or are you a fellow artist?"

"I paint but I would not call myself an artist. Someday I'd like to go back to school and earn the title." My laugh is self-deprecating.

A shaggy white eyebrow lifts. "So you define artistry by education?"

"Um, no..."

His eyebrow lifts higher. "Well, lass, then how does one earn the title of artist?"

Feeling like I have planted my foot in my mouth, I consider his question at length before answering. "Anyone who creates should be considered an artist."

"But you don't consider yourself an artist?"

"No one has ever paid me for my art."

"Many artists go their whole lives without ever earning a cent," he counters.

"Why don't you tell me what makes an artist? You're the gallery owner." The words come out snippy. He grins.

"Did you bring your paints to the island? Are you working on anything here?"

"Actually yes. I'm working on a mural for my sister's cottage and a small seascape."

"Finish a piece. Bring it on by and let me hang it. The only requirement we make of our artists is they have the guts to let others see their work."

"Oh, no. What I paint isn't comparable to what you have here." My face flames.

"Are you one of 'those' artists, you know, who paint a straight line and call it art? The crap those fancy New York galleries display is enough to make me blubber! Spilling over your paint cans or cleaning your brush on a canvas is not art." He shakes his head with disgust and I cannot help but laugh at his vehemence. "The real art is passing that manure off as valuable."

"There tends to be a bit more than just one line to my paintings. I dabble a bit with scenery but honestly, I fall in love with body parts. If I see interesting hands or beautiful shoulders in a magazine or on a movie, I'll try to paint the individual feature against a back drop of brilliant colors. I'm partial to portraits."

He clicks his tongue on the roof of his mouth. "Sounds like art to me but you see, it doesn't matter if I like it or think it's good. My opinion of your work does not give it legitimacy, gallery owner or not. Let me expand on this a little more. It's like meeting people. Some people will like you, and some people will hate you. If I decide right now you are a worthless human being, will you leave believing me?"

"No. You don't know me."

"Exactly. You don't get your self-worth from strangers. So why do you fear me seeing your art? Ability, even if raw and undeveloped, has value. Maybe there is something unique and original about the way you paint, but we won't know unless you bring something in."

"If you'd spend as much time trying to sell art as you do pontificating about it, we'd be wealthy. Michael, not every visitor passing through our doors is looking for a lecture."

Caught up in the discussion, I had heard no one approach. I recognize Michael's wife from the painting, even though she is older than depicted.

I offer my hand in greeting. "I liked hearing his perspective. I'm Skylar. I heard of your gallery and stopped by for a peek."

She takes my hand briefly. Her icy green cat's eyes, almost expressionless, rest on her husband. She is tiny and ageless. Her cappuccino skin is creased and her hair falls to her waist in long black curls. Whereas Michael is all electricity, passion and bluster, this woman is calm, cool and regal. The relaxed mood Michael and I shared evaporates.

"She's an artist, Tracina. The discussion is appropriate," he says, defending himself.

"I'm Tracina and this is my husband, Michael. I doubt he introduced himself." She raises an imperious eyebrow. Michael grimaces, guiltily.

"I was behaving. Was I not the perfect gentleman?"

Tracina waits for my response; her coldness is a sharp contrast to the warmth of her husband. Fidgeting under the directness of her stare, I race to answer. I can't help feeling as if I am being accused of participating in something inappropriate.

"Um, yes, of course!"

"You'll have to excuse my husband; when he's off his leash, he gets into trouble."

Reaching out, Michael snares his wife's wrist. "She likes my lack of manners. She's a prude, Skylar, on the surface anyway, but why'd she marry a raunchy bastard like me?"

Tracina's eyes flare open and her jaw clenches. Michael flinches from a well-aimed punch to his arm. Tugging Tracina towards him, Michael slaps her bottom. Stepping forward, my hands raised in a gesture to calm, I say, "I've come at a bad time..."

"Michael, don't you dare." Tracina's threats are useless as he bends her backwards and places a passionate kiss on her lips.

I change course and inch towards the door. When Michael lets Tracina up for air, her face is flushed, swollen lipped, and smiling.

She shoves him away. "You can't resist pushing my buttons can you, you brute? You should be neutered." Tracina spits out the words but ruins the attempt at indignation with a giggle. This isn't a lover's spat rolling out of control. They are teasing. A smile tugs at the corners of my mouth.

Michael holds up his hands in a gesture of repentance. "She wouldn't dare, Skylar."

"Don't be too sure. Now because you've acted the ass in front of our guest, you can go and start cooking lunch while I try to repair the impression we've made. I'm surprised she hasn't left, thinking we're crazy." Tracina smiles at me, green eyes warmed by a smile so genuine I don't know how I ever thought her cold.

"I uh… actually wasn't sure there for a moment. I'm a school counselor and I was considering which de-escalation tactic would be best to calm the situation," I admit.

Tracina snorts out a laugh. "I'm so sorry, Skylar, I don't mean to laugh." Tracina tries to contain her mirth. She loses control.

"It's okay. I'm too relieved to be offended," I say, chuckling.

She gathers me for a quick unexpected hug. "You have a sense of humor and you are a painter. Wonderful. That finishes it. I like you and I believe I am going to keep you." She taps me on the cheek and then turns to leave the room. "You will stay for lunch. Look around a little more while I go and crack the whip on my husband. Every room has art. Feel free to explore. Meet us in the kitchen when you are done."

I'm not going anywhere. Something inside me clicks into place. I am inundated with the unusual sensation of having come home. It's an emotional reaction I try to attribute solely to meeting people with a shared love of art. However, Tracina's hug moved me as much as Michael's offer to hang one of my paintings. Spending time with these two people is guaranteed to lead to more roller coaster emotions but it's too good an opportunity to pass up. I am compelled to stay.

Chapter 6

I am engrossed by the plethora of artwork until the smell of freshly baked bread drives me in search of the kitchen. Michael and Tracina are working side by side in the obvious center of their home. Mismatched chairs of metal and wood circle a polished oak table. Colored bottles of sand fill the space from the top of the aged wood cabinets to the ceiling. Garlic and onion hang in mesh baskets above the sink. A bowl overflows with ripe bananas. The windowsill is filled with fresh potted herbs. Newspapers are stacked on a nearby chair.

Michael is drying his hands on a towel. "All done are you? We're about ready. Tell us a little about you while we finish up," he suggests, pulling out a chair. I take the offered seat, and drop my purse by my ankle.

Tracina sets the table. "Yes. Where are you from, Skylar?"

"I live in the city of Edmonton. It's in Alberta, Canada. I have a thirteen-year-old daughter and you already know I am a school counselor. "

Michael stirs a pot on the stove before moving it to a hot plate on the table. "I want to know how an artist chooses to be something other than an artist."

I laugh. "They get pregnant in college and get a practical paying education."

"Got a picture of her?" Tracina tosses a full breadbasket on the table.

"Of course." I lift my purse on to my lap and pull a photo out of the protective plastic case in my wallet. "This is Rachel. She's back home with my sister."

"Pretty girl, just like her mother. Where's her father?" Tracina asks, passing the picture to Michael. After a glance, he hands it back.

"We divorced a few years ago. What about you, any children?"

"We were never so lucky." Michael squeezes Tracina's shoulders as he passes by. It's a small contact, but it straightens her back. She gives him a watery smile. I regret the sadness I have brought to their eyes, and apologize.

"Don't be sorry. We've been very happy, traveling and painting. It wasn't meant to be." Tracina is sad but philosophical; there is pain but also acceptance. "So what is your medium?" she asks, returning the subject back to me.

"I sketch occasionally, but I love painting. Acrylics, oils, watercolors, I love them all but I don't always know what I am doing. I've never had formal training."

"It's just as well. Those academic assholes confuse people," Michael growls, his accent deepening. "Don't go to school. They'll just fill your head with manure!"

"I enjoyed art school. Just because it wasn't for you... she'll make her own way." Tracina wags her finger at her husband. Sitting in a chair next to mine, she leans toward me. "Michael did not do well in art school."

Michael huffs and joins us at the table.

"Are you here for very long? We could paint together once this weather improves." Her casually-dropped offer stops my heart.

"Are you serious?"

"Very. It will be fun, if you can come back?"

"I'd love to. I'm here for the month of July and even though time is passing quickly I am sure there will be plenty of time for me to come back. I'm staying with my sister who just bought a cottage in Double Bay."

"Is she the doctor?" When surprise registers on my face, Tracina explains. "This island is like a small town. A female doctor buying a house in Double Bay is big news. About the painting, let's pick a day and commit or time will pass and it won't happen."

"Lexie will be arriving tomorrow afternoon. I should first spend a few days with her. Is Monday okay?"

"Monday's fine. Feel free to bring her along. She can visit with Michael."

I eat a bowl of creamy seafood soup, three fresh rolls, and a banana for desert before Tracina suggests we visit the studio she shares with her husband. Michael stays behind to handle the lunch clean-up. It is still raining. Pelted by thick drops, Tracina and I dash from the back door to a small building across the yard.

The studio has windows for walls. Even with an overcast sky, the single room is filled with natural light, making it an artist's dream. Art supplies clutter cupboards, shelves, and tables. Several easels, bearing canvases, are set up around the room. I study several works in progress, including another nude portrait of Tracina.

"How palpable your love is. I can feel it move between you," I marvel. "I can see it in the way he paints you."

"We are a couple of old fools." She passes me a container of her paint brushes to examine. Her hands are delicate but lined and her knuckles are slightly swollen. I wonder if she finds painting painful. "It wasn't always so. At one point, Michael was the one person in the world I hated most. Marriage isn't easy. You know that, of course, if you have been through a divorce. But as the saying goes, what doesn't kill you only makes you stronger." Tracina pulls a stool near a shelf and begins organizing paint tubes as she speaks. "There were miscarriages, a still-birth. And we made some mistakes out of pain, fear, and stupidity."

I am surprised by the open turn to the conversation. She speaks to me with the honesty of a lifelong friend. She lacks the affected social mask which most people cling to in order to keep their flaws hidden. Her willingness to be open and vulnerable knocks me off guard.

"So tell me what the secret to a happy marriage is. With a divorce under my belt, I obviously have lots to learn." My question is delivered with a light laugh.

"Anyone can have what we have, Skylar, if they are willing to take risks and work hard. You can't get complacent. Even after twenty-five years, we have arguments. Sometimes I get angry enough to sleep on the couch." Her hand falls to my knee and we share a conspiratorial chuckle. "But we don't play games. We always tell the truth, even if it hurts. There is security in the knowledge that Michael has seen everything dark and ugly about me and still thinks I'm beautiful. I wish everyone could have what we share. Oh, listen to me! Other than painting, my husband is the one topic I can go on about forever. How about you, is there anyone in your life?"

"Not even close." Normally, I would say this with a touch of proud defiance, but today these words are tinged with loneliness. Tracina's open honesty inspires the same in me. I don't feel the need to hide behind bravado. "I have kind of put that aspect of life on hold since the divorce. Life is complicated enough."

"Men are great complications. Oh look, it's clearing up," she says. The sun has broken through the clouds, and seems intent on pushing them away.

"I've monopolized your day." I am reluctant to leave but politely offer an opportunity to end the visit. I do not want to overstay my welcome but I can't fathom ending the visit one second earlier than I need to.

"Not at all. Spend the rest of the day with us if you have nothing better to do. In fact, we could do a little painting."

"I'd love to watch you paint but I'll wait until Monday to join in."

"Would you mind running up to the house and getting Michael?"

Brushes meet canvas. Paints mix. The air is filled with oil and turpentine. I bounce between them, soaking up their movements like a sponge. My fingers itch for my own brush. More than once, my hand lifts with the urge to practice the techniques they employ, but today is about discovery. I watch them paint; I listen to their banter. The afternoon disappears.

In return for their hospitality, I take them out to dinner at a local restaurant of their choosing. It is a short drive in the jeep to the crumbling concrete building with peeling paint. They assure me the food is the best to be had in Tarpum Bay. I note the prices are very reasonable. Two bottles of wine disappear over the course of the meal; most of it into Michael's glass. He flirts outrageously with all of the women in his vicinity. Tracina laughs and pours him more wine. She enjoys his appreciation for women. Instead of being jealous, she takes pride in it.

Mouthfuls of food are the only reason for conversational pauses until Tracina begins yawning. "Would you like to stay over?" Tracina asks as we leave the restaurant.

"It's lovely of you to offer, but I'll be fine. I barely finished my wine and once my last coffee kicks in, I will be wide awake for hours."

"I better get this lush home. We'll walk." Tracina gestures to Michael, who is singing and dancing his way down the sidewalk. "He's going to have a big head tomorrow and I'll get to paint while he recovers."

"You're a devious woman, Tracina."

She heads off after her husband, stopping to wave. "I have your number and you have ours. We'll get together next week for sure," she calls out.

I reach the jeep. "You bet. Thanks for today."

After the long day, I should be tired and dreading the drive but instead I am wired, sparking with excitement. I can't wait for Monday. For the first time in my life, I have met people who are like me, who get me. They share my need to create. They understand how, in the act of creation, I am at my happiest.

I reach the cottage and try to call Lexie and Rachel. There is no answer, which is disappointing. There is no one else with whom I can share the details of my news. I met actual artists. And if I can finish a piece, I could have a painting hanging in an art gallery. This is huge!

My excitement is overrun by sadness. There is no one else I can call.

Nancy did a great job cleaning but tonight the cottage seems more barren than beautiful. The kitchen is sterile with cleanliness. There is too little furniture. I sigh and admit to myself that it is the fullness of the day which has left me empty. I'm hollowed out by loneliness. Several times during the day, I witnessed Michael touching Tracina. Unconsciously she leaned into and welcomed every one of his caresses. They held each other's gazes when they spoke, and returned each other's smiles. I was a voyeur to intimacy; I breathe against my own bitterness. I don't remember Rand ever looking at me with unabashed desire. I don't think I ever looked at him that way either, even in the beginning. He was a horny young man and I was a lonely young woman; the only thing connecting us was our needs.

I envy Michael and Tracina's connection, marveling over the discovery that some people really do fall in love, for good, forever. I don't begrudge them what they have, but I want it for myself. I want to know someone the way Tracina knows Michael. I want to be known. Long ago I convinced myself being alone is fine, even necessary. It is a fallacy which will not hold up to scrutiny. I feel what I have been missing. After four years with barely a thought of a man, I have a sharp craving for touch. I want the intimacy of someone holding me in their eyes, in their arms, in their heart. I twist with the knowledge that I was not built to be alone.

Normally solitude is a friend; a precious commodity for a single parent who rarely has the opportunity to do as she wishes. Tonight solitude is an enemy. My fantasies of the future are crumbling. I can see when Rachel begins her life as an adult, living to please only myself, is a novelty that will wear off. What will I do without the daughter who comes first in my life? Who will I be? I fear I will feel like I do tonight, disconnected and self-pitying.

My need doesn't magically make anyone materialize in front of me. I push the longings aside. They have surfaced but I do not have to deal with them right now. My sister arrives tomorrow. She is a master of distraction, and an expert at holding feelings at bay. Lexie is exactly what I need.

Chapter 7

"Yo, ho, ho, and a bottle of rum, here I come!" Lexie shouts, before letting out a long coyote howl. Dropping into the passenger seat of the jeep, she slams the door, props her feet up on the dashboard and drums her hands on her thighs

"You might want to yell a little louder. I'm sure the fishermen on the other side of the island didn't hear you."

My sister sizzles with energy. "I refuse to let your sarcasm penetrate my relief. I am just so fricking happy. Let's get going."

"Yes, ma'am," I answer, backing out of the airport parking lot.

"Christ! What a week. I need to blow off some steam. I sure as hell hope you don't think we're just staying in tonight?" Lexie runs her fingers through her cupid-like halo of ebony curls. "There's a fish fry in Governor's Harbor every Friday. I went the last time I was here and it was a blast. It's an all-out party on the edge of the Caribbean with people, dancing, and plenty of booze. It's positively dripping with sexual possibilities." She slaps my thigh hard. "Stick with me, kid, I'll get you laid."

I wince as much from her words as from the slap. "You scare me, Lexie."

"For three weeks, you're mine. Before you leave, I want you flat on your back with some gorgeous hunk making you feel like a woman."

"I think I want to go home."

"Okay. I'll settle for getting me laid and you having an actual conversation with a male. Don't ever say I don't compromise." We both laugh.

"Actually, I spoke with a man yesterday."

My sister's head swivels with interest. "Who? Some waiter at a restaurant?"

"No. He is the owner of a gallery. We had lunch and dinner together. He even offered to hang one of my paintings if I can complete it before we leave."

"Holy shit! No kidding. Is he attractive?"

"Hmm, he's kind of like a slightly younger, shorter Sean Connery with the sexiest Scottish accent."

"You are shitting me, right? I mean, how slightly younger than Sean Connery is he? Not that I'm judging. If he's male and sparked your interest, I couldn't care less if he's a hundred. It's a beginning."

"Somewhere in his sixties."

"I've dated men that age."

"There's only one problem though. Maybe you can help me with it?" I resist the urge to laugh. "You'll have to help me bump off his wife."

Lexie looks perplexed for a moment and then she sticks out her tongue. "You are such a phony. I should have known better than to believe you'd ever have anything going with a man. You're going to shrivel up and dry out," she proclaims, looking over her sunglasses, which have slid down her nose. "Why you won't admit you are as horny as the rest of us. Somewhere inside you is a little voice screaming 'Skylar, please get me some.'"

"If there is, you'll be the first to know."

"The first to know should be some great, hulking, sex god of a man but I will want all the gory details."

"Oh, grow up already. You are supposed to be a doctor. Doctors are supposed to be intellectual and serious minded. You know, respectable."

"I hate to shock your maidenly sensibilities but …newsflash, Skylar; doctors fuck. After what I see in a day, the last thing I give a crap about is respectability." A shadow crosses her eyes.

"You worked this week?"

"Yeah. Rachel spent two nights with Amanda while I picked up a couple of shifts. The last one I could have done without." Lexie so rarely complains about her job, any admission of difficulty tells me it was bad. "I lost a couple of patients. One was a baby, in a car accident." She wipes at her face as if to rub the memory away.

"Do you want to talk about it?" My counseling hat slips on.

"Living it was enough. Thanks, though." I don't push. Lexie handles her job stress very well. Her methods are outrageous but effective.

"So, tell me, how has your week been going? Isn't this place great?"

"I can't thank you enough, Lex. It's been… I don't have the words… If I wasn't driving, I'd hug you and kiss you again."

"I got enough loving back at the airport. You just about knocked me on my ass."

"This trip has been an incredible gift. My head is clear, my shoulders are light, and I am only missing Rachel every other hour."

"I expected daily phone calls. I couldn't believe you only called once."

"I have been very busy. Besides painting, I had a great day with Michael and Tracina, the people who own the gallery. They are so different from anyone I have ever met. I think they are the last happily married couple on the planet."

"No one is happily married. Spend more time with them. You'll see the cracks appear," she warns.

"Cynical. You can see for yourself. We are going to visit them Monday."

She shrugs indifferently.

At the cottage, we lug her baggage out of the jeep. As soon as we walk in, she sees the mural. "Did you paint this? Of course you did. It's beautiful, when did you get so good? It's been years since I've seen anything you've painted."

Her reaction makes me beam. "I hoped you would like it. I've also been working on a seascape of the view from your deck." I point to the easel a few feet away.

"This is what is different about you. There is a light in your eyes again. Painting is 'it' for you, and you're a fool if you don't stay with it."

"Don't pick on me." I warn her lightly, stopping her before she gains momentum for one of her she-knows-better-than-me lectures.

"I'm not picking on you. I like seeing you this happy."

"Let's get you settled."

For once she lets me end a conversation. We make short work of getting her unpacked before she drags me for a walk on the beach.

Walking in the sand is hard work. Our feet keep sinking so we slip off our sandals and walk along the water's edge where the sand is firmer, the trek easier. Occasionally a warm wave tingles and bubbles to our ankles. Several hundred feet down the beach is Lexie's neighbor. His house is huge, and every day that I have walked on the beach I have taken a few minutes to stop and admire. I point up at the house as we walk.

"That has got to be a million dollar home."

"My cottage cost that much. That one has to be triple that amount."

I gasp a bit at her revelation. "Wow. George said he's a nice guy. Maybe he's good looking as well as being rich. Sounds like a match for you, if he's not married."

She shakes her head. "You need a sugar daddy more than me."

"I've had fantasies of a rich man coming along but that level of wealth scares me.

"He is no better a person than you because he has money. Rich guys can be as bad or as good in the sack as poor ones. Trust me."

"The differences in backgrounds would be hard to overcome. How would a guy know if you liked him for himself or his money?"

"You like him for both," she laughs. "Sky, rich people just have bigger bills."

"Easy for you to say."

"Hey, I remember. Money makes some problems go away and gives you a whole set of different ones. You need to get past the 'I'm not good enough because I have no money' thing you have going on. It's a beautiful house Skylar, but it is just a house." She knocks the chip off my shoulder and turns us back in the direction of the cottage. "I don't really want a long walk. I just wanted to come and say hi to the ocean and the sand. C'mon. Let's get ready to go out."

After showering and shaving my legs, I dry off and rub in scented lotion until my body is soft and smooth. "What does one wear to a Fish Fry?" I ask, walking past Lexie's open door.

"Party casual. Stick to sandals for the feet. Pick some tunes to get us in the mood. I'll make us warm up drinks and call a cab. It can take a while to get one. We're not driving."

Lexie emerges from her bedroom wearing a bath sheet. Similarly wrapped in a towel, I make my way to the living room. I sort through my CDs and select AC/DC, cranking up the volume. Lexie lets out a howl of approval from the kitchen. Seconds later, on the way to her bedroom, she shoves a drink in my hand. The rum and coke is sweet and familiar. I follow her to her room and she drops her towel. She shimmies into red thong panties before shaking her head in time to the music, belting out the lyrics.

"Boy, does this song bring back memories." She lifts a brilliant red spaghetti-strapped dress and slides it over her body. It ends mid-thigh, prominently displaying her long legs. "What are you going to wear?" I lift my shoulders with uncertainty. "It better be something hot!" The order comes as she shoos me out of the bedroom.

I've never been one for dramatic face painting, but tonight I don't want to look like a mom. My wide grey eyes pop once I run some brown liner around them and stroke on mascara. Naturally deep pink, my lips require nothing more than clear gloss. For a touch of color, I brush a light dusting of blush on my high cheek bones.

Damp from being wrapped turban style in a towel, I let my hair spill out, giving it several vicious rubs. I contemplate blowing it out straight but pile it all on top my head instead. A few long tendrils escape. I curl them into slender ringlets.

I dropped a few pounds in preparation for this trip so I'm closer to curvy than to lumpy in my black boy-cut lace panties and matching bra. A white off-the-shoulder peasant style blouse contrasts with my newly acquired tan. The bra will be pretty visible under the gauzy shirt, but I decide the look is sexy. I pair it with a skirt made from yards of light shiny black material. A silver belt cinches my waist. I apply a quick drying silver polish to my toes before donning simple, black leather sandals. To finish off, I step under a spray of perfume.

"Wow, holy wow!" Lexie says as I join her in the kitchen.

"You look incredible," I return the compliment, "but for once I'm not going to feel like the plain younger sister."

"You've always been beautiful, Sky. You are going to have to beat the men off with a stick. About time too, you are practically a born-again virgin."

"After you have a kid that's impossible."

"Well, let's face it you haven't gotten any since your divorce. So if you don't rate born again status after four years, I guess no one ever will. Shit, there's the cab. Wave and let 'em know we'll be right out. I'll shut off the stereo. You're bringing a purse? I want to throw in my cellphone and lipstick. C'mon, we got to go."

Chapter 8

We step out of the taxi in front of Haynes Library and into the heart of the Fish Fry. The street is the dance floor. Our taxi creeps forward, disappearing as the displaced dancers reclaim their spots. I follow Lexie through the crowd to the curb. Two wooden steps down from the street and our feet hit the sandy beach of Anchor Bay. The Caribbean laps at the shore nearby. Under several large trees, a makeshift kitchen is dispensing food to a long line of people. From the other end, drinks flow out at an even faster rate. Loud reggae blares from a large sound system, set up on a long table on the library side of the street. Behind gigantic speakers, a young Bahamian shouts out encouragingly to the dancing crowd.

The night is just being birthed but I can already feel its potential. This is a night when every drink will sail down my throat with ease. There is a sway to my hips, a delicacy to my steps. I am hyper-aware of my body. My breasts feel full, tingly, and heavy. The sensation reminds me they have another function besides getting in the way when I exercise. The resurrection of my libido, which began last night, appears to be continuing. Tonight, I am a free young woman who is thousands of miles away from being a mom or a counselor. I give myself permission to engage in harmless flirting if the opportunity arises; and by the looks of the huge crowd, opportunities are everywhere.

The weekly party is in full swing. Bahamians mingle with tourists. Everyone has drinks in hand. The smell of deep frying food overshadows all else. I line up for something to eat, Lexie for drinks. She rejoins me in time to select rice and peas with deep fried fish. It's gutted but the head, skin, and bones are intact. I decide on BBQ chicken and ask about the ingredients in the conch salad. I'm warned the chopped vegetables and sweet shellfish are doused with a spicy orange and lime dressing. At an open picnic table, we eat with relish. The food and fruity rum drinks disappear with no thought to calories or modesty.

"I couldn't eat another bite. I am so full." Lexie pushes her plate away. "Want a beer or another Bahama Mama?"

I want to soak my tongue in a glass of ice. I pick up my napkin, wipe my mouth and toss it onto the plate. "How about water? The Bahama Mama was potent," I answer.

Lexie is gone in a flash. Left to play with my fork, I feel conspicuously alone. I better get used to it. Lexie loves to mingle and will probably disappear all night. I once made the mistake of going to a Christmas party with her and spent the evening babysitting our handbags. I cast a few glances around, trying to rally positive feelings. Lexie would not sit alone feeling uncomfortable. She'd start a conversation with someone.

My eyes stray to the street, tonight's makeshift dance floor. It's been years since I danced anywhere but in my kitchen. The reggae music is unfamiliar but the slow easy lyrics and sexy vocals are growing on me. The dancing couples are not performing any complicated steps. Their hips sway to the rhythmic beat. I glance around.

My eyes stop when I see him. My heart stops when I see him.

For tonight I am ruined. No other guy is going to measure up because never before have I seen so many sexy attributes attractively rolled into one package. The delicious blond hunk is tall enough to pass the six-foot mark. I've always gone weak at the sight of broad shoulders and muscular biceps, and he's got both. I gauge my body's reaction. *Yup, I'm definitely feeling a little weak.* His hips are narrow but not so slim he could fit into any of my jeans. His stomach is so flat I'm certain, under his tucked-in, white T-shirt, there is washboard abs. I've never seen washboard abs in person before, but I'd love an introduction. He laughs and rocks back on his heels; his thigh muscles shift under the blue denim, and I am suddenly aching in forgotten places.

He lifts his hand and pushes back a full mane of tussled curls streaked gold and platinum by the sun. The motion is smooth. His face erupts in a smile. I am lost. Now that is a face I'd love to paint. He has the most wide-open, mischievous grin I ever remember seeing; his eyes dance and laugh, they shine and tease. I'm enraptured by his dimples as they appear and disappear. His thick eyelashes, full lips, and very white teeth would be almost pretty if they were not offset by the rugged masculinity present in his other features. His nose has a slight hook to it and it is a touch crooked. Laugh lines crinkle out from the corners of his eyes. He is a man who smiles frequently. A light growth of facial hair covers a strong jaw and firm chin.

In the center of a circle of people, he is totally comfortable and completely in the moment. I like that he isn't glancing around, checking people out or measuring himself against the other males present. Each time he talks, I can almost make out what he is saying, just by taking in his body's movements. When someone else speaks, he stops moving and listens with undivided attention. I wonder how it would feel to be the recipient of his undivided focus.

Then it happens.

He is scanning the crowd absently when his gaze passes over me. It returns. He sees me. He sees me seeing him. Embarrassment at being caught staring has my heart pumping blood through my veins in a torrent, but I can't tear my gaze away. Awareness arcs between us. My stomach flips in response. I drop my eyes, my cheeks get hot.

When I look up, his eyes are waiting. He gives me a wink and a knee-melting grin. He raises his beer in a salute. My face flames even more as everyone in his group suddenly turns to see who has his attention. My sister reaches our table.

"Hello? Earth to Skylar? I've been calling you. What's up? You're smiling like an idiot and blushing like a virgin."

"I'm just a little flushed from the heat." I press my open palms to my cheeks.

"You're also full of it. Here's your water. Maybe it will cool you off." I press the cold, moist bottle to one flaming cheek then the other. After a swallow of water, I risk a quick glance at "the babe." I'm disappointed he is no longer looking in my direction.

To pacify Lexie, I say, "A girl can't even keep an embarrassing moment to herself. I just got caught staring at a cute guy." I take another gulp of water.

"Really?" Lexie's head whips around. "Where is he? Point him out."

"God, you are as subtle as a bulldozer. Why don't I just send a flashing sign to perch above his head? He's on the edge of the crowd, by the bar, the tall blond in the white shirt and jeans. Looks like a surfer."

"Mmm. He is fuckable. Go introduce yourself. Maybe you'll get lucky and he'll give you a ride." Lexie wiggles her eyebrows and pumps her hips suggestively. "On his surfboard," she clarifies without any pretense of truthfulness. "What are you waiting for? Give him the old 'hello what's your sign?' Ask him to dance."

"I don't think so. What if he says no?"

"What if he says yes?" She purrs the question into my ear. "Bat your eyes, bounce your tits and you'll be flat on your back before you know it."

I choke on a laugh. "I wouldn't know what to do with that much man."

"As a doctor, I can safely assure you there are few men in this world who would be physically too much man for any woman."

"Does everything have to be sexual with you?"

"Does everything have to be chaste with you? What you are feeling is sexual attraction. It's perfectly normal. I'm proud of you. You are loosening up. We may get you laid yet!" Lexie roars and heads turn in our direction.

I close my eyes. "You just don't ever stop."

"No, I can't. C'mon, I met some guys, cute hockey players from the States. They are younger than us but beggars can't be choosers. If you're not going to go after him, you might as well come with me." Lexie pulls me up. "It's time to let loose, little sis."

I don't want to go. I'd rather sit here and cast the occasional furtive glance at the 'babe,' but with no reason to stay where I am, I let my sister tug me into the crowd.

“I’m not sleeping with anyone, Lexie,” I threaten, yanking her to a stop.

“We are having a drink, not sex.” She enunciates each word. Prodding me forward with a hand on my back, she hisses in my ear, “If you can’t tell the difference, I will arrange a remedial Sex Ed class for you later. Relax. Here they are. Smile and pretend you can have fun.” She smiles and I fight the urge to grimace. Lexie reaches for the arm of one of the approaching men, wrapping her fingers possessively around his bicep. “Skylar, this is Calvin.” The young man beams at Lexie. I am not sure if he is smitten or sensing an easy lay. We exchange nods. “And this is Devon.”

Buried in muscle, Devon is almost missing a neck. Resembling a football linebacker, he towers over me, slowly assessing whether I am worth his time. Feeling like a piece of prime rib on a platter, I retaliate by similarly checking him out. I decide that although he is clean-cut, he is too well dressed. A silk shirt matches his blue eyes exactly. His black slacks are tight and his flashy gold chain obvious. I suspect he waxes his eyebrows. This guy tries too hard, and can’t even get my pulse up. The blond hunk took my breath away without trying at all.

We sit at a table. I sip a fresh drink. Calvin is solicitous. He asks eager questions and listens with focused attention. I feel an urge to warn him. My sister has a short attention span when it comes to men. He’s just the lay of the week. I push aside my disloyal thoughts even though I know Lexie’s going to eat him up and spit him out. Devon the sullen hustler is more her usual speed but they are oblivious to each other.

Lexie pulls Calvin to his feet. “I bet you are great on the dance floor. Sorry, Devon, I have to steal him away.”

“How ‘bout a dance?” Devon trumpets in my ear.

“I’d love to dance,” I reply because it is a better alternative to sitting here watching Lexie sizing Calvin up with predatory speculation. I follow Devon up onto the street, relieved when he leaves a comfortable space between us in spite of the soft and sexy music.

“Where are you from?” he shouts again, louder than necessary.

“Edmonton,” I answer.

“Home of the Oiler’s, the City of Chumps.” He thinks he is funny but I am a big fan of my hometown hockey team. If I had hockey gloves on, I’d be throwing them off and the fight would be on.

Instead I ask, “Who do you play for?” He names his team. “Have they ever won a Stanley Cup?” His grin fades. “Didn’t we kick you guys out of the playoffs last year?”

I regret showing off my hockey knowledge. Understanding I am no neophyte, Devon launches into an in-depth analysis of last season’s games; each and every game. He dominates the conversation, at times shouting above the music. I am unable to contribute a thing beyond nods and murmurs. After our third dance, I use thirst as an excuse to return to the table. Devon fetches another round of drinks but I decide to let the drinks pile up on the table. There is something about this guy that I don't like.

I catch glimpses of the blond babe in the crowd. Every so often, the hairs on the back of my neck rise and I know he is looking my way. He probably assumes no-neck-Devon is my boyfriend. Songs change, the night passes, and he does not approach. After more hockey talk and additional dances with Devon, I begin to think of leaving. I'm tired of trying to keep my eyes from glazing over.

Just a couple of hours ago, I was feeling young and energized. I really thought that we would spend the night having fun, meeting people, dancing, and relaxing. My sister has abandoned me to Devon. She has hardly even returned to the table except for quick swallows of alcohol and water. This night was never about us hanging out. It was always about getting my sister laid. Lexie is plastered all over Calvin. His hand cups her ass; their lips are locked. I'm not surprised. It looks like the night's mission has been accomplished. I no longer need to be here. Even though it is the middle of a song, I stop dancing and turn to walk away.

Devon's hand snares my wrist. "Whew, look at those two go!" He points at Lexie and Calvin. "I wouldn't mind a little of that. How about it, Skylar?" He slurs the 'S' in my name, pulls me close, and nuzzles my neck. My skin crawls. He is more inebriated than I realized.

"Uh, Devon, why don't you get me another drink?" I make the suggestion as I try to extricate myself from his grasp.

"You have three on the table. You're not drinking very fast."

Damn. He's not as drunk as I thought.

"Come on, give me a little kiss. Let's see what happens," he coaxes, pulling me tightly against his body.

"I left my purse sitting on the table." I try to turn away from him as he tugs me forward. He is stronger. I lose my balance and fall forward into his chest.

"I can see it from here. It's fine." His hold is unbreakable.

"Look, I'm flattered but we don't really know each other."

"I know enough," he answers. "I bet you're a great fuck." His hands reach down and squeeze my ass, in imitation of Calvin's grip on Lexie.

"Enough, Devon!" I push futilely at his chest. "I am not interested in going to bed with you and I would appreciate it if you would keep your hands to yourself."

With a cajoling smile, he says, "Ah, don't be that way." Then he is kissing me. His tongue tries to force its way past my clamped jaw. I push against his chest but I can't break his hold. Devon's feet are planted firmly apart, braced against my struggles. His mouth mashes mine; his teeth are digging into my lips with bruising consequence. My eyes tear in frustration. I'm done being polite. I bring my knee up as hard as I can, grinding it squarely into his groin.

Chapter 9

"YOU BITCH!" Devon slurs. One hand protectively covers his groin, the other holds my wrist in a bone-crushing grip. He's recovering and I am scared.

"Take a hint and keep your hands to yourself. LET GO OF ME!" I yell. Using a trick my dad taught me, I point my index finger and twist down hard, breaking his hold. He begins a stumbling advance. I back up but not fast enough to evade his long reach. He snares my left hand. Reacting instinctively, I close my right hand and launch my fist into his nose. My hand explodes with pain, but I have the second I need. I whirl free of him.

Thunk!

I run straight into another solid male chest. Warm hands find my shoulders, steadying me on my feet. My escape blocked, I shove against the firm male body. I look up into amber and jade eyes, soft with concern. A second rush of adrenaline sweeps through me when I realize it's the blond guy I admired, coming to my rescue.

"Let me handle this," he says, placing me protectively behind his body. To Devon, he says, "The lady is not interested."

"Nobody hits me and gets away with it," Devon snarls.

"You'll have to go through me to get to her." My rescuer is lighter than Devon, but at least half a dozen drinks more sober.

Lexie joins the ruckus. "What's going on?" she demands.

I step forward. "We had a disagreement. I'm apologizing for hitting Devon."

"Why did you hit him? What did you do to my sister?" Wild and indignant, Lexie jumps towards Devon. Calvin grabs her.

"He was groping her. She told him to stop. He didn't," the blonde man explains.

"You son of a bitch! No one lays a hand on my sister."

"I'll take him home, Lexie. He's drunk. Let me take him home." Transferring Lexie to me, Calvin grabs Devon by his shirt. "You're coming back to the pad and you are going to sleep it off! Sorry, Skylar. He gets stupid when he drinks."

"She kneed me and then she punched me," Devon whines.

"Looks like she broke your damn nose. Move! Before this guy kicks your ass worse than she did," Cal rebukes. "Your brains are full of beer. You can barely stand. I'll be back in ten minutes. Don't leave," he says, casting a pleading glance over his shoulder at Lexie.

She shrugs off my hold. We watch as Devon is loaded into a distant car. I release the breath I didn't realize I was holding. It is as if I've just stepped off a vicious tilt-a-whirl. My hands are shaking and my knees are knocking. I hardly feel qualified to stand.

"I was so into Cal I didn't watch out for you. Are you hurt? You're trembling."

"I'm okay."

"She handled herself very well." I look up into those green eyes with yellow flecks and I am back on the tilt-a-whirl. Any calm I gathered is lost. He is taller, broader, and even better looking up close.

"Um, thank you, um...." I struggle to piece together enough words to make a coherent sentence. He assumes I am fishing for his name, rather than for lucidity.

"Mack," he supplies. For the second time tonight, his smile hits my stomach, making it loop.

"Well, Mack, thanks for stepping in when you did. I'm not ashamed to admit I was very relieved to have a man intervene."

"You rocked him pretty damn hard with your punch, Slugger." He delivers the nickname with a wink which instantly brings a blush to my cheeks. "Just wanted to make sure you knew someone had your back ...um?" Several seconds pass before I realize he is waiting for an introduction.

"Sorry. I'm Skylar." My cheeks flame hotter. "This is my sister, Lexie."

"Pleased to meet you, gals." He shakes Lexie's hand. Instead of shaking the one I offer, he takes my sore hand. "Get some ice," he orders someone in the crowd and examines my hand. "Can you move your fingers? You can't move them, can you?"

I look down at my hand cradled in his, being stroked gently and manipulated by his long tanned fingers. The throbbing seems to have ended. I suspect it is being drowned by the pounding of my heart in my ears. I try to snap myself back into thinking mode.

"I think I can." I wince from the attempt.

"It might be broken. We should get it looked at."

Lexie pushes him aside. "Let me see. I'm a doctor." She dismisses his examination and begins her own poking and prodding assessment. "I don't think so but I'd need an x-ray to be sure."

"Look, everything is moving. It hardly hurts at all. I'll just put some ice on it and go home and take it easy." I am not lying, the discomfort is easing. The skin is slightly red but unbroken.

"Where's that ice?" Mack disappears into the crowd. My eyes follow his retreating figure, and I decide his ass is fantastic.

Lexie grabs my face. "You're in shock, you idiot, that's why you aren't feeling anything."

"I am not in shock. Honest. I'm fine." I do my best to clear the dazed look from my eyes. I wish I could make my flushed cheeks disappear as easily.

"I was going to leave with Cal. Thank God I didn't."

"I don't need a babysitter but I do want to go to the cottage. I've had about all the excitement I can handle."

"Here comes Mack. You don't want to leave now. Let's get him to have a drink with us. I'll disappear later."

"Lexie…" I growl under my breath in warning, but it's too late, Mack is upon us.

"I'll get you laid yet," she whispers into my ear. My sister smiles sweetly up at Mack as she takes the plastic bag of ice from him and drapes it over my hand. I hop up onto a nearby picnic table, throwing a warning glare her way. She pretends not to notice.

"Mack, thanks again for coming to my sister's rescue. We are buying you a drink. It's the least we can do for all your help." Lexie is the picture of innocence, but I see through the façade to the devious mind at work. "Beer okay?" she asks and he nods. She is off.

Alone at the table with Mack, I self-consciously blow a breath at my bangs. "Good luck on getting your beer anytime soon. Lexie is easily distracted."

"And what are you?" Mack climbs up to sit beside me on the picnic table. His hand curls around the edge of the table inches from my leg. I meet his gaze and give myself a mental pat on the back when I am able to return it without blushing.

"I'm the quiet one."

He breaks into laughter. "You knee a guy in the groin and punch him in the nose, and you are the quiet one? Remind me to keep a close eye on your sister."

"You should. It was her idea to come here tonight and look where it got me. I know enough to avoid doing anything Lexie thinks is a good idea."

"You seemed to be having fun. You danced often."

"I didn't think you were paying attention." The words are out before I can stop them.

“I’ve been paying attention since the moment I laid eyes on you.” His slow southern drawl is a caress.

I turn a darker shade of red. *Is he flirting? Teasing?* I haven’t a clue. I am decidedly out of practice at interacting with the opposite sex. I decide to take the statement as a compliment. I file it away in my memory for a later examination.

“Where are you ladies staying?” he asks.

I try to sound casual, even though I am pleased he is asking. “Lexie owns a cottage in the Double Bay area.”

“She’s the Canadian doctor. You’re my neighbors.”

“Oh! Are you Mr. Mackenzie? Nancy works for you.” I realize he is the owner of “the house.”

He nods. “I’ve been meaning to stop by and introduce myself but I have company from the States staying with me.”

Lexie returns, sets a loaded tray of drinks on the table and starts passing out small plastic cups with a clear liquid inside.

“Tequila,” I groan.

“Mack accepted one. Don’t be rude.”

I let the sarcasm drip from my voice. “Lord no. I wouldn’t want to be rude. It might create a scene. Oh, that’s right. I caused one of those already.”

“Shut up and drink. Forgive my sister, Mack. She can be fun. I’ll pour a couple of these down her and she’ll be a hoot.”

“She’s fine the way she is,” he smiles.

I decide tossing back a shooter is better than blushing. I squeeze my eyes shut, and don’t open them until I’ve swallowed every last bit of tequila. I lift a wedge of lemon to my lips, biting down before choosing a beer from the tray. I pass it to Mack. Our fingers brush.

“Guess what, Lexie? Mack is your neighbor to the north.”

“That would also make you the person hogging Nancy. I tried hiring her on a more permanent basis but she said she’ll only work for me until she can find someone else to take over.”

Mack shrugs. “Whoever she finds will be great.”

“Sorry about that, guys.” Calvin reappears, apologizing profusely to everyone. “I should have kept a closer eye on him. My only excuse is your sister had me distracted.” Lexie welcomes him back with a forgiving hug.

"Don't think about it again." She passes him a beer.

"So I already know you're a doctor, Lexie. What do you do, Skylar?" Mack asks.

"I am a school counselor."

Calvin chokes on his beer. He clears his throat and laughs. "You'd think she'd have better conflict resolution skills." He nudges Mack.

Mack grins. "I want to take an anger management session from you."

I give them each a dirty look. "Tonight was an aberration. This is exactly why I don't go out with you, Lexie. You get me into trouble."

Mack pats my shoulder. "Relax. We are just having fun with you, Skylar. You had every right to do what you did. "

"I can't believe I punched him." I cover my face. "I could have been arrested! What was I thinking?"

"You were protecting yourself, as you should. You don't go to jail for fighting off a sexual advance. Devon should know better. You could've called the police and pressed charges. It's not over. I will be talking to him tomorrow," Calvin says, reassuring me.

"He hit the booze pretty hard. He may need alcohol counseling," I suggest.

"No problem solving. You are on vacation," Lexie interrupts. "More shooters for everyone." She passes another round out.

"One was plenty. I'm going to need rehab after this trip," I argue but she shoves a drink into my hand.

"You can't come to the Bahamas and not have a 'Sex on the Beach.' What shall we drink to?" Lexie pretends to ponder briefly, eyes lit up with mischief. "Oh, here's an oldie but goody. To future bed partners!" she announces wickedly.

"Here, here." Cal taps his glass with Lexie's.

"Skylar made that one up years ago."

My cheeks burn. My sister would have to remember that little fact right now. Mack and I exchange gazes as we swallow the concoction.

"I need to dance." Lexie sets her glass down and tugs at Calvin's arm. "Finally the alcohol is hitting me in all the right places." She kisses him deeply, in front of us, for several long seconds.

"Get a room!" I snap.

Lexie pulls her lips off of Calvin's. "I will if you will," she laughs.

When they are safely on the dance floor, I apologize. "About my sister, Mack. She's, well… she's Lexie. You never know what she is going to say or do. She loves to shock people. She will get worse as the night goes on, even if she does not have another drink. If you want to rejoin your friends…"

"Actually, I sent my brothers back to the cottage when I grabbed the ice for your hand. They took a taxi load of girls with them. They'll be plenty busy for the next few hours. If it's all right with you, I'll stay on the off chance I might be able to persuade you to dance?" He holds his hand out to help me down off the picnic table.

"Um…yeah." I give him the lamest response possible.

It was hard to string sentences together while we were sitting side by side on the picnic table, but now he wants me to move to music? It's a daunting task but I don't refuse. I set my beer on the table. My hand is swallowed by his. It tingles in response to his touch as I follow him up on to the street. A slow ballad is playing. His one hand easily finds my waist and the other gently cradles my punching hand. I am sure I am going to trip or stumble awkwardly, but lubricated by the drinks and skillfully guided by his gentle nudging direction, I move easily. Groping for conversation, I tell him he is a good dancer.

"I had an excellent teacher. My mom made all of us boys dance with her."

I melt. "That's sweet. You would have been hugely popular at my high school. Most of us girls were stuck dancing in groups while our boyfriends watched. Any guys brave enough to get out on the dance floor never sat down again."

"I'll let you in on a little secret. We hate looking like idiots. Once we know how, we love to dance. It's one of the few socially acceptable ways a guy can touch a woman without having been first introduced. I mean, we barely know each other and here we are..." His words trail off as he presses our bodies closer for a turn. "I can feel your whole body against mine in front of all these people and no one even bats an eyelash." His voice hums against my ear as we fit snugly together.

God, he feels good. My overburdened senses struggle to keep up with the effect of his nearness. His body radiates heat. The shoulder under my hand is rock hard. A few inches away are the golden curls at his nape. I want to play with them, to see if they are as soft as they look. I'd like to run my fingertips along his jaw and feel the rasp of stubble on my fingertips. He smells clean and he smells salty. I want to bury my face in his neck and take one deep yummy breath after another.

He pulls back suddenly and I am jerked out of enjoyment. "I'm sorry, Skylar. An asshole used dancing as an excuse to grope you earlier; now I'm doing the same thing."

"No you are not." I reassure him quickly. I don't equate him with Devon in the slightest.

"I like dancing with you too, Slugger." As the song ends, he spins me around.

"More shooters!" Lexie yells into our ears, shocking me out of Mack's embrace, breaking the mood. I follow Mack back to the table.

"Honestly, Lex, I've had enough. I've drank more tonight than I have in the last five years. I'm done."

"Yeah, I'm good," Mack also declines.

"What a waste of good booze! I'm very disappointed in you, Mack." Lexie splits the drinks between herself and Cal. "You can make it up to me by doing me a favor. I want to leave with Cal but I don't want to leave Skylar alone. Would you mind if she hung out with you?"

"I'm ready to go, Lexie," I interject as I see a ploy developing.

"Cal and I were hoping to be alone for a while at the cottage by ourselves. I guess we could go back to his place but I can't promise I won't beat the crap out of Devon while he's passed out."

"Stay, Skylar, for a bit?" Mack gives my hand a squeeze and I realize we are still attached. "I didn't bring a vehicle but we can catch a taxi later. I'll get you home safe."

"Perfect!" Lexie digs in my purse, pulls her phone out, turns it on, and tucks it into my bra. "I'll call you," she says. "I can see I have left you in very capable hands. It's up to you to decide where you want him to put them."

Lexie gives Mack's cheek a quick peck. "You've been a savior tonight. I'll have you over for dinner one night this week, if you are not having breakfast at my house in the morning." She gives us a saucy grin and is gone.

Chapter 10

I want to dig a deep hole in the sand, crawl in and die of embarrassment. Maybe I'll bury my irrepressible sister instead. It would serve her right. I'll admit to having lustful inclinations toward Mack but they are firmly restricted to fantasy.

"Want to buy a sister really cheap?" I retort.

Amusement crinkles his eyes. His grin widens. "She's a character. Only interested in a good time but she's honest about her intentions. Now you, I haven't figured out."

"Really? Compared to Lexie, I am easy." As he laughs, I race to correct my blunder. "I mean I'm not complicated. What you see is what you get. No murky waters or deep layers here." I am babbling.

"The second I saw you, I thought to myself there is one pretty party gal out looking for a good time. Then you blushed and wrecked my assessment." He points to my flaming face and I cover the offending cheeks. "Who blushes like that?"

"Someone who doesn't get out often. Do not confuse me with my sister. I am not in the habit of partying and I am not on the prowl," I sputter.

His shrug strikes me as disbelieving. "Eleuthera has a funny effect on people. Many come looking for a little rest and relaxation; soon they're looking for company. The Fish Fry is the hottest hook up spot on the island. You arrive as a single, you leave in a pair."

The cocky proclamation irritates me. "Talking from experience?"

"Excuse me?"

"I'm just saying… This is the place to find women who are looking for more than just a drink and a dance. Could be, you show up here happy to oblige them." I don't bother to hide my smile as he flinches.

"You think I'm here to pick up someone?"

"I'm just connecting the dots."

"Not the right ones. My brothers wanted to meet some of my friends and check out the Fish Fry. I'm not looking to get laid."

"And I stayed to avoid being the third wheel in my sister's latest sexcapade."

"Fair enough. No more judgments. The party is just getting going. C'mon. You can meet some of my friends and we'll dance. I'll take you home in a while."

I follow as he winds his way through the crowd, surprised when we end up at the bar and I'm introduced to the bartenders, who tease Mack about missing out on working a shift. The next thing I know we are donning aprons and mixing a huge vat of fruit juices and rum. After brief instructions on the drinks and the prices, I am taking and filling orders.

"I hope you don't mind. We really don't have to do this if you would prefer to go and dance or mingle?" Mack asks as I drop change into a waiting hand.

"Are you kidding me? This is fun! I just chatted with a couple from Italy."

The crowd seems to be growing. Even with our additional help behind the counter, the line up for drinks doesn't shrink. Before I know it, Mack is plucking my apron strings and passing the garment to my replacement. He leads me from the sand up to the crowd of dancers and introduces me to a group of young Bahamians. The blaring music prevents conversation. Nods and smiles are exchanged as we join in with the dancing. The music has shifted from the unfamiliar reggae to more contemporary music. Akon and Rihanna are not normally what I listen to but they are familiar and the familiarity inspires greater exuberance in my movements.

A beautiful braided young girl on my right begins to sing. She gives me a coaxing elbow to my side, a nudge to join her. I do and she claps encouragingly. She then tries to get me to perform some of her hip shaking and butt wiggling moves. I get the hang of a few. More often than not, I end up doubled over, laughing at my attempts. Mack easily mimics the young male dancers. He has obviously danced with them before. They egg him on until his moves send the young men into peals of laughter and prompt the young women to point and giggle. He laughs with them, exaggerating his movements before returning to his own simple, fluid steps.

Everyone on the street is dancing. Most are also singing. The party atmosphere is contagious. It's that perfect point in the night when everyone is well lubricated. Time speeds up as I become more interested in having fun than worrying about looking like a fool. A new song begins and the crowd goes wild. It's a line dance and I don't know the steps. I intend to sit out but I am thrust to the front of the crowd for instruction. A smooth-moving, young Bahamian leads everyone through the steps. Mack, standing on the edge of the crowd, catches my eye and points to the bar. I mouth the word 'water.' He disappears while my instruction continues.

The song is played over and over until everyone on the dance floor can make it through the whole song without any missteps. The crowd cheers. Dying of thirst, I search out Mack and spot him waiting at the picnic table with two bottles of water in hand. I reclaim my perch beside him. His golden curls are dark and damp. Moisture beads his brow. I accept a water bottle and unabashedly finish it in several long swallows.

"I can't remember the last time I had so much fun. You've given me the night out I wanted to have with my sister. Thank you for staying with me."

"Hardly a hardship."

"I believe you. You really do love to dance."

"Yeah, good music should make you want to dance don't you think?"

"Do you come here often to dance?"

He shakes his head in response. Water bottle at his mouth, I've asked him the question as he is in mid-swallow. He replaces the cap. "The Fish Fry is a lucrative community fundraiser and so I volunteer frequently. The dancing is just a bonus." He catches me stifling a yawn. "I better get you moving."

I check my watch. "I'm sure it'll be safe to head back now."

The Fish Fry is winding down. The crowd has begun to thin.

"One more dance?" he asks. "I like this song."

It's not a song I know. A steady, throbbing drum beat and a crooning guitar swirl out of the speakers, lifting me to my feet. Thick bass forces its way past my ribs until it changes the beating of my heart. The music begs for movement. A sexy male voice sings of kissing, dancing, and holding. It's a slow song, an end of the night finisher.

The heavy moist air has its own sensuality, increasing the sheen of sweat on the mingling bodies; it heats up heat-seeking bodies. The only movement to the air is in the waves of vibrating bass. Caught up in dancing, my awareness of him was background noise, my attraction almost reduced to a mosquito-buzzing-by-the-ear distraction. Back in his arms, I am hit with full-on awareness. One of his hands is resting low on my back, the other nestles mine against his chest. His jean-clad thighs brush against my bare legs. I don't know where to look. He is too tall for me to see over his shoulder and looking at his chest is asking for trouble so I stare up at his lips. He catches me, smiles, and tucks me in even closer to his body. I allow myself a temporary leave of good sense and enjoy being held. Soaking in his warmth I rest my head against his chest, and breathe in the salty smell of his skin as his body moves me.

"You're vibrating," he says into my ear.

You bet I am, I think, before realizing he is referring to Lexie's phone which is still trapped in my bra. I answer it but can't hear her over the music, even when I walk away from the music back to the table where it is not so loud.

Regretfully I announce, “I guess it’s time to go.” I grab my purse off the picnic table and drop Lexie’s cellphone into it as Mack pulls one out of his back pocket and dials a number. He talks briefly.

“You don’t have to leave.”

“I’m good to go but it’ll be a few minutes. Why don’t we start walking? If we head this way, the taxi will come across us.”

The Fish Fry falls away behind us, the music getting more and more distant. The calm Caribbean runs parallel to the road and to our steps. We say nothing for a time. I am willing myself to forget I am walking near a beach, on a hot night, with a gorgeous man at my side.

“How long have you been here?” His voice breaks the silence.

“Almost one week down, three to go. And you?”

“Six years.”

“Really? You are so lucky. Photographs don’t do this place justice. Everything is so vivid. The sky is bluer, and the plants are greener.”

I admit I have only dipped my toes in the ocean when he asks if I have tried snorkeling or diving. “You have to get into the water. It’s just as beautiful underneath the surface.” He guffaws at my look of disbelief. “Scared? Don’t be, I’ll take you.”

I smile at the possibility of seeing him again. “Where are you from? I love your accent.”

“My accent? Oh, it’s pure Bahamian.”

“You wish. I think maybe there is a little Texan in your background?”

“There is a whole lot of Texas in my accent,” he confirms.

“I think a southern drawl is quite sexy.” As soon as the words leave my mouth, I gulp, wishing I had the ability to reach out and grab them back.

“Do you think anything else about me is sexy?” He grasps my hand and pulls me to a stop, waiting for me to respond.

All I can think about is how small my hand feels inside of his. I try to keep my answer light. “You’re obviously a good-looking guy, but I don’t think I should mention it. I’d hate to contribute to any further swelling of your head.”

“I’ve no fear as long as you are around, Slugger.” Mack resumes walking, pulling me into sync with his stride. His hand grips mine firmly.

“So you’re from Canada and you are a school counselor. What’s that like?”

“Stressful, and much too serious a job to talk about on vacation.”

"Okay, what do you do for fun?"

"Better. I paint. I've spent almost every waking moment I've been here with a brush in my hand. What about you? What do you do for a living?"

"Uh-uh. I'm not done hearing about painting. Your eyes lit up for a second. It's more than just a pastime."

I would rather hear about him. Too much talk about me will allow good sense to intrude. I don't want to think about what I should or shouldn't be doing right now. I am enjoying my little escape from reality. I like walking with my hand firmly tucked into his. I like it too much. There it is. Good sense has found me. Before the flirting goes too far and one of us starts getting ideas, I decide to throw a little cold water on the situation.

"No, it really is just a pastime. I'm too busy being a mother to have serious aspirations in an artistic direction."

"You're married?" He drops my hand as if he suddenly realized it might be a rabid animal.

"No, not anymore. I'm divorced."

"Oh. I'm sorry." He begins walking again and I can feel his relief. Mack does not reclaim my hand. Even if it is for the best, I miss his touch.

"Yeah, well, me too. It was rough on my daughter, but he's remarried now and is much happier."

"And you? Are you happy?"

"For the most part." I answer maybe a little too quickly. I shake off my current doubts in that regard. "My life back home is very simple, and completely focused on my daughter. I guess that's why I bristled earlier. I am anything but a party girl. I work and I parent. I'm not very interesting."

"Bullshit. You're plenty interesting. You have an important job and a child. That is much more interesting than being a partier."

"I disagree. Parenting a teenager is all about team sports and proactive supervision."

His forehead wrinkles with surprise. "You don't look old enough to have a child who is a teenager."

"Rachel is thirteen. I'm well into my thirties. There are plenty of years between us, but thanks for the compliment. Occasionally we are confused for sisters. Drives her crazy, I love it. What about you? Do you have a wife, girlfriend, or kids all over the world?"

“I date occasionally, no one seriously, at least not lately. Never been married and no children but I do want both. Why are you looking at me as if I suddenly just sprouted a second head?”

I let out an unladylike snort. “A guy like you is only alone out of choice.”

“A guy like me?”

“You have to know you are good looking.”

“I do?” he blushes.

“Every week I bet there is a fresh batch of tourists at the Fish Fry vying for you to be their vacation fling. With your looks and your house I am sure it would not take much to convince one of them to join you for more.”

“Fling is the operative word. There is nothing serious going to happen with someone who lives somewhere else.”

“Exactly. So if you really want more, you wouldn’t still be here after six years.”

“Saved from answering by the taxi, here’s our ride.” A car approaches, slowing to a stop. I reach for the door handle. Mack brushes me aside and opens the door for me. I get in and slide over, realizing he is going to join me in the back.

“We’ll drop the lady off first.” Mack provides the location and the two men begin a conversation while I enjoy the wind blowing through the open window. After a few minutes, I’m hypnotized by the drive and the late hour. I fall into a light sleep. Mack says my name as we come to a stop. Tossing the driver some money, he says he’ll walk the rest of the way home. I scramble out of the car. All the cottage lights are off. The door is locked. I knock but there is no answer. Mack peers through the windows.

“Where is she?” I ask when it is obvious she isn’t going to answer.

“Maybe she left a message on the cell phone?”

I check the voice mail. Lexie tells me she and Calvin decided instead to stay at his place and she’ll be back sometime in the morning.

“That witch! She locked me out and left. Crap! She has the keys!”

“I’ll try the patio doors.” Mack disappears around the corner. He returns in a few moments. “I tried the windows, they are all locked. There used to be a spare key.”

“I took it from the hiding place when I got here last week and put it on the ring with the jeep keys.”

“And those are- ”

“Inside. This is just great. I have to use the bathroom!” I growl in irritation. “It would serve her right if we smashed a window!”

"Have you ever tried to smash shatter-proof glass before?"

"You are kidding me?"

He laughs. "Nope. I owned this cottage before Lexie bought it from me. I installed these windows myself. Very expensive and meant to stand up to hurricanes." He points to the ocean. "We could try it. It could work... although my place is just down the beach." He bounds down the steps and picks up a heavy looking rock from along the flower garden. He holds it up to me. "You can have the honors. Or...." He holds out his hand to me. "I have plenty of spare bedrooms. You can borrow one."

"I can just sleep out here on one of the loungers"

"I'm not leaving you alone."

I'm not going to go pee in the bushes while he hangs around. I step down and take his hand. He tosses the rock away. I guess I'm going back to his place, if only to use his bathroom.

Chapter 11

A sliver of moon is not enough to light the way but Mack's house is a glowing beacon in the distance. We walk towards it, accompanied by the sounds of the Atlantic Ocean alternately crashing and lapping at the shoreline. The warm wind whips the loose tresses of my hair around the nape of my neck. I am taking chances. Walking barefoot on a beach, my sandals are in one hand, a stranger's hand is in the other.

As we reach the steps leading up to his deck, I stop Mack.

"I'm just going to use your bathroom and head back and wait for my sister."

"Sure and I am going with you. Do you want to meet the party crowd? I love my brothers but their friends I could live without. Or we could slip in through the patio doors to my bedroom. You could use my bathroom while I sneak into the kitchen and grab us a bite to eat and something to drink. We could picnic on the beach?"

I am scared this night won't end, but I am more scared it will. "I'd prefer the beach," I say honestly. I don't want to join the group inside. I would rather sit on the beach and listen to the waves and his sexy voice. Before long I'll be back at Lexie's; for now, I will enjoy a vacation from good sense.

"Awesome. We'll avoid the horny, drunk, college kids." His description makes me laugh. "I'm serious, they are driving me nuts. When they aren't eating all my food or drinking all my booze, they are fornicating in my bed! You wouldn't believe how many of my condoms they have gone through."

"Do you buy them by the case?"

He pauses to clear his throat, realizing his misstep. "Stuff here is expensive. You'd think they'd have brought their own. Damn moochers!" Mack slides open the patio doors. "Anyone in here?" he calls out to the darkened room. I giggle, hoping someone is 'fornicating' in his bed so I can watch him flounder but the coast is clear. I drop my sandals by the door and follow him.

He switches on a light and disappears through the bedroom doorway. I quickly make use of the toilet. Catching a glimpse of my face in the mirror as I wash my hands, I almost don't recognize myself. My eyes are sparkling, my cheeks are flushed. Opening my purse, I unfurl a large string of cellophane packets. Mack might be out of condoms but it looks like I am well stocked, thanks to my meddling sister. I shove the condoms to the bottom of my purse and withdraw lip gloss. A quiet knock on the bathroom door tells me Mack is back.

"I'll be right out," I whisper before glossing my lips and closing my purse.

"You better have a good appetite, this basket is full. Grab a blanket from on top the closet. We'll need something to sit on," he directs.

"There are two. Does it matter which one I bring?"

"Bring both in case you feel cold."

"Why do I get the feeling this isn't your first middle-of-the-night picnic?" I ask, once the blankets are in hand and I am closing the patio door behind me.

Faking insult, he huffs, "Are you suggesting this is some well-executed seduction scene I do with every girl I take home from the Fish Fry?"

"Aha! I knew I wasn't the first!"

"Smart-ass! Keep it up and I'll pounce on you the way I pounce on all my Fish Fry conquests!" He turns on the flashlight he has in his hand and waits for me to catch up. We make our way side by side down to the beach. He points to a spot and I spread out one blanket, dropping the other. I kick off my sandals and sit. He sticks the flashlight into the sand, and sets the basket in between us on the blanket. I dig in my purse and call the cottage as Mack lays out the food. There is no answer.

"What did you bring?" I ask, tucking the phone away.

"Bottled water, red and white wine, some cheese, bread and crackers, potato chips, left over fruit salad from lunch, and some cold cuts."

"Sounds good, I'll start with chips and some water."

"Ugh! I was hoping you'd be a wine and cheese gal."

"There's always dessert," I joke.

I help myself to the food. Music from his house drifts out, filling the gap in our conversation. I sip the water and then, to be sociable, I let him pour me half a glass of white wine. Some women claim wine goes right to their head. It tends to hit me a little farther south. After only a few sips, I can feel little alcohol-induced licks of sensation spread from my belly. Mack glances at me often and with each look, I grow more heated.

I grope for a safe topic of conversation which will not increase the electrically-charged awareness arcing between us. "So are you going to tell me anything about yourself or are you going to deliberately remain mysterious?"

"Not much to tell. I'm from a small town in Texas. It's a farming community. My mom still lives there. Dad passed away quite a long time ago, when I was in high school."

"I'm sorry. How did he die?"

"He had an aneurysm. He was a banker. He went to work one day and didn't come home. Mom was left alone to raise five boys."

"How many?" I ask, incredulous.

"Five. Ethan and Aiden are inside," he points to the house. "They came down here to celebrate finishing college. Ethan, the baby, finished an education degree and Aiden finished law school. Then there's Samuel. I'm the second oldest. Max, the oldest, is a banker like Dad, back in Brenham."

"Wow! I admire your mother! I can't imagine how difficult it must have been to raise five boys alone."

He doesn't hide his fondness. "She's terrific. The best. She did a pretty good job too, if I say so myself." His pride is unmistakable. "We all head home for Thanksgiving and Christmas and they try to make it out here a few times a year. I never miss an opportunity to see my family, even those two lunatics inside." He offers me some cheese. I take a slice. "What about you? Do you have a close family?" He holds out the bowl of fruit. I take a few pieces. The watermelon is swollen with sweet juice.

"Sure but that's easy because there is only my daughter Rachel, Lexie and I. We lost our mom when we were young and we don't get along with our father. Enough. No more food." I ward off his attempt to pass me more fruit. He packs up, placing everything in the basket but the wine. He tops up our glasses.

"With the vital statistics out of the way, we can talk about the fun stuff."

"Like what?"

Settling himself back on the blanket beside me, he takes my hand. Examining it by touch, he traces each finger, then flips it over, tracing each line mapping my palm. He folds my hand in his. "Do you put out on first dates?"

I laugh. "This isn't a first date."

"I'm asking for future reference." He reclines. "Let's look at the stars. I make a great pillow," he says, patting his stomach.

Feeling brave, I rest my head on him. "I still don't know what you do."

"I'm not trying to be secretive. There is not much to tell. Not anymore. I used to be in real estate development and construction. It was a family business." As he speaks, his stomach lifts and falls.

I smile in response to the movements. "Was?"

"Hmm. Max and I were attending college and Sam was going to join us. Mom was complaining our dorm costs were more than her mortgage. I got the idea to renovate an old house for us to live in instead of renting an apartment or paying dorm fees. I found an inexpensive house that needed work. Mom took out a mortgage and Sam, Max, and I did all the work. When it was completed, we sold it for a very nice profit. We were hooked. Max, with his business degree, was in charge of the finances. Sam became a journeyman carpenter. I had a degree in construction management. Mom was a silent partner. Together we created Mackenzie Construction and began building houses and then apartment complexes from the ground up. Before long, we had several employees and we pursued large scale developments. We were very successful. Our biggest project was our final one. It was a huge development of new homes just outside of Los Angeles. It took us three years to lay the groundwork. In a little over a year, we put up 50 houses."

"50 houses in Los Angeles? You were very successful."

"Yeah but it came at a price. For ten years it was all I did. After the big development, needing a break, I booked a trip to Eleuthera. One month passed and then another. After three months, I bought a house here and fixed it up on my own. Sam and Max wanted to move on to another project. Instead, I bought another house, here, to work on. Finally I realized not only did I not want to go back but I wanted out completely."

"That must have been hard on the family closeness," I speculate.

"You'd think so but there weren't any hard feelings and now we're all very relieved. We sold everything and split it up. It was just in time, before the housing bubble burst in the States. We would have lost everything we built and maybe more. Financially I am okay but career wise, all I know is building construction. I want to go back to it eventually, but never at that scale again. Now there is no great demand for my particular talents back home. I am left trying to decide what to do with the rest of my life. Have you ever heard the saying… idle hands are the devil's tools?" His supposedly idle hands have in fact been very busy removing all the pins and clips holding my hair in place. Now he is smoothing the free tresses across his stomach. "What? No snappy comeback?"

The pounding rock music emanating from Mack's house has switched to slow sultry songs. I want to groan in frustration as everything; the darkness, the ocean, the wine, and the music, all seem to be leading me in the direction of sex. I rise from the blanket. As he stands in front of me, I can't think of a damn thing to say. I'm silent for a long time. He waits.

"No. I'm not sure what to say and I sure don't have the slightest clue what to do with you," I eventually blurt out.

He throws back his head, laughing. "Is that what's got you bothered, darlin'? I have plenty of ideas. You just figure out if you want me and I'll handle the rest." He steps closer and for a second I am sure this is it, he's going to kiss me. Towering over me, the light is to his back. His face is just shadow but mine is lit up for him to see. "God, you blush prettily." His hands sandwich mine.

"You have that effect on me," I answer. I drop my eyes and look at the ground. Our feet point towards each other, denting the sand. I am incredibly aware of his height and his broad muscular frame. Every inch of him radiates an encouraging heat. He makes me feel small, delicate, and in need of warmth.

There is no teasing in his tone when he asks, "Is that the only effect I have on you?"

I nod "no" and my body responds. My hand begins to tremble in his.

"Are you cold?"

"No," I whisper.

"Scared?" His hand cups my chin and tilts my face up to his. The light is to his back. I can't see his expression but he can see mine. If he's looking for a refusal, he won't find it. His mouth lowers. I lift mine.

I expect his kiss to be as direct and confident as his conversation. Instead, his lips whisper delicately over mine, tasting me lightly. His sweet, sexy kiss starts a gentle answering ache within me. In my sheltered little world back home, men like Mack don't cross my path and kiss me senseless. Maybe if they did, I would have built some resistance, but I have none. Before this kiss is even over, I already want the next.

Chapter 12

"I will walk you back if … when you are ready?"

It is not the question I am expecting. With his mouth inches from mine, his hands on my face, I believe he is really asking me if I want to stay.

"I don't want to go. Not yet."

His hands fall to my waist, tugging me closer. I raise myself up on my toes. Again he kisses me, with a mouth that is firm and only slightly open. Tantalizing and teasing, his mouth barely brushes, barely tastes me. I exhale frustration. I'm feeling too much or maybe not enough. Both possibilities seem true. He finally deepens the kiss, gently tearing me open with his mouth. I lean into him; my legs are incapable of supporting my weight. I am limp, wasted.

I told my sister I didn't need or want sex, but tonight, with this man, I can visualize the possibility. Behind me, in the darkness, I can hear the waves moving. They move closer and pull away, not unlike what I have been doing with Mack all night. I am rolling back and forth between what I should do and what I want to do.

Sometimes I'm just sick and tired of being responsible. For years my sexual side has been on hold but it doesn't want to remain that way.

Why should it? There are condoms in my purse. Who is ever going to know? I think before I am carried away by another slow, drugging kiss. He is not immune. I feel the hard ridge of him, growing and pressing against my belly. His arousal increases my hunger for him. My fingers tighten in his hair; I open my mouth and find his tongue with my own. I press myself into the full hardness behind the denim fly of his jeans. He needs to know the way I want this to go.

"In a hurry, babe? I'll catch up," he drawls against my open mouth. With a suddenness that expels all the air from my lungs, he crushes me against him. His tongue plunges and retreats, darting in and out, teasing and taunting. His teeth bite, the stubble on his jaw scratches, his hot tongue soothes. These stronger, more forceful kisses match my body's need. His hands cup my breasts; his thumbs brush across my nipples. *Ah!* His mouth finds my throat and I almost crawl up his body with the pleasure of it.

His mouth continues to make me mindless. He kisses me as if it is his favorite pastime, as if he could do it forever, as if it isn't just a prelude to a fuck. My throat, ears and collarbone all receive attention before he buries his face into my cleavage, nipping the tender skin. He lowers our bodies to the blanket-covered sand, and settles himself between my thighs. There is sweet friction where our bodies meet. My fingers dig into his shoulders. He shifts, bearing all his weight on one arm to push my blouse further off my shoulders, off my arms. He flicks open the front clasp of my bra. I tug his t-shirt from the waistband of his jeans. My fingertips tickle and stroke his smooth skin. Firm muscle ripples against my splayed fingers.

"We can go up to the house."

I shake my head. If we stop now I will have second thoughts. "No, here. Now."

He sits back, and resting on his heels, pulls his shirt over his head, and tosses it off to the side. Then he steals the words from my thoughts. "You are beautiful," he whispers, his voice a smoky whisper. I sit up and reach for the front enclosure of his jeans. Impatiently he pushes my hands away and heads straight for my breasts. The air has sensitized my nipples. His tongue and teeth are overkill. "I don't have anything here to protect you," he whispers against my skin.

"My purse," I say, pointing to where I left it. "Lexie put condoms in my purse."

"I'll thank her later." He leans over, plucks it up and drops it on my stomach. The strip of foil packets is in my hand when he stretches out beside me, minus his jeans. "I don't know what is turning me on more, this beautiful mane of hair," he reaches out and covers my breast with a lock of my own hair, "your perfect breasts, or the way I can feel you looking at me, nervous and hungry."

I ignore the rush of pleasure his compliment sparks. I don't want his compliments. I don't want to think this could be more than a fast, dark joining. *There is nothing beyond this moment. This is simply sex. There is nothing special about the way he has brought my body alive, the intensity of my response is a result of extended celibacy,* I mentally reassure myself.

I am grateful for the darkness. Up until this point, I can say I have been carried away by the moment, by booze, by him. But I am lucid, and he is waiting. There is nothing like a rock hard penis pressing against your hip, and a condom in your hand to make you realize you are truly about to have sex. I am overly aware of the rushing and pounding in my ears. His hand reaches under my skirt, tracing the lacy edges of my panties, running his fingers over my waist. I lift his hand to my breast; I don't want him feeling the stretch marks, the soft bulge of my stomach. I cringe inwardly as his hand stubbornly returns. He traces a stretch mark with a fingertip.

"Pregnancy scars a body," I whisper self-consciously.

"You feel like a woman to me," he says. "Are you okay?"

I nod. "I'm nervous. I feel like an idiot, coming on to you so hard. I don't do this. I haven't done this in a long time, but I don't want to stop." I force the words past the block of fear in my throat.

"Are you sure?" he whispers the question huskily.

"Yes," I answer, knowing the instant his lips hit mine I will stop thinking. I am right. He kisses me again and all I feel is drugging, languid desire. I am hot, and achy and empty. His hands stroke my thighs, creeping closer to their apex. Reflexively, I close them. I feel him smile against my mouth.

"I'm not going to just jump you."

He pets me delicately as if he has all the time in the world. I don't and so I let my thighs fall apart for him. He doesn't take my open thighs as a direct invitation. Instead he kisses my throat, working his way down across my body. His lips and tongue are everywhere. His teeth nibble at tender areas until I am panting and writhing beneath him, wanting him inside me. I find his hot, hard length. I stroke him expertly. I want to shatter the control which prevents him from moving between my thighs. He groans in response. We both struggle to control our breathing.

"You keep it up a second longer and I'll be done. Help me put this on." He takes a condom from my hand, opens the foil packet and hands it to me. I slide it on. He moves. He slips into me. I feel full.

My body knows this dance. I've done it in the back seat of a car, between crisp white sheets, and on the floor of a bathroom with cold tiles pressing up into my back. But I have never danced under a starlit sky with the wind on my skin. I've never done this dance with Mack. I'm surprised by the fierce pleasure coiling within me. I'm overcome by his ragged breaths, his husky praises. His breaths are deep and fast in my ear, telling me he is close. This beautiful stranger won't let go until I do. I don't expect to unravel but I do. I come apart in his arms. Only then, does he collapse on top of me, burying his face in my throat.

Pleasure recedes and sanity returns. I am buried under the pleasing weight of him.

"I must be getting heavy for you?"

I shake my head, not because he isn't heavy but because I have gone from a state of pure thoughtlessness to a vortex of whirling thoughts and emotions. I don't want to face what has happened. My head is twisting with too many questions.

What happens next? Will there be an awkward struggle back into our clothing, and an even more awkward goodbye? Do I kiss him? Shaking hands seems absurd while he is still nestled between my thighs, and my hands are still gripping his shoulders. He shifts suddenly, lifting off of me.

Kissing my cheek, he whispers, "Let's head to my bedroom." He is wearing a satisfied smile. "The wind is dying down. The bugs are coming out. My ass just got bit." The last sentence makes me grin. It's not awkward. He is the same Mack after the sex as he was before. He tugs his jeans up and sits up, fastening the fly. "Wait. Hold that thought. The sun is rising." He motions with his chin. Black has faded to grey, a slash of red breaks through the clouds, lighting the water. He returns, lying next to me. The second blanket covers our bodies. He pillows my head with his arm and rests his chin on my shoulder. We watch the sun rising together.

I swallow the dry lump in my throat, trying to concentrate on the sea of colors exploding before us and not this sweet intimacy. It's a beautiful sunrise but it is his tender touch which tugs at my insides. His fingers lazily stroke my hip. His soft kisses on my bare shoulders move my heart and stall my body. I'm stuck to this blanket in the sand when I should be moving on, even if only in my thoughts; but I am in the moment, fully with him. He satisfied my body and now my heart has been touched. I wanted it unaffected.

When the last of the pink sky is gone, Mack says, "Let's go up to my house. The bugs have not been fooled by this blanket. They know we are under here and are planning an attack." He nudges me up. "C'mon lazy bones. Wrap the blanket round you. I'll get the basket, and the rest."

It takes a second to wiggle my bra back into place. I slide on my blouse, smooth down my skirt, and slide on my panties before standing. I flap the blanket, shaking the sand out of it. Mack doesn't put his shirt back on; he tucks a chunk of it into a back pocket, passes me our shoes, loads his hands and leads the way up to the house and into his bedroom.

"I'll use the bathroom first if you don't mind. I've got a little something to dispose of," he says, without looking my way. I blush. He disappears and everything is silent for a moment. I hear the shower start. He hasn't closed the door. "You can join me if you like."

Showering is too intimate an activity. I wait for him to emerge. He is out quickly. A towel hugs his waist, another he rubs over his hair.

"It's all yours."

I slide past him into the bathroom, shutting and locking the door behind me. My hair is disheveled, my lips are swollen. Sand has worked its way into places it has no business being. I shower quickly but not fast enough to stop myself from thinking too much. *Am I leaving? Should I leave? Do I put my clothes back on?* I dress and walk out of the bathroom. There is no mistaking the look in Mack's eyes. In the darkness, his eyes were hidden, his face shadowed, but it's morning and I can see he wants me. My mouth goes dry and I stop in almost mid-step, caught like a deer in the headlights of a car. He lifts his hand out to me.

"I should probably get going. Lexie might be worried," I say lamely, casting my eyes around.

"Darlin', you're not going anywhere." His drawl is more pronounced and it sends a shiver through me. He gives me a boyish smile. My reservations melt. I can't go when he makes me feel wanted with just a look and a line. I like that someone as sexy as him wants me. I like the notch of him in my belt. Shyly, I take the few steps which separate me from him. He lifts the sheet in invitation.

"When you smile, I stop thinking," I admit. My thighs hit the edge of the mattress.

"If you were thinking of leaving, that's a good thing. Come here, babe."

The room is too bright for my comfort. I walk to the window and close the blinds. Once the room is nearly dark, I undress and slide next to him. The semi-darkness is no protection. What happened on the beach was a flash flood of need and passion, but this time he takes my mouth and body with slow deliberation. Watching the sunset together was intimate; it is nothing compare to what happens next. Mack studies every wave of pleasure crossing my face. He drinks every moan and gasp from my lips. He whispers encouragement and tells me again that I am beautiful. Afterwards, he wraps himself around me. One of his hands cups my breast possessively and the other strokes my hair.

"I'm glad you decided to stay," he says simply, before drifting off to sleep.

I have never been more awake in my life. Every twitch he makes might as well be happening to my own body. After several long minutes, he turns over onto his back. I turn with him. My hand reaches up to stroke his abrasive chin and to caress his chest. *God damn this man! How I have lived so long and not been loved so well?* How is it a stranger could take me on a beach with such intuition and insight, I am left vulnerable and stripped of all defenses? Not once did my ex-husband ever make me feel this way. Mack is dangerous. Obsession and adoration; for the first time, I understand what these words mean. It's time to go. I creep to the bathroom and dress.

As I begin the walk back to Lexie's cottage, my eyes are pulled to the spot where we made love. The sand holds the dent of our bodies, physical proof of the night which passed. Residual excitement courses through me then I am hit by the first impact of guilt. He asked me to stay. Leaving does not feel right but neither did lying in his bed, waiting for him to wake. As hard as leaving was, I had to go before I left pieces of myself behind in a stranger's bed. It makes no sense to attach meaning to any moment I shared with Mack. I need to be as cold blooded as my sister. Hopefully, somewhere in our shared genetics, I also have her capacity for detachment. Someday, I hope to look back on last night as a sweet memory of sex on a beach, but this morning, I can't find a frame that fits. I can't label what I shared with Mack. I will not examine how he made me feel.

Chapter 13

A hangover is a hell of a way to start a day.

My body is damp from a shower, my mouth has been dried by a piece of unbuttered toast, and my face hovers over a steaming cup of coffee. I consider taking a sip but I'm not sure if it will stay down. All efforts to restore my body to something closer to normal have failed, causing me to suspect I am struggling with morning-after regret and not a hangover. I shouldn't have slept with Mack and I definitely shouldn't have compounded the mistake by sneaking out of his bed like some guilt-ridden wraith.

I consider going back.

Maybe he is still sleeping. Yeah, after six hours? Doubtful.

How can I possibly salvage the rest of this trip? I can't imagine leaving the cottage and risking the embarrassment of seeing Mack around. Maybe he wouldn't care? I want to crawl back into bed, bury deep beneath the covers, and sleep it all away. When I wake up, I want it to be time to fly home. From the nearby bedroom, I hear my sister stir.

Great, now I have to deal with the Spanish Inquisition.

Wearing only a T-shirt and panties, Lexie emerges from the bedroom, her hair a mess of black curls, her eyes sleepy. She stretches and her t-shirt pulls tight across her breasts and lifts to reveal her little red thong. My sister yawns and scratches one perfect buttock before making her way to the coffeepot. She refills my cup, pours herself one, and sits down opposite of me.

"You're up pretty early, for having crawled in at dawn."

"It was nice of you to lock the door."

"Oh! That was an accident. I came back as soon as I thought of it."

"You're full of shit. You set me up.

"Well…?"

"What?" I evade her question, blank faced. I am not ready to share. It is too fresh, too raw.

"What happened? Did you sleep with him?"

"We aren't teenagers any longer, Lexie. I haven't swapped sex stories with you since we lost our virginities." My index finger draws a brown wet circle, on the table with a dot of spilled coffee.

Lexie continues probing. "You admit there is a sex story to be told?"

I rest my forehead on my hand. I shoot her a warning look but I am sure the tinge of embarrassment coloring my cheeks robs my glare of any serious warning.

"Oh c'mon, Sky. I'm not going to ask for stupid details like his length and circumference. I just want to know if you fucked him and if you are going to see him again? It went okay. He didn't hurt you or anything…?"

"No, Lexie." I push my hair back out of my face. "We had sex. I had fun." I recite the words as if I'm reading a grocery list. The silence is uncomfortable. I rise and put my coffee cup in the sink, thinking I've shared enough information.

"You finally have sex and 'I had fun' is the best you can do?"

"I'd rather discuss length and circumference." I turn the faucet on, adjust the water temperature and add soap. I scrub the dishes fiercely. They need little more than a rinse.

"I'll take what I can get."

"It was no big deal. I certainly don't want to see him again." The cowardly lie falls easily from my lips. My gaze out the kitchen window is unseeing until I realize I am staring in the direction of Mack's house. Does he know I am gone? Does he care?

"That bad?"

"No, but it's not something I want to repeat. I had a little fun. Now it's over."

"You sound like me." Lexie grabs a tea towel from a drawer and wipes the dishes.

"Maybe I am more like you than we thought." I want this to be the truth but we both know it's not. "Where'd you leave Cal?"

"Here. He is taking me out for breakfast. You want to come?"

"I had toast. Breakfast the next morning, huh? Sounds serious?" I tease lightly.

She pins me with a look. "You expect me to answer your questions when you won't answer mine?"

"I answered your questions, Lexie."

"You think I don't see this is bothering you? I don't like being shut out."

I almost choke on a laugh of incredulity. "You're kidding me, right? Join the club. When have you ever really let me in? How about this, Lex? When you share, I'll share."

She throws a dismissive hand in my face. "Fine. Sit and stew in your foul mood. I'm taking off. Maybe a little solitude will improve your disposition."

I don't try to stop her. I retreat to my room and listen to the sound of her and Calvin leaving. They take his vehicle. Once they are gone, I dress. I am fearful Mack might show up. I'll have to go somewhere else. The jeep is still in the garage. I fill it with my easel, painting supplies, and a cooler. After a few tries down roads which go nowhere or become impassable, I find a deserted beach with crashing waves. I unload my easel and spend what is left of the afternoon painting. I stop only to drink water, reapply sunscreen, spray on bug repellant, or eat from the cooler. Too soon, the light falls and I must pack up.

I'm relieved to find the cottage empty when I return. I call Rachel and fall asleep. In the morning, I find a note on the kitchen table. Lexie has come and gone. I am free to lose a second day in painting.

* * *

By Monday morning, the sick, guilty feeling in my stomach is overshadowed by nerves. The prospect of showing Michael and Tracina a completed work is exciting. The little seascape is finished and it will accompany me to the gallery today. Given more time, I could produce better, but I think it is a fair representation of my skills. Lexie is in her bed when I remind her of our planned outing.

"Yeah, I'm coming but you are going to have to drive. I am exhausted, not enough sleep last night." She throws the covers off her body and stretches lazily.

Lexie sleeps for the entire drive, including a stop at the bakery for muffins and coffee. When we reach the gallery, I give her a little shake. She accepts the coffee I offer and guzzles it greedily from the jeep to the gallery. Tracina greets us, wearing a loose, flowing blouse, khaki Capri pants, and brown leather sandals. Her hair is held back from her freshly washed face with a white hair band.

"Skylar, you came." She enfolds me in a welcoming hug then empties my hands of the coffee and muffins. I introduce the two women.

"Welcome, Alexandra. I am so glad Skylar brought you. We heard about the new doctor on the island." Tracina squeezes both of Lexie's hands in greeting. "Skylar, why don't you hunt Michael down while your sister and I get to know each other? We'll take a little tour. He's in the studio. Do you paint, Alexandra?"

"Nope. I have never been creative, other than in bed, of course."

I growl a warning at her, but she ignores me. She sees no reason to humor me. The tension between us is still present.

"We can't all be painters." I hear Tracina laugh.

Michael doesn't look up when I stick my head in the door of the studio. He waves me in, and continues to paint. I plunk down on a chair to watch him work. Loading a brush, he delicately dabs at the painting in front of him, carefully creating a dimple in the cheek of a child. I get a vision of Mack's smile, his deep dimples.

"Did you bring me a painting?" Michael barks, startling me up on to my feet.

"Actually I did. It's a small piece. I'm not sure how good it is, but it's done." Insecurity creeps into my voice. "It's in the car."

He begins cleaning his brush. "Go get it. I'll meet you inside."

I retrieve the small painting, ignoring my desire to give it a final look over. My palms are sweating and slide ineffectually on the door knob until I tighten my grip. This moment is huge. I've never seriously considered doing anything with my art but Michael and Tracina have sparked a hope that I am terrified they will now extinguish.

Michael takes the canvas and holds it up. Tracina looks over his shoulder. I feel the urge to vomit. My face must reflect this feeling because Lexie is there, with a comforting arm. Her support makes me feel worse. I owe her a swift apology at the first opportunity for the recent rupture between us. Michael and Tracina continue with their perusal, faces unreadable. The silence grows my insecurity.

"Um…I think I can do better. I am sure I can do better. I'm rusty and my technique is too simple and basic, amateurish... with dedication, I will improve."

"Skylar, love, shut up. You really are a distraction." Michael puts up a hand. I am forced to wait several more agonizing seconds before he finally says, "I would be more than happy to display and sell this little piece of work for you, Skylar."

Relief cuts through my anxious anguish. "Really? You like it?"

"It's rough and raw, simple and basic, but that is part of its charm." Tracina nods in agreement. "I'm not going tell you this is the greatest masterpiece I've seen, but I will say it is a very good painting. The way you handle the light is inconsistent, and some of your strokes could use more fullness, more depth, but I do really like it. I wish we had more paintings of this caliber."

Michael nods. "Not everyone in this world can take what they see and translate it into something recognizable on canvas with realism. You have ability. You also have a unique way of using your brush and color. If you develop your skills and work hard, I think you have a chance at making an income, especially with the right connections." Michael points to himself and Tracina. Lexie hugs me. I close my eyes and expel a breath of relief. "Don't go quitting your day job, lass, but I guarantee I can sell this piece. After some instruction from us, you'll be even better. I'll set it up in the studio to finish drying. In a few weeks, it will be varnished, framed and I'll find a place to hang it." His eyes twinkle when I hug him. He gives my shoulder a paternal pat.

"Skylar, we should get painting while the light is good. Are you going to join us, Alexandra?" Tracina asks.

"Lass, you just stay here with me and forget about going off with those two. I'll find something interesting for us to do." Michael's brows wiggle suggestively.

"Hmm, an offer I can't refuse."

"I think leaving these two alone is just asking for trouble," Tracina predicts. "But I want to paint too much to be stuck babysitting."

"Run along, ladies. So, Michael, what you got to drink around here? Every Scotsman I have ever met has a supply of well-aged honey. I need a cure. You know, hair of the dog that bit me last night." Lexie rubs her hands together.

"I have just the thing to fix that problem of yours. It'll put hair on your chest and fire in your belly. I don't suppose you know any card games, gin rummy, cribbage, or poker by chance?"

I am incredulous. "It's morning. You're not going to start drinking already?"

"I thought you were leaving," Lexie says, shooing me away.

I grab my painting supplies from Lexie's jeep and meet Tracina in the studio a few minutes later. She gathers what she needs. "Let's paint on the beach. Not too far. Any piece of beach is as good as another," she says.

We set up our easels side by side and then examine each other's paints, brushes, and canvases. Tracina is a vault of information. I wish I had thought to bring a pen and paper. I pay attention and try to soak up every word. Her explanations come in short spurts. I watch and listen before picking up my brush. Tracina encourages input and is heavy handed with praise. My confidence grows. Lexie arrives a couple hours later with sandwiches but she does not stay. After eating, Tracina and I retreat into our separate canvases.

"We're losing the light," I say, a long while later. The air is getting moist; my back is stiffening from my upright posture. "I'm done for the day. Thank you, Tracina. I owe you too much already but I have to ask if I can come back again before I leave?"

"You're welcome. And thanks for allowing me to teach you. I have to say I enjoyed it and I'll be upset if you don't come back."

"Tomorrow?" I suggest hopefully.

She laughs and throws her arms around my shoulders. "I'll be waiting. Let's pack up this stuff and see what those two rascals made for dinner. We are having another friend drop by. It'll be a dinner party. Lachlan is like an adopted son. He'll be delighted to meet two beautiful visitors."

We join Michael and Lexie in the kitchen. A rich beefy aroma makes my mouth water.

"What is that?" I ask, inhaling deeply.

Lexie answers. "Authentic Scottish stew and dumplings."

"Which means they dumped a bunch of whiskey into it," Tracina informs me. "Is Lachlan here?"

Michael checks the clock on the wall as he ladles out a plate of stew. "No, he's a bit late. We'll start. He'll be here soon enough."

"I made the dumplings," Lexie announces.

"And I performed open heart surgery on the beach today. You've never been able to follow even the simplest of recipes. You burn water." I take a heaping plate of stew from Michael and join Lexie at the table.

"Michael showed me. C'mon. Try a bite."

I eye the dumplings on my plate suspiciously. "You go first."

"The dumplings are perfect. Your sister is a fast learner. I taught her a thing or two today."

"Yeah, how to make Scottish stew and how to cheat at cards," Lexie tattles.

"Michael! No one is ever going to play with you if you don't stop cheating!" Tracina admonishes.

"She's too smart to cheat. How about you, Skylar? Did my sweetheart teach you a thing or two today?" Michael asks, changing the subject.

"Yes! Tracina is a wonderful teacher," I say, before biting into a dumpling. It is fluffy and buttery. "Okay, these are the best dumplings I have ever eaten," I concede.

"Did you hear that, my love? It's good to know we could always fall back on teaching painting and cooking if the gallery stops making money."

"If I had students as gifted and willing as Skylar, it would be a joy."

"You had more fun than me. I'm sure this one sharked me." Wagging a finger in Lexie's direction, he explains. "I trounced her several times at chess. She pouted after my final victory and insisted we switch to cards. I walloped her soundly at rummy and cribbage and then we played a bit of poker. Who loses poorly at all those other games then wins as soon as money is involved?"

"I was just lucky," Lexie says, feigning innocence.

"You cheated. I can't prove it, but I am sure of it."

"You're just being a sore loser," Tracina reprimands Michael. "We've already established you're the cheat at the table. Why do men always accuse women of dishonesty when we get the upper hand?"

Suddenly a familiar male voice joins in from behind me, capturing everyone's attention. "Because, Tracina, unlike you, most women are liars."

All heads turn towards the newcomer, including my own, even though I don't need confirmation that the voice belongs to Mack. Every word finds and hits its mark. Blood rushes in a raging river to my head, pounding in my ears, reddening my face. I flinch physically as his gaze sweeps past me. There is no recognition, no trace of warmth.

"I don't know if I would go that far, Mack, my friend," Michael says. "Someone shit in your cornflakes this morning? Pull up a chair, fill a plate, and help me put these women in their place. Nicely though, old man. No need to offend."

"It would be impossible to offend these two. They can chew a man up, spit him out and not miss a step. Wouldn't you agree, Skylar, Lexie?"

Lexie's mouth opens to blast him. An elbow to her ribs stops her. Tracina's glance sweeps with puzzlement back and forth between us.

"I'm sorry I am late. I should have called. I didn't realize you already had company. I'll leave you to your visit." Mack inclines his head slightly in Tracina's direction.

Michael continues on, unaware of the charged atmosphere. "You know better. There's plenty of food and lots of wonderful company."

"I'm definitely going to pass." Mack snorts scornfully.

"Lachlan, behave yourself. Whatever has gotten into you?" Tracina says, reprimanding him.

"Tracina said she was expecting someone named Lachlan. If I had known it was going to be you, I would have left. You were invited; we've overstayed our visit. " I slide my chair back and tug my sister up. Tracina stops me with a gentle hand. I give her a small negative shake of my head and squeeze her hand before removing it from my arm.

"Why does anyone have to go? Are you all nuts?" Michael demands.

"Never mind, Michael," Tracina snaps.

"Why are you yelling at me? What the hell has got everyone in a dither?"

I can feel tears at the edge of my eyes. My head drops down; my voice is husky as I speak. “I had a wonderful time today. Tracina, Michael, I’m sorry to leave so suddenly but I’ll call you later.” It is cowardly to leave without explanation but I wouldn’t know where to begin. “I really am sorry.”

Bravely, I look to the amber and green eyes I have been avoiding. I want Mack to know he is included in the apology. He looks through me as if I am not there.

Chapter 14

"Now that was a bloody awkward situation!" Lexie says when we reach the jeep. "I'll drive and you can explain just what the hell went on back there! I thought things ended on good terms with you two?"

I climb in the passenger's side, find the keys in my purse and start the engine for her. Lexie slides behind the wheel and shifts into reverse. My fingers are trembling. I may have put the scene behind me literally, but my body hasn't quite recovered.

"I never said that. Fuck! I made a mess out of things." I hang my head. "I panicked and behaved like an idiot."

"Whoa, slow down and start at the beginning."

"From the moment I saw him, Lexie, I was attracted to him. Honestly, I never expected to end up sleeping with him! But I did. Afterwards, he was very sweet. He asked me to stay. I waited until he fell asleep and I hightailed it out of there. I thought I could handle casual but I couldn't."

Lexie's frustrated groan is punctuated by her palm connecting with her forehead. "You were in good hands. Mack doesn't do casual either."

"How would you know?"

"He left with you and not me. Don't glare at me. Listen, we are equally attractive, but I advertise that I am an obvious, no-strings-attached, sex partner. He went for you rather than the potentially easier lay. He isn't interested in casual sex. A guy like him can get that at the drop of a hat. If he asked you to stay, it was because he really wanted to spend more time with you. So go over later tonight and apologize. Fix things."

"I don't want to fix anything with Mack."

"Skylar, you were not built to be alone. You think you are but you are not. I am a selfish animal but even I need people occasionally. I need a warm body in my bed, reminding me that I am a woman and that I am alive. Feeling passion and desire is fun, it's intoxicating." Lexie tosses her head back and lets out a throaty scream of triumph.

"No, it's not. I've felt sick to my stomach since Saturday morning."

"That's just nerves. Feeling something, Sky, is what life is all about. It's what we wake up for, what we work for. You can't tell me in the time that Rand has been gone, that you haven't fantasized about someone coming into your life, blowing your panties off your body, and rocking your world?" She howls again. I shake my head at her antics. "It doesn't make sense to just shut up a part of you and pretend it doesn't exist!"

"Yes it does, Lexie. It is all part of the parent-child contract. Rachel comes first."

"Don't tell me you are still on that 'not dating' kick?"

"Scoff all you want. It's best for Rachel. I don't expect you to understand but I made that resolution with a clear head, and a great deal of common sense."

"Plenty of single parents date."

"This one doesn't. If it was five or six years from now and she was off to college, it would be a different story. I never would have left his bed."

"You've done four years hard time with no touch, no sex, and no connection. Are you really willing to give up another five years at a minimum? That's a bloody long sentence."

"I have Rachel. She is enough."

"Is she, really?"

It's obvious she doesn't believe me; and after Friday night, I don't believe me.

"Well, I give up trying to make sense of the senseless. I wanted you to step outside of that boxy, little life you hide in. You want to go back to it; you can. I don't know about you but my stomach is growling. It's a freaking shame to have missed out on the stew and dumplings. Let's stop and grab a bite to eat."

After a quick dinner in Governor's Harbor, we spend the evening hanging out at the cottage. I call Rachel. Lexie and I watch TV. Before heading to bed, I call the gallery and speak to Tracina. I apologize and ask if our plans to paint are still on for the morning. I wonder if Mack is still there and what, if anything, he has said. She promises to meet me bright and early in the studio. She isn't angry, just terribly curious.

The next morning, I leave to paint. Lexie is expecting Nancy to drop by and chooses to stay behind. While Michael minds the gallery, Tracina and I work side by side. I've been trying to figure out just how much to reveal, and she has been shooting me one expectant look after another. Eventually, I give up on the very unproductive session to sit on the sand, wrapping my knees with my arms.

"Do you mind if I talk while you paint?"

She stops. "It's about time.' She places her brush in a plastic wrapper and joins me on the sand.

"I'm sorry about last night. What all did Mack tell you?"

"Not much. He just made some cryptic remark to be wary of you."

I drop my forehead to my knees. I keep my head there but turn it slightly to meet her eyes. "I've given him good reason to feel that way. I know we don't know each other very well, but I think of you as a friend. What I am going to tell you might impact whatever good opinion you've formed of me," I begin.

She reaches out and gives my hand a reassuring squeeze. "Skylar, you don't owe me any explanations, but I do hope you feel that you can confide in me?"

"I had sex Friday night with Mack."

Tracina's green eyes widen in surprise. "Oh. That is a news flash."

"I handled it all wrong, I am afraid. He expressed an interest in seeing me again, and I made it clear I was just interested in the sex, after the sex."

"Ouch!"

"Yeah, it wasn't one of my finer moments. It's been years since I've been with anyone and I let myself get carried away. Afterward, well… there is no point in starting something with a man who lives thousands of miles away. More importantly, I made a choice to avoid any romantic entanglements while my daughter is growing up."

"And you never explained any of this to Lachlan?"

"No."

"I can't divulge any confidences but he really is the wrong guy for a fling."

I nod, chastised. "It never really came up. He did tell me that his first impression of me was that I was looking for a good time. I denied it but I guess his original assessment of me was right. It seems calculating. That's not who I am, even if it is how I behaved."

"If you know the truth, does it matter what he thinks?"

"I shouldn't care but I do. He is going to be very hard to forget."

* * *

My painting time with Tracina ends before the sun reaches its zenith because it becomes too hot to sit unexposed under the sun. I return to an empty cottage. A scribbled note informs me Lexie is with Calvin. She will be gone until the next morning. I spend the afternoon playing solitaire with a deck of cards, listening to music, and avoiding the beach. After barbecuing a steak and throwing together a salad, I sit and eat in front of the TV for company.

The sun drops below the horizon and still the night is uncomfortably warm. The air is heavy with humidity and I am driven outside to the swimming pool. A bikini and an ice cold beer are my battle weapons against the heat but neither is having an impact against the sticky moist evening air. I dangle my feet over the edge of the pool. The water is as warm as the air. Every inch of my skin not covered by the bathing suit, glistens with sweat. Now and then a breeze teases me with an insincere promise of relief as I wait for the temperature to drop.

I've always had a gift for repression but it fails me tonight. I am alone with my thoughts and all my thoughts are of Mack. This night is so similar to the night we met, it is impossible not to think of him. The smell and the taste of the air are identical. Waves crash nearby on the very same beach where we made love. In my memory, he is whispering in my ear and caressing my skin. His hot mouth is on my body. My insides tighten. I had forgotten how sex starts out making you feel so empty, hollow and aching, and then so full, swollen and satiated. Before that night on the beach, Rand had been my only lover, and sex with him usually left me feeling vaguely hollow. I finally understand what all the hoopla is about. All orgasms are not created equal. When there is a strong attraction, sex is intoxicating and potently addictive.

Unfortunately, my memories of that night are all tied up with shame. It would be nice if I could dust my shame off, dive into the water, and emerge clear of regret. Taking a long pull from my beer bottle, I damn myself for the night of uncharacteristic impulsivity. I've never been much of a risk taker and that is probably why I fell into bed so easily with Mack. My life is boring, so predictable I couldn't help but leap at the first bit of stimulation that came my way. Someday, when Rachel is gone, I will look for someone who makes me feel what Mack did. I can't have that kind of passion in my life now but there are other kinds of passion.

I need to make my own fun, to find my own pleasure. My sister is right. I need to start living outside of my boxy little world. I refuse to spend one more second moping. It's time to stop wallowing and start swimming. I stand. Before I dive into the pool, a ridiculous thought enters my head. I scan the shrubs, the yard, and the ocean. Satisfied that I am alone, I release the closure on my bikini top. I push my bottoms down my hips. They land poolside as I jump in the water. Self-consciously, I break the surface. Nothing below my shoulders pops out of the water.

I have never skinny-dipped before. My heart is pounding as if a thousand eyes are on me. The urge to reach out and tug on my suit is huge. I want to clothe myself but I ignore the instinct. This is what I need, a little more courage, and a little more adventure. Nude swimming is not in the same league as sex on the beach with Mack but it is an activity free of emotional entanglements. It's a start. The risk is small. The only person who may find me here is my sister, and she wouldn't even raise an eyebrow. She'd probably strip and join me.

After a few tentative forays around the pool, I can swim without stopping to furtively look and listen. Eventually I relax further into a backstroke, presenting my breasts to the night. Once my anxiety dissipates, I find skinny-dipping delightful. Unconstrained by wet clothing, I enjoy the warm, slick water against my skin. I allow my body to rise up and float.

It's good for the mind and the body to feel the blood pounding through the veins now and then, I decide. Maybe I should try rock climbing? I've always wanted to take a yoga class-

Through water-filled ears, I hear the murmur of a voice. My eyes fly open and my feet drop to find the pool bottom. My hands cover my body.

I am not alone.

Chapter 15

"I said nice weather we're having!" Mack repeats blandly, his tone completely at odds with the situation. I flounder for the side of the pool, cowering against the wet tile.

"You scared the shit out of me!" I accuse him angrily. It's bad enough to be caught swimming naked, but to be caught by Mack makes it ten times worse. Why is it every time I take a risk on this island he is involved?

"It's a little late for modesty. Seriously, Skylar, why bother covering those beautiful breasts. I've seen them. Heck, I had them in my mouth." The words roll out of his mouth like thick honey, sweet and slow. I know better than to trust the sudden change. His smile is a smirk.

"Screw off, Mack, or should I say screw off, Lachlan?"

"Mack is short for Mackenzie, my last name. Tracina and my mother are the only two people in the world who call me by my given name."

"You might have mentioned that sooner."

"I think we both forgot to mention a few things."

"Maybe. Look, will you just leave? This isn't a free show."

He crosses his arms and stares me down, unfazed by my anger or shrill demand. "You're swimming naked, outside, where anyone passing by can see you. If that isn't a free show, then I don't know what is." He lifts his T-shirt up over his head and drops it to the poolside. My breath catches in my throat as his smooth bare chest and tight stomach are revealed. He reaches for the button fly enclosure on his jeans. "At the very least, it is a bloody invitation in neon lights." The first button falls open.

I press closer to the side of the pool. "You're not getting in here with me!"

His fingers work the second open. "That's exactly what I am doing."

"What the hell for? You are mad at me. You think I am scum, remember?"

His fingers stop. Any relief I might have felt is undone when he cruelly retorts, "I don't have to like you to fuck you, Skylar."

The sharp blunt words render me speechless with indignation, but when the third button falls open, I find my voice. "Mack, we had fun, and I am sorry I behaved badly.

Let's just leave it at that." I make a pathetic attempt for my bathing suit. He beats me to it, tossing it onto a nearby chair, hopelessly out of reach.

"We have unfinished business. Right now is the perfect time to sort it out because you aren't going anywhere without your suit, are you?"

"Mack, you've embarrassed me enough; just let me get out," I plead.

I see a flash of emotion pass across his face. It disappears too quickly to identify. "I've embarrassed you? I felt like an ass, waking up alone."

"I'm sorry. I'm sorry. I am sorry. I don't know how many times I have to say it, because I really do mean it. I mean it. Now please, just go." My words have had no effect. There isn't an ounce of pity in his eyes.

"Nah, I don't think so. What kind of gentleman would I be if I left you swimming by yourself? What if you slipped and fell? Come on out." He picks up my towel and holds it open. He seriously expects me to just walk out of the pool into that towel and back into his arms. I glare at him. He leans over, offering his hand.

Through gritted teeth, I demand, "Pass me my swimsuit."

"Fat chance, darlin'." He draws out the vowels longer than necessary, laying his accent on, real thick.

"Don't call me darling!"

"Sorry, babe." He grins and this time, the smile reaches his eyes. I'm trapped and he is enjoying every second of my vulnerability. "Stop being a prude and take my hand."

Enough is enough, I decide. I reach out for his offered hand, but instead of tugging myself up, I brace my feet against the side of the pool and I yank on him for all I am worth. His eyes widen in surprise as I viciously pull him forward. He tries to regain his balance, but his momentum and my weight are too much. He hits the water as I make for the edge. I am up and out of the pool in a flash. The towel is wrapped around my body by the time he has wiped the water from his face.

"I suppose I deserved that." He climbs out of the pool completely drenched. He lifts one soggy, sandal-covered foot, sets it back down, and gives me a rueful grin. It emits a squishy slurp. Pool water streams from his jeans. I should be running from his likely retaliation, but I am laughing so hard, I can't even walk. "You know for a little gal you sure are strong."

"You should have seen your face when I yanked on you!" I giggle. "Your sandals are leather. They're ruined. I hope they weren't favorites."

"Nah, I've only had them for a few days. Just breaking 'em in."

"Even worse. I'll pay for them."

"There's plenty more where they came from. I deserved to get dunked. I was being a pest. But you know, it's not every day you come across a pretty lady swimming in the altogether. I couldn't resist."

"Swimming in the 'altogether.' That must be a Texan description. I do love that accent of yours." Silence falls and tension builds. Our anger has dissipated, leaving us groping for what comes next.

He speaks first. "Sky, I am sorry for being such an ass tonight. Truce? I really do want to talk to you. You do owe me that." The shyly delivered apology is irresistible.

"Come on in. I'll get you a towel and we can throw your clothes in the dryer." He follows me into the cottage. I'd like to dress but good manners force me to grab him a towel from the bathroom first. He closes the patio door behind him and turns. Our eyes meet, and I can literally see the arrogance build in his. His fingers flip open the last copper fastener on his button fly denim jeans.

I throw the towel at him. "I thought we had declared a truce?"

He catches it and begins drying his wet chest. "We are negotiating terms. No treaty has been signed. You've seen me naked, what's the big deal?"

His coarseness fuels my own. I make a point of directly looking at his crotch and then looking away dismissively. "You are right. It's no big deal."

He crosses the room in long fast strides, leaving me nowhere to go but in reverse. The cool wall hits my back. His hot body collides with mine. From my breasts to my thighs, our bodies are compressed. The towel is poor protection from the heat of his skin.

"Now we both know that you are lying." He is cocky and assured.

"I've had bigger," I flip back hotly. My mind tries to cling to anger but my body is in collusion with him. It knows how good he can make it feel. My mouth goes dry.

"But the question is, have you had better?" He speaks the words almost against my lips, just a hair's breadth from touching them. Our eyes are locked. I can see the gold in the green of his irises. Arrogance is replaced by lust. "Have you ever come so fast or so easily, darlin'?" He drawls. "I saw the surprise in your eyes. I felt you tighten around me. The nail marks on my back still haven't healed."

I flatten against the wall, closing my eyes. It's a last ditch effort to keep him at bay. I want him again.

As if he knows what I am thinking, he whispers into my ear, "It looks like I arrived just in time. You need another good fuck." His words register and I want to slap him. I want to hit him hard enough to wipe the brazen, knowing look off his face. Bruised blue from the impact of his words, I struggle against him ineffectually. He has me pinned to the wall. I sob with acute frustration.

"Aw shit, Skylar!" He takes my crying mouth. "I'm sorry." He breathes the words into me. "I didn't think I would hurt you. I didn't think I could hurt you. I'm sorry."

Bewildered and defeated, I sag back against the wall. "What do you want from me?"

"I want you, Sky. I'm sorry. I just want you."

I don't respond to his kisses. I'm scared. He pushes apart the towel, baring my breasts. I will not let it fall away and cling to the inadequate barrier, which does not prevent his mouth finding my breasts. It can't keep his fingers from between my thighs. The strength leaves my knees; my anger is replaced by deep need. I pull his mouth to mine for a long, drugging kiss. My mouth is as greedy as his.

"Do you still have those condoms somewhere?" he asks. I nod weakly, raising a hand towards the bedroom. He scoops me up into his arms, carries me into the darkened room, and places me on the bed.

"My purse, it's on the floor, there." This time he doesn't pass it to me. He opens it and finds the foil packets himself. My leather purse hits the floor. He shoves his jeans down and off his hips, kicking them away. Our bodies are enmeshed; our hands are clasped. He moves within me. It happens again, the same crazy race to release. The tension builds within me, tightening my core until I am taut and straining. The hoarse groan in my ear tells me he is as far gone as me. I snap with pleasure, clutching and dragging him with me to release. Like the first time, I'm of two minds, wanting to hold him tighter, and needing to push him away. I am left immobile by the lingering hum of pleasure rippling through my body.

"It's time for a little honesty." His words slice through my contentment. He kisses my mouth lightly. I scurry under the blankets as he turns on the bedside lamp. He disappears to the bathroom before returning to the bed, settling under the covers beside me. "I didn't mean for us to end up in bed like this. I hoped we could talk first."

Defensively, I snap, "Well, I didn't plan it! This is the last thing I wanted."

"Take it easy." He grasps my hand and brings it to his lips. His hold is tight, his kiss delicate. "You have the same scared shitless look in your eyes that you had the other morning. This time we are going to hash things out." The demand is softened by a coaxing grin.

"Okay, fine." I join him on the pillow so that we are face to face.

"Why did you leave, Skylar?"

"It's complicated."

"If you'll explain, I'll listen."

I focus on our entwined hands, my small pale fingers in his large golden grasp. It's a safe place to look while I try to figure out what to say. "I don't do casual sex, Mack. I don't believe in disrespecting myself or letting somebody use me that way."

"Whoa! I was not using you. I think you have us confused." He rolls onto his back, away from me. His eyes sweep the ceiling and his jaw clenches in irritation.

"I'm saying it wrong." I place a gentling hand on his chest. "After my divorce, I made a decision to avoid sex. You made …" I shake my head and correct myself, "you make me forget that decision."

"The subject never came up but, Skylar, I don't do casual sex either. It's been well over two years since I've been with anyone."

My mouth falls open.

"And it was pointless to tell you because you don't believe me and I can't prove it, but it's true. I told you Friday night, I am at the stage in my life when I want more. That's why I asked you to stay. My interest in you isn't only sexual."

I sigh. "Mack, I made a decision after my divorce to not have anyone in my life until my daughter is grown and gone. My husband remarried very quickly after our divorce and shoved the new woman down Rachel's throat. I swore I would not do the same. Since Rand left, there hasn't been anyone. I don't date, ever. I won't."

Propping himself up on one arm, he reaches out and brushes my hair away from my face. "I understand. You made a choice not to date until your daughter is grown and I made a choice that I wouldn't have casual sex, but here we are."

"I know. It doesn't make any sense."

"But here we are," he insists.

I don't know how to respond. His gaze is intense, his statement serious. I change the subject. "So you are saving yourself for marriage?"

"Hardly. I just made a series of bad choices and took some time off from dating. I figured time would help me clear my head and discover what I was doing wrong with women. Didn't learn a thing. I seem to have fallen back in to my old pattern."

"Which is?"

"I am undeniably attracted to unavailable women and women who don't want the same things out of life that I do. When I wrapped up the last Mackenzie Corp. development, I was engaged. She dumped me when I pulled out of the company. Thought I lacked ambition. I bailed on the lifestyle she wanted, so she bailed on the lifestyle I wanted. The next woman I dated rented a house here for a summer. She loved the island but not children. She was a dedicated career woman. The one that ended dating for me," he pauses sheepishly, "was all for marriage and children. In fact, she had a husband and kids at home."

Covering my mouth, I gasp, "You have got to be kidding me!"

"Before she left, she confessed her marital status and suggested she'd be willing to change it for me. I said thanks, but no thanks. It was about then I realized my selections were getting progressively worse and it was time to take a break. So, contrary to whatever you may believe, I avoid racking up Fish Fry conquests. I volunteer there occasionally, but always leave alone. At least, I did until you came along."

"And I turn out to be one more unavailable woman. You have a problem."

"Tell me about it. I think I need counseling, Counselor." He kisses my shoulder.

"I work with children and teenagers."

"Make an exception. I want more time with you."

"I'm here for only a couple more weeks. I'd like us to be friends."

"Skylar, that's a little like closing the barn door after the horse has been let out. I can't just be your platonic friend. Sexually, you blow me away. Look at tonight."

I give him a smile of agreement. "I know so little about you, Mack, and what I know I really like..."

"It's not every day you find the chemistry we have. Let's hang out and see what happens? We can go into this as adults, knowing where we stand. Come on. Yes or no?"

I know the smart thing to do. I know what I should do, but I don't want this to end. If he wasn't naked in the bed, if he wasn't so damn easy to talk to, maybe then I would have a hope of turning him down. The best I can do is issue us both a warning. If there is a price to be paid for this time with him, I am willing to pay it.

"Here on the island. This is all I have to give."

"I'll take it."

"We are asking for trouble."

"You can agree or I will keep you in this bed on your back until you leave. Neither of us really has a choice," he says, returning the warning.

Chapter 16

Mack sleeps soundly next to me as if the experience is not new. The novelty of his presence in my bed interferes with my ability to sleep but I awake surprisingly energized. Throughout the night, when our bodies became separated, he reached out and tucked me in close. Would he treat any female body in the same manner or is he reaching specifically for me? I puzzle over this question until I am forced out of the bed, in urgent need of the bathroom.

Upon my return, I am stopped by the sight of him, stretched out. He is a sleeping statue of gold, lit up by the first batch of morning sunshine. The sheet covers him from the waist down. One arm is behind his head, the other rests along his side. The lines of his face and body are smoothed by the light and his stillness. I don't control what happens next. A kitchen chair and my easel are quietly smuggled into the room. A drawing pencil materializes in my hand. On a canvas, I begin a quick sketch of his body, aware that each pencil stroke represents a decrease in the time available to me. He'll soon wake.

"Skylar?" Lexie's knock interrupts my work. "Can I come in?"

Mack cracks an eye open then closes it. He turns over and buries his face under an arm. I stand and toss the sheet more fully over his body, and then call for her to enter.

Smiling wickedly, she says, "Looks like somebody got some."

"I fought hard but she overpowered me. It was totally against my will," Mack mumbles sleepily.

Lexie flops down on the foot of the bed, giving it a few hard bounces. "You can't rape the willing, big guy."

"Are you going to pull the big sister routine and threaten to beat me up?"

The last thing I need is Lexie and Mack dissecting how he ended up in my bed so I interrupt. "What's up, Lex? Just being snoopy?"

"I admit my curiosity was killing me. I suspected from the clothing in the hallway you had company. Cal made breakfast. Hmm... what's this?" My sister notices my easel. I'm not fast enough to keep her from seeing the canvas.

"It's just a beginning sketch. We'll be right out." Lexie winks at Mack and surprisingly leaves without comment, closing the door behind her. Mack sits up and swings his legs over the side of the bed. He stands. The sheet falls from his hips. *God he is sexy!*

"Good morning," he says, kissing me fully.

"Good morning," I answer.

My chin is rasped by his morning-after stubble. His fingers find the hemline of the shirt on my body. He begins to raise it. We've only been together in darkness. He's never really seen the silver stretch marks zigzagging across my stomach, breasts, hips and my upper thighs. My breasts are large and heavy. My lower stomach is soft. Not wanting my flaws revealed to him, I stop his hands, hoping to distract him with my words.

"I have been sketching my next painting."

Ignoring me, he continues his attempts at exploration. "I love you in my shirt. You have absolutely nothing on underneath?"

"I've been sketching you. I want to paint you. Don't worry, you're not nude."

He stops. I'm not sure what to make of the look on his face but I swear his cheeks darken. "You are sketching me? Can I see it?"

"Um..." I hedge. "It's not much to look at yet."

"I can't see you naked in the light of day and I can't see your sketch. You sure are bossy." He tries to sound casual but I can hear the edge in his voice.

"And you are pushy." I feel as if he is trying to chip away at my barriers. I can't allow that if I am going to leave this island with my heart intact. I turn away. "You won last night. You're here with me. But I need to decide for myself what I will let you see of me."

"You can trust me. I'll have you naked in the sunlight and you will not regret it, Skylar. I promise to find you beautiful."

"Don't make a promise you can't possibly keep." I stroke his lips lightly with my fingertips. I speak to his mouth because his eyes miss nothing. He kisses my fingertips.

"I wouldn't think of it. I promise to be honest. What else can I promise you?"

I press myself against him. I pull his mouth to mine. I kiss him deeply. "I really want to try to get you down on a canvas. Morning light would be best. I don't know what your schedule is..."

"Since you asked so nicely, I'd love for you to paint me. My schedule is what I want it to be. That's the beauty of being unemployed. I'll let you know if something comes up but otherwise, assume the mornings are yours."

"Wow! You are easy."

"Not so fast, Slugger, my time is valuable. I expect you will make it worth my while. I believe you owe me a sitting fee for this morning. I'd like payment right now." His moist, heated lips graze mine.

Breakfast is waiting out on the deck when we finally join Lexie and Cal. They are polite enough to not mention the lengthy delay. It should be an awkward foursome, but the conversation and banter flows fast and furious. Through it all, Mack can't keep his hands off me. When he is not playing with my hair, he is holding my hand. The attention is intoxicating.

"Cal, could you give me a hand with the dishes while the ladies enjoy the sunshine?" Mack begins stacking our empty plates.

"I figured you'd be the type to stick us with the dishes," Lexie taunts.

"Nah. My libido is way more important than my male pride. A happy woman is a woman who wants to have sex."

"You know it! I cooked Lexie dinner last night. She was very appreciative. Nothing says thank you like a good-" Cal catches the orange Lexie throws at him.

"Don't even think of finishing that sentence," she warns him, arming herself with the fruit bowl.

"Okay, okay." Cal holds his hands up in surrender. He grabs the fruit bowl and carries it into the house. Mack trails after him with the last of the dishes.

"You are glowing," Lexie says, teasing me when we are alone.

"Shut up!" I laugh dismissively. "That's what people say to pregnant women."

"I'm serious! There are astronauts in space being blinded by the shine in your eyes. Somebody likes somebody!"

I shrug and take a drink of orange juice. "I'm taking a page from your book and living for today. You should be proud. He agreed it's only until I leave."

"What a waste," she chides.

"What's a waste?' Mack asks, rejoining us.

"This day, we are wasting valuable sun time. Let's do something."

"The dishwasher is loaded and running. Sky, babe? I still have company at my place. I really should get back and see my brothers. Tomorrow they go back to the States. Do you want to come over, maybe go for a boat ride?" His invitation includes us all. "I have a sailboat I keep docked at South Palmetto. We could all spend the day out on the water."

"I'm going to hang out with my sister today," Lexie announces. I'm relieved. I want to spend every moment I can with Mack, but meeting his brothers would be weird.

"They are gone in the morning; then you will have my undivided attention," Mack promises. I walk him to the beach. We kiss goodbye. When I come back, Cal is gone.

"I hope you don't mind hanging out with me today? It might be our last chance to do so for the next few days. Cal has decided to extend his stay. We might do some island hopping. I know this was supposed to be our trip, but you've got Mack and I've got Cal. If you don't mind, I will take him up on his offer."

I am being dumped but I am not upset. I was trying to think of a way to wheedle time away from her to spend with Mack. "We have today."

"Yup, let's go explore this island."

We skim an Eleuthera vacation guide. Lexie tells me the Glass Window Bridge was damaged in the last hurricane and is under repair. We consider seeing the Hatchet Bay Caves until we read it is recommended to take a guide. We have no interest in locating one. In the end, we decide to pack a cooler and check out some other beaches.

It is late morning when we arrive at Surfer's beach. The beach is empty but out in the water, two people sit facing each other, bobbing up and down on their surfboards. The waves on this beach are loud, pounding events. As we split a soda, Lexie explains that in a series of waves, there is one bigger than the rest. The surfers are waiting for this wave. When it comes, they paddle furiously, before springing up onto their boards and riding the wave in. They repeat this performance a couple more times before they come ashore and settle against the shade of a bluff, out of our sight.

"We've come at a bad time. The tide is changing. The waves are too small to ride," Lexie explains, standing and tugging me to my feet. "Let's get to the Queen's Bath. The tide is getting lower and that is the best time to check out the tidal pools." We hike back to the vehicle and continue on. The sun is directly overhead when we reach the rocky cliffs. We climb carefully down to the clear and pristine tidal pool, strip down to our bathing suits and soak. After our swim, we snap pictures of white waves crashing against the cliffs. This part of Eleuthera is very narrow. Just across the road from the pounding Atlantic Ocean is the Caribbean. We spread our towels, eat lunch, and doze on the quiet, sandy beach.

Later that evening, during dinner back at the cottage, I tell my sister I enjoyed the day. Lexie raises her glass of wine to me. "I had a good day with you too, Sky." We clink glasses. "It is a rare day that we aren't picking at each other about something."

I set down my glass and tear open a fresh roll, purchased from a bakery we passed on our travels. Oven warmed, it melts the generous dab of butter I spread over it. "Yeah, you want me to loosen up and I want you to grow up."

"I am grown. I just don't want the same kind of life that you do. Marriage and kids would tie me down and bore me crazy." Passing me a bowl of salad, she asks, "I'd be a terrible mother, don't you think?"

"No. You are a great aunt. Rachel thinks you are the best thing since sliced bread. I complain about how difficult and thankless being a mom is, but I am glad I had her. Don't you wonder if you are missing out?"

"What about you? Don't you want more?"

It irritates me how expertly she deflects all conversation away from herself. I barely know Mack and I've had more intimate conversations with him. Lexie is never willingly open with me. "I asked you first."

"No. I really don't."

I admit I regret not having another child. "I wanted a big family. But that is not going to happen. Rachel has to grow up and then the right guy has to come along. I'll be almost forty. The biological clock is pounding, not ticking. I will have to settle for the right guy at this point. I think you were right. I'm not meant to be alone."

"Does Mack have anything to do with this sudden change of heart?"

"I'm not going to lie. I like him but the timing is off for us. It's a shame too, because he claims to want a family and to settle down."

She draws a line in the air. "Score one. Told you he was the settling down type."

"Don't you want a relationship that lasts longer than a few weeks?"

"Does such a thing exist? I've never found it."

"Michael and Tracina seem happy. Mom and Dad were, weren't they?"

"Look how that ended."

"Maybe that's our problem. The way we grew up, it was bound to have long term effects. If Mom hadn't died, I think we'd have had happier love lives. We were lucky to escape our childhoods without being alcoholics, but there was still fallout. I was too needy and you never let anyone close to you."

Lexie splits open her bread and then brushes the crumbs that cling to her fingers. Her gold bracelets tinkle vigorously, warning me of her growing annoyance with the topic. "Is this a therapy session? I don't remember signing up for one?"

"I'm not trying to counsel, I'm trying to explain something in me has shifted. I used to be as jaded as you. Until recently, I never believed it was possible to live happily with someone. What examples did we have? But you know, Lexie, some people are very happy together. Some men want to get married and spend their lives with one woman. Some men want to be fathers."

"Are we talking about anyone in particular?"

Swallowing a mouthful of wine first, I clear my mouth to explain. "I am just saying not all men are like Rand or Dad. It's possible for us to find someone someday and be happy. Don't you want to leave it behind, grow beyond what we know?"

"You don't remember the way it was. Sometimes I wish I didn't. They were crazy about each other. I remember being jealous. On their own, they were great parents but when they were together, we stopped existing." She's never told me this before and caught up in the memories, she looks softer, almost wistful. Then the edge returns. Her eyes flash as she hacks into the chicken breast on her plate. "For months after she died, Dad wouldn't even get dressed or take me to school. It was like he was gone too. It scared me. I never want to be that lost."

"We've been through rough times and came out the other side stronger for the experience. What happened to Dad, well, I've often wondered if he had a mental illness and Mom's death was just a straw that broke the camel's back."

"Why are you making excuses for him?" She gives me one of her I-don't-know-where-I went-wrong sighs. "You know what makes me angry? I see people die, people who don't want to die. He chooses to slowly kill himself every day."

"Sex or booze; both can be used to self-medicate."

"I'm not taking anyone down with me. I'm selfish. Maybe I take after Dad that way. I'll own that. He was a damn selfish bastard for the way he raised us. I'm better than him. I've never let anyone down who needed me. I love life. I take very good care of myself, I pursue every interest I have, and I love my job. I like being in the E.R., adrenaline coursing through my veins, piecing bodies back together. No one has come along who is more interesting than that."

"So you admit you do think about it?"

Her eyes narrow as she thinks about her response. I'm surprised by her answer. "Sure. But I also think I'd eventually get bored by the same old penis day after day. If the right one came along, who knows? Maybe I would move here and spend my days engaging in blissful sex."

"It can be weeks at home between visits for us. If you moved down here, we'd never see each other."

"I would miss you and Rachel."

"I talked to her yesterday afternoon on the phone. I don't think her visit with Rand is going that great. She was kind of quiet. I wish she were here with us."

"Next time. I'm enjoying seeing this side of you. You're a woman again, more than just a mother."

I nod. "A part of me is back. I didn't know it was gone. I feel whole. I'm curious to see how many of these changes I will carry with me when I return."

Chapter 17

Lexie is gone when I wake in the morning. There is a note and a rose on the table.

Skylar,

I stopped by to see you. Lexie wanted to leave you her car so I offered to drive her to town. She says she will call you in a few days. I'll be at my place by ten. Meet you there.

Mack

It doesn't take me long to dress. After choosing a pair of red shorts and a simple white tank top, I blow dry my hair until it falls in a soft shiny curtain down my back. A light application of makeup makes me feel pretty. I slip sandals on my feet and grab the keys for the jeep. I don't want to arrive at Mack's place in a sweaty mess.

Two lions carved from stone stand at the entrance to Mack's driveway. One of the lion pillars bears a plaque with the name *Mack's Abode.* The cement drive winds out of sight. I follow the tight curves until the house appears, nestled among short, fat palm trees. Numerous flowerbeds break up the expanse of green carpet lawn. I'd hardly call this place an abode. Many of the homes on Eleuthera are concrete, square dwellings vibrantly painted. Mack's home is sand colored and has been constructed from wood and poured concrete. I park at the foot of a great stone staircase. Each step has been inlaid with marble. Flowers overflow white stone planters on either side of the stairs.

I can't reconcile the laid-back Mack that I know with this house. It looms large, proof of the disparity between us. I ring the doorbell and take a few deep breaths. *This is just a fling. The size of his house doesn't matter,* I remind myself. He answers the door and his old denim jeans, faded t-shirt, bare feet, and big smile put me at ease. He wants me here. "You look great," he says, welcoming me with a kiss. It is not a quick peck, but a long slow taste that curls my toes.

"I wasn't sure where to park?" I motion to the jeep parked at the bottom of the steps.

"There's fine. Come on in. Did you have a good sleep?" he asks. I slip off my sandals. He shuts the door then wraps his arms around me.

"Yes I did. It was sweet of you to drive Lexie."

"I wanted to slide into bed with you but sanity prevailed. I realized the sooner I got rid of your sister, the sooner we'd be alone." He nuzzles my neck. I tilt my head back. His pleasure-provoking mouth takes advantage of the increased access to my throat.

"This house is amazing and the grounds are stunning."

"It didn't look this good when I bought it." Lifting his head, he looks around. "It was damaged in a hurricane. The previous owners were divorcing and neither wanted to spend the money to fix it or to buy the other out. Trying to renovate here is difficult. Materials have to be shipped in and few people have the patience to renovate on 'island time.' I saw the value in an underpriced property I could fix and sell for a big profit."

"So you are going to sell it?"

He shrugs noncommittally. "I made the mistake of remodeling for myself as opposed to doing it for a quick sale. It would be hard to let go. At this point, I like living here."

"I envy you. You have a beautiful home and the ability to do what you want. I hate my apartment. I work two jobs and sometimes I still struggle to make ends meet. If you don't have to leave, you shouldn't."

Laughing, he says, "Two jobs huh? Way to make me feel like a slacker. I have a pretty nice set up but I don't intend to spend the rest of my life sitting on the beach."

"Why not?"

"Because it's not enough. I came here to get myself refocused and pretty soon I will go back to the real world. I've learned what I needed to know. I like working with my hands. I love building homes that people love. I get the odd project to tackle here but not enough work to sustain me. Money is not a driving force so I'm considering low-cost housing projects."

"That would be a wonderful use of your skills, very altruistic."

"Not entirely. I still want to turn a profit, but they can be small profits. C'mon, I'll give you the official tour, but be prepared. It's a bit of a bachelor pad."

The foyer is separated from the great room by a massive staircase leading to the second floor. I follow him up the stairs into a massive empty open area.

"I've considered lining the walls with built in bookshelves, adding some couches, and a desk. This would make a great library. Out through these doors is a balcony. It's a shame there isn't a view of the ocean from the back of the house." Mack closes the doors behind us after we get a bird's eye view of the yard. "Off this room over here are two bedrooms and one bathroom." I peer into the doorways of each room to see simple furniture, bare white walls and hardwood floors. We cross back over to the other side. "These rooms are also furnished," he says. There is no art on the walls, no personal touches in either room. A queen sized bed, a pair of dressers, and two nightstands fill each room. The bathroom on this side has a jetted tub. The fixtures are sleek and shiny.

Back down the stairs, we go into the great room. Three leather sofas and two recliners dominate the huge room, edged by several matching end tables. A large fireplace fills one wall. An entertainment system, with a flat screen television, fills the opposite wall. A wall of windows looks out over a swimming pool three times the size of Lexie's.

"The pool looks as if it is part of the ocean!"

"Infinity pools are pretty cool. It is a neat architectural feature. This," he motions, "is supposed to be a formal dining room. I'm using it as my office space." There is a large desk and computer visible, both cluttered with paper and books. "The kitchen has a breakfast nook. That's where I usually eat. It's just through here."

Wooden doors separate the kitchen from the rest of the house. A chef's dream, the space is larger than my entire apartment. In addition to the walk-in freezer, there are two wall-mounted convection ovens and dual dishwashers. The cupboards are the color of honey; the countertops are black granite. Furnished with a table and chairs, the breakfast nook has French doors leading out to the backyard.

"Two sinks?" I exclaim. One sits under a window and the other is centered in an island.

"I thought it might be a good idea."

"You have thought of everything! Cooking in here would be a dream!"

"I mostly barbecue outside." Taking both of my hands in his, he pulls me forward until my body collides with his. My heart picks up speed. "This place could use a woman's touch. You're artistic. I bet you could give me some ideas to turn this house into a home."

For a millisecond, I imagine living here and arranging it with beautiful things. The loft would make an excellent studio... I stop the stupid fantasy. I will not leave my imprint on this man's home.

"Decorating is not my thing. You have done great so far. Fill it with things you love."

"I'd love one of your paintings. The mural at Lexie's is wonderful."

"You can have your portrait when I am done. It will be a more realistic rendition. Speaking of which, can I coax you into posing for an hour or so? I left my stuff out in the jeep but it will only take a second to bring it in." He agrees. When I return, he is waiting in his bed with only a sheet across his hips.

"That's the way I like a man, obedient and subservient," I tease.

"How about bored? If I am going to lay here naked, the least you could do is get rid of your clothes. Give me something to keep my mind busy."

"I'll turn your TV on for you."

"I don't want to watch TV. I want to watch you."

He's forgotten the deal we made. He's pushing again. I busy myself with my easel and paints. I don't want to say yes or no so I say nothing. He sits up and turns to plump and pound the pillows behind him.

"What is it with women? I swear you are all brainwashed from infancy to hate your bodies. I have scars on my body." Mack lifts a leg free of the white sheet and points to white zigzags on his knee. "They don't repulse you or turn you off. They are just there and part of my body, right?"

"I don't know. I guess I just feel that if you saw me fully, completely in the light of day, you would be..." I can't finish the statement. "Other than me, have you ever been with a woman who has had a child before?" I watch as he gives me a negative shake of his head. "Exactly. As good looking as you are, I bet all you have known is perfect figures, flawless skin, flat tummies and tight tushes."

"For all the good it did. Those women aren't here and you are. Insecurity is a bigger turn off than a few stretch marks ever could be."

I have a strong urge to walk out the door. No one likes to be called insecure or a turn off. "It's pretty hard to feel good about yourself when the only man who has ever seen you naked leaves you for a twenty-two-year-old kid with a perfect body."

"You can't believe your husband divorced you because of your appearance?"

"Intellectually, of course not. We had been dating for several years before I got pregnant accidentally with Rachel. Rand was pressured by his family to do the right thing when he asked me to marry him. I wanted to create the family I never had for Rachel. Our sense of responsibility wasn't a strong foundation for a marriage. I know that."

"You weren't in love."

"We weren't passionately in love, but who is? I cared for him. He was my husband, the father of my daughter. He was the one person in the world I discussed everything with until the day he walked out the door and did not look back. He went from my bed to another woman's bed without hesitation or explanation. He rocked my confidence and my pride. I am left to fill in the blanks. All I can think is I wasn't enough."

"He was a fool. I'm not him. Nothing about you could turn me off. I see you and I want to see more. You make me hard, Skylar. I can't fake that reaction."

I throw my hands up helplessly. "In the dark, between the sheets, it works." I stop speaking, unwilling to reveal any more. Fear is making this decision, in more ways than he realizes. I'm scared he won't like what he sees but I am even more terrified he will. If he sees me naked and he accepts me flaws and all, another barrier is broken between us. I need my walls up. I am trying mightily to keep my heart encased.

"Come here." He pats the bed when I don't move. "Come, you stubborn woman. I don't want to fight with you. Well, actually I do want to fight with you but I can see you don't."

I comply although I remain irritated. Stretching out facing him, I know he isn't going to win this battle. Mack props himself up on one elbow. His other hand searches for mine to hold.

"I don't take you sharing your body with me lightly. Not even a little. I understand I'm not being fair. You shouldn't be the only one taking a risk so I'm going to tell you a little story." Mack pauses. He has my complete attention. "I'll trust you to keep this to yourself. A woman, who is very dear to me, started dating a man. One thing led to another and they slept together. He never talked to her again. She was humiliated. Months later, I was with her when she ran into him. He was with a much younger woman and didn't even acknowledge her. She insisted we leave immediately. I eventually got the story out of her." Mack's grip on my hand tightens. I hold my breath, waiting for him to continue.

"I wanted to find him and kick his face in. I ranted and raved until she asked me if I had ever slept with a woman just for sex. She told me women don't have sex lightly. It always means something to them. Always. And if I had ever had sex with a woman and did not look back then I was as ignorant as the man who used her. The thought that I could hurt anyone, like the bastard hurt my mother, was life changing."

"Your mother?"

"Uh-huh. After Dad died, she couldn't contemplate dating another man, never mind sleep with one. So when this happened, it was awful! I didn't think she'd ever recover."

"Did she?"

"It took a while but eventually my step dad came along. I don't want to know the details but somehow he managed to convince her that she was a desirable and beautiful woman. And I learned a valuable lesson. Skylar, I don't get involved with women that don't attract me. You are incredibly beautiful, in face, body and personality. I want you naked in front of me. I want you to know that you turn me on. I don't want you ever thinking I find you wanting. Trust me, and trust yourself," he says quietly.

He tugs on my shirt, pulling it up and over my head. He undoes the snap of my shorts and slides them down my hips. I begin to tremble when he unclasps my bra. My eyes are too scared to meet his as he tugs my panties off. He lays me bare to his gaze and to the sunlight. He makes love to me in the brightness of the sunshine and then carries me outside and loves me in the warm waters of the ocean. The sky, the sand, and the water are the only witnesses to our developing intimacy.

Chapter 18

I no longer believe I can sleep with Mack and emerge emotionally unscathed. I guess I am more like his mother than I am like my own sister. I can't take sex lightly, he makes it impossible. I wake in his bed every morning, believing I will return to Lexie's cottage. When the night rolls around, I end up asleep in his arms. Mack consistently devises a reason for me to spend each day with him. We spend another Friday night dancing at the Governor's Harbor Fish Fry. The next day, we work in his yard, cutting the grass and weeding the flower beds. Two days are devoted to helping a neighbor build a garage, another to cleaning Mack's sailboat. I spend no time at Lexie's cottage except to make quick calls to Rachel and change my clothing. I speak with my sister on the phone a couple of times. Lexie is enjoying her tour of the Bahamas with Calvin. I'm grateful she is in no hurry to finish the vacation with me as I greedily devour every moment with Mack.

My heart is involved and, for a while, I avoid wondering about his. As we grow closer, it is harder to not think about what he is feeling, especially as he seems intent on dismantling more and more of my protective emotional walls. He does so slowly. I don't even realize what he is doing at first. His questions are discretely spaced and casually asked. My two jobs are of great interest to him. Over time, he learns what I like about each position and what I hate. Questions about my father are deflected until after an encounter with an inebriated tourist at a restaurant, I find myself talking about my childhood. Mack has no personal experience with alcoholism or poverty in his family but he listens and asks the right questions to encourage me to say more.

Rachel is another frequent topic of conversation. Every day I miss her a little more. Saying her name and talking about her eases my discomfort. I share with Mack how difficult and lonely motherhood is sometimes but mostly it is fulfilling and necessary to me. During a picnic at Lighthouse Beach, I'm shocked when I hear myself admitting how much I now want to pursue a career as an artist when Rachel is grown. I have barely admitted this realization to myself but he wriggles the confession out of me. Effortlessly, Mack learns more about my life than I ever intended on sharing.

It is hard to remain closed off when he is so forthright. I have yet to stumble across a topic or question he won't answer. I learn how his father's death brought his family closer, but also how sometimes the absence of his father could not to be filled by his mother and brothers. Mack misses his dad like I miss my mother. We are comforted by the mutual understanding each has for the loss the other has experienced. It is a connection we've not found anywhere else.

One night in the darkness, Mack confides he often worries marriage and children are not in the cards for him. Such a future would be daunting, he says, because he does not want to be alone. His older brother is married, one younger brother is married, and another is engaged. One of these days, he fears the baby of the family is going to announce he too is engaged. Mack feels he is losing common ground with his family, becoming a third wheel, or a single among doubles.

Beyond the long talks, the sharing of secrets and sexual intimacy, I am drawn closest to Mack by my painting. True to his word, the mornings are reserved for me to capture him on canvas. His willingness to be vulnerable with me, in front of me, for me, makes it impossible for me to keep any emotional distance between us. Regardless of the length of my sleep the night before, I crawl from bed as early as possible, anxious to commit more of him to memory. I foolishly embed him deeper within me. I paint Mack in comfortable silence; I paint him through deep conversations. More often than not, I paint him while he sleeps. Each day his form has emerged more clearly on my canvas, until finally, this morning, I am done. I turn the easel so his completed portrait will be the first thing he sees when I wake him.

"Mack," I whisper, kissing his mouth as my finger strokes his cheek. His sleep-messed curls are a mane on the pillow beneath his head. His long, thick lashes rest on his cheeks. Looking every bit like a slumbering tawny lion, Mack stretches. He opens his golden eyes momentarily. Sleepily, they close again. "It's done," I say simply.

"I'd say it's just beginning," he corrects me with a raspy morning drawl. His hand pushes my shirt up, baring my naked bottom. As each of his hands cup a cheek, his mouth searches for mine. "Your portrait, I finished it," I persist, avoiding his mouth. I point. He wipes his eyes and sits up. I eagerly await his honest reaction.

His eyes widen. He smiles. As wonder and pride cross his face, I feel myself relax. I am not sure which was more anxiety-provoking; the first time he saw me naked in the daylight or these past few seconds.

"I don't know what to say, Sky. It is incredible!"

"I am terribly proud of it. It came out better than I hoped. It's quite an intimate painting. Where do you think you'll put it?" My excitement keeps me talking. It would be perfect in here."

"It is egotistical to love a painting of myself but I do. When can we hang it?"

"It could be a couple of months. Oil paintings take a very long time to dry, plus it'll need to be varnished and framed. Michael is finishing my seascape. We could ask him to do this one, if you don't mind them seeing it?"

"I'll call and see if we can drop by later."

"You didn't tell them I would be coming," I reprimand him when he hangs up the phone. "You are a shit disturber."

"It will be a surprise. Hey, let's sail to Tarpum Bay. Today is as good a time as any to get you out on my boat. We could be gone until late tomorrow though."

"I'll go pack a bag and check in with Rachel. I'll be back," I promise.

* * *

A couple of hours later, Mack's hands rest confidently on the helm. I sit beside him, watching the ocean and the passing land. As it turns out, I'm not the best sailor. My hands clutch my seat as the boat rises and falls over the waves. I feel no nausea, but I am a little terrified by the feeling of being adrift on the powerful ocean. Mack keeps up a steady stream of conversation until I calm and adjust to the new experience. After a few hours, the warm sun lulls me into a nap. Mack continues sailing, landing us at a dock in Tarpum Bay in the late afternoon. We walk to the gallery. To their credit, Michael and Tracina hide their shock when they see me at Mack's side. Their composure remains intact even when Mack presents the carefully carried portrait to Michael.

"You think you can throw a frame around it?" Mack asks.

Tracina's mouth opens. She covers it with her hand, her eyes flipping back from my face to Mack's. "What a wonderful job," she says finally.

Michael gives an appreciative whistle. "Lass, you have talent. Not only is this a well-executed portrait but Tracina tells me she's already had a few inquiries about your seascape on the website."

"You're kidding me."

"As soon as it is dried and framed, it will fly out of here," Tracina assures me.

"Speaking of which, how much should I make the check out for on this one?" Mack pulls a wallet out of his back pocket and removes a tattered but intact blank check.

"I'm not selling it, Mack. It's a gift," I answer.

"I won't take it if I don't pay for it. You put a great deal of time into this portrait. Hours of your vacation have been spent on it."

"Those hours were for my benefit."

"Sky, if you want a career as an artist, you have to be willing to separate friendship from business," he chides.

"I will not take money from a man I am sleeping with."

Michael clears a choked cough from his throat. "Hard to argue with that, old man."

"Okay, fine. But I will pay for the framing." The stubborn thrust of Mack's jaw eases when I nod my agreement.

"Come down the hall with me to the office, Skylar. I want to show you the website and the inquiries I received. Mack, do you mind if I add a description of your portrait to her online portfolio. I don't know if you would be comfortable with me taking a digital photograph of it..."

"Go ahead."

Tracina takes the portrait. Leading me to the office, she says, "You did such a lovely job, Skylar. Having a portrait and a seascape shows your range. It would be a shame not to include it." In her office, Tracina powers up her computer and then, using a digital camera, she snaps a picture of the portrait. Once it is uploaded, she walks me through the process of adding and editing my portfolio. "Your portfolio can be found in the 'New Talent Section.' I put together a brief biography which I'll need you to embellish and edit. I'll give you your own password so you can make changes from your home. All you need is a computer and a digital camera. Do you have any other completed paintings?"

"A few. I could dig them out of my storage room. I doubt if any are good enough."

"Photograph them all. Let me assess them."

"Sure. This is incredible! I can't thank you enough."

"No thanks are required. Let's get this out to the studio where it can dry properly."

The men are missing from the gallery and they are not to be found in the studio. Tracina is not concerned; she suspects they are off inspecting Mack's boat. We hang out in the studio. I experiment with her brushes and paints while she tidies up.

"It was wonderful to finish the portrait but it was hard to show it to him," I admit.

"They are our creations, and to be finished means we must admit the work is the best we can do at the time. It was done," Tracina comforts. "It demonstrates the depth of your skill, and also the feelings the two of you share. I'm very glad you and Lachlan managed to work things out. You are good for each other."

She cares for him. This could be awkward. I stop painting and wipe the excess color from the bristles on a piece of old newspaper. Tracina takes the brushes from me. She dips one into a small glass container of poured paint thinner, swishes the brush around, and passes it back to me. I walk to the studio sink, turn on the tap, add soap, and begin to work the color from the bristles.

"I leave in less than two weeks. It'll be hard to say good-bye."

"Does he know that is what you intend?" Tracina passes me several more brushes.

"Mack understands my limitations."

"Your concerns, Skylar, about distance and your daughter, those things can all be worked out if you are both willing, don't you think?"

The last brush is rinsed. I lay it on a nearby rack to air dry, smiling in an attempt to lighten the conversation. "It is just as well. Mack is almost forty. He's been footloose and fancy free for a long time. I'm not up to the training."

"Men are all fixer-uppers," Tracina laughs, "including my husband. If you could see what I started with."

"Tell me." I sit on the small wingback chair and pull my bare feet up.

"Look at the brushes he used and didn't clean! He can't find a thing to save his life. He has the manners of a hog. That's after thirty years of training. When I first met him, he was cocky enough to believe the bloody world revolved around him and that a woman's place was in the kitchen or in the bedroom. Oh Lord, we had some fights! But he is everything I've ever wanted." Tracina pauses as she gathers her hair, pulling it all forward over one shoulder. She circles the thick mass with her fingers, smoothing it in long sure strokes. Her eyes are soft but there is a gentle warning when she speaks. "Lachlan is like Michael, Skylar. I firmly believe when he meets the right woman, she better be ready. He'll fall hard, he'll fall fast, and he will make an incredible husband. Love doesn't come along every day."

"I like Mack an awful lot," I admit, "but my daughter is the love of my life."

"Some day she will be gone."

"Yes. And things will change. I will have to build and shape a life without her as my primary focus." I appreciate Tracina's honesty but she doesn't really understand my situation. "I only get one chance to raise Rachel right. I may have countless opportunities at relationships. Even if Mack were interested, I wouldn't be."

"All I have to do is look at the portrait, Skylar, and I can see you care for him. I'm a painter. I've been painted. I know the link that is built between an artist and a model."

"The connection to my daughter is much more powerful. Tracina, I've seen parents do awful things in the pursuit of a relationship. I know mothers who have lost their children because they moved a drug-dealing boyfriend into their home. I know fathers who stop paying child support and visiting their children when they start a new family. At least half a dozen kids on my caseload every year end up homeless because they don't get along with the new step parent. These aren't isolated cases. Blended families don't work. They are extremely difficult relationships, almost impossible to navigate."

"You are a counselor, you deal in problems. When would you see the successes?"

"True. But statistics don't lie. Second marriages are notoriously unsuccessful. It is not a risk I am willing to take."

"I guess I am a little naïve. Forgive me for being so pushy. It's tough to see people I like not end up together. Are we going to be left behind as well?"

"That reminds me… here, for you and Michael." I dig a piece of paper out of my back pocket. "It is my address, phone number and E-mail. I don't know if I'll get a chance to come back. Mack is keeping me pretty busy."

"I refuse to allow him to hog you all to himself. I will insist he bring you back. I guess we should go find them. I don't know about you but I am starving. I do believe it is my night to cook. You can give me a hand."

The men are in the kitchen. We all visit over dinner and then Mack and I head back to the boat. Michael and Tracina offered us a bedroom but Mack passed on the invitation. He intends on sailing as soon as the sun comes up. It's a beautiful night and before going below, we sit on the bow, watching the stars and sipping wine.

The conversation with Tracina is in the back of my mind. A seed of worry has been planted. I've known from the beginning that I will not walk away from Mack unscathed. Tracina has suggested Mack will be similarly affected. I can only hope she is wrong. I shake my thoughts free of the earlier discussion. There was too much talk about leaving. I want Mack while I can still have him. I turn in his arms and whisper his name in his ear.

"Lachlan, is it?" He raises an eyebrow.

"I wanted to try it out. You're Mack to me. Always will be, but I love the name Lachlan."

"I could get used to you calling me Lachlan if you say it like that, all husky and throaty. It would sound even better if you were moaning it."

He is teasing but I am not. "Lachlan," I purr sexily. Just in case he doubts the seriousness of my intentions, I run my fingers under his shirt, skimming the waist band of his jeans.

"You say that again, you do that again Babe, and you going to find out just how big the bed below is." He growls his warning. I want him to carry out his threat.

"Lachlan," I repeat.

He takes me down into the belly of his boat.

Chapter 19

Mack wants to know if I want to go out for dinner. Naked, he stands at the sink shaving. After he left a trail of red skin on my neck and breasts, I was unable to convince him that I like both the look and feel of the two day growth of stubble. I join him as he rinses his face and splashes on aftershave. A thick white towel blots the excess moisture from his skin. I am lifted onto the bathroom countertop. Mack steps between my thighs and frees my towel-bound hair.

"I have absolutely no energy," I complain.

"I tired you out?" He gives me a cocky smile as he opens my towel. Our clean, naked bodies meet.

"No. Cloudy days make me lethargic."

"Good thing we don't have many of those around here. Have I told you that I like to be naked with you? I'm not talking about sex." At my doubtful look, he continues. "Our tussle in the shower was terrific but I'm talking about touching you, smelling you, holding you. It feels good in a way that is not sexual."

"You're cuddle reflex is emerging." I kiss his chin. "You can't stay to your side of the bed and you use any excuse to touch me. Classic signs of being a cuddler. Rachel was a great cuddler. Her body was a warm little oven. She'd press her cheek against mine so hard it hurt, like she couldn't get close enough to me. I barely remember the last time she hugged me, never mind cuddled."

Mack's arms tighten around me. "Sounds like you need to stock up. I'll throw some pizza in the oven. Later we can watch movies and I'll make my world famous popcorn. We'll spend the evening in bed, indulging our cuddle reflexes."

"Ah, the decadence of having a TV in the bedroom. Sounds perfect. Let me head back to Lexie's for clothes and to call Rachel."

"Clothes are not required for an evening in my bed. As for calling your daughter, use the phone by my bed." He lifts me from the vanity and sets me on my feet, before pushing me out of the bathroom. On the way past his closet, I snag a t-shirt.

"I'll be quick."

"Don't be. Talk as long as you need."

Grateful for the privacy, I dial the number. Sherry picks up. I ask for Rand.

"Hey, it's Skylar. Is Rachel around?"

"Oh. Hello. How's the beach?" he asks.

I guess I have to make small talk first since we are back to politely speaking again. "Great. How's Calgary?"

"Hot, dry and windy."

"And Rachel? Can I talk to her?"

"She is gone to the Stampede. I'll get her to call when she is back."

I almost drop the receiver. "She went alone?"

"Of course not. Candace is with her."

Candace is Rand's niece, a child I have never much liked. She has always had a bit of a mean streak, and I always made a point of watching her closely when she played with Rachel.

"Oh? You let two thirteen year olds go alone? I feel so much better."

"Don't start with me, Skylar," he warns. "Sherry wasn't up to it and she needed me here. Candace has a cell phone. They'll be fine."

I take a deep cleansing breath but it does not clear me of the desire to reach through the phone lines and give him a shake. "What time are they supposed to be back?" I throw my gaze heavenward when he does not answer. "You never gave them a curfew? They could be back in five minutes or in five hours! That's real smart, Rand."

"I didn't think about it. Christ. Mothers. If your kids are not attached to your tits, you're not happy." His voice is rising and his breath is coming out in short puffs over the phone line. "How's she ever going to grow up if you never let her do anything? I'm her father and if I want to let her go to the Stampede alone, I will!"

"Yeah, I guess you will. Have her call me when she gets in." I swear softly and set the phone back in its cradle. My stomach is knotted with worry when I join Mack in his kitchen. He is putting together a salad and there is a frozen pizza in the oven.

"Uh-oh. You are not the same sexually satisfied woman I left in the bedroom ten minutes ago." I give him a weak smile and sit at the island. He passes me a can of soda. "What's wrong?"

I run a hand over my face, but it does not loosen my worried frown. I explain what I learned from the phone call.

"What's the Stampede?" he asks.

"It's a huge… I guess you would call it a fair. There are rides and games, a big rodeo. Tens of thousands of people go to it every day."

"Sounds like fun."

"I guess. Edmonton has its own similar event. Do you think I am being over protective?"

"You're asking the wrong person. I'm not a parent. When I was thirteen, I did a ton of things on my own without my folks around but I lived in a small town."

"Did he explain what to do in the case of an emergency? Would she know enough to ask for help, or even where to go? More than anything, I'm pissed Rand didn't want to be with her. They don't get much time together." I tuck a strand of hair behind my ear, deciding to change the subject. "Is there anything I can do to help?"

"Nope. Salad's done. We're waiting for the pizza now."

We eat, wash the dishes by hand, and then take a short walk on the beach. Even the powerful waves are unable to distract me from worrying. I keep visualizing my daughter caught in the worst case scenarios. Rain starts and we run back to the house, entering through the patio door into his bedroom. While Mack makes popcorn, I tidy the bathroom and make the bed. I am punching and fluffing the pillows when Mack enters carrying a large bowl.

"What did those poor pillows ever do to you?"

"Sorry. I'm imagining they are my ex-husband right now."

"Why don't I make some tea? I'm sure you are not in the mood for a movie."

"Yes I am. Bear with me. I don't want to sit and stew. I need the distraction."

Mack selects a movie from his entertainment stand. I absently munch a handful of popcorn. Returning with the remote control, he snuggles next to me as the movie begins. After two hours of flying bullets and over-the-top car chases, the credits roll. The empty popcorn bowl is on the floor. I notice the darkness out the window.

"It is after nine o'clock back home. Surely she is back by now? Shit! She probably called Lexie's cottage and I wasn't there."

"Call back and leave this number for her."

"You don't mind?"

"Not at all. I'll give you a minute," he offers, leaving once again.

I let out a deep gust of relief when my daughter answers the phone. She immediately breaks into sobs. "Can I go home?" she asks.

"What's wrong? Are you okay?"

"I'm okay but I want to leave. Candace met some boys at the Stampede. They wanted us to go to their place. I wouldn't go. She left me there. I called Dad to come and pick me up and now Dad's mad at me because I don't know where she is."

"Where is your dad now?"

"He went looking for Candace. I don't like her. All she wants to do is party and hang out with guys. I tried telling Dad what she is like but he said I was being rude."

The urge to race home and swoop in and save her is strong. However, she is not a couple of hours drive away. And I don't want to leave. Maybe I can talk them through this. "After this episode, I am sure your dad will send her home."

"I don't care. He and Sherry will still be blaming me. Why is this my fault? I didn't do anything wrong. Can't I just go home and stay by myself until you get back? I can't stand listening to Sherry whining or lecturing me about how I should be more grateful. Grateful for what? That they don't want me here? Mom, he has broken every promise. He hasn't spent one day with me. Please, can I leave?" Rachel dissolves. Her heartbroken cries fill my ear.

Part of me is ready to move heaven and earth to get to her; the other hopes it won't come to that. "I have to talk to your dad. He'll have to agree. Plus, it will take me time to change my tickets and arrange the flights. I can't guarantee when I'll get there."

"Try, Mom. Please. I got to get out of here. Please. I miss you so much."

"I know, baby. I love you. I'll call back in a bit and talk to your dad, okay?"

I am fully dressed except for my sandals when Mack finds me hunting under the bed for the missing footwear.

"What's wrong?"

"I need my sandals. I'm going to go back to Lexie's. I've got to talk to Rand and I don't want to tie up your line. This could take a while to sort out."

"Something happened?"

"Candace took off with some boys and left Rachel alone at the Stampede. I knew something like this was going to happen! I never liked that little brat! Rand is oblivious to anything but Sherry. He wouldn't see trouble coming if it was bearing down on him in a semi! Where are my sandals?"

"They're on the deck." Mack retrieves them. "You don't have to leave. You're welcome to use my phone for however long it takes."

"It's sweet of you to offer, but it's better if I go and deal with this."

Warm hands on my shoulder stop me. From behind, his body molds to mine. "If there is anything I can do to help, you will ask?" His arms feel good around me. For a moment, I let him hold me. I brush his cheek with a quick kiss and leave. The phone is ringing when I get to the cottage. I race to answer it.

Rand doesn't bother to say hello. He launches straight into an attack. "Rachel said you are coming to get her? We just had an argument; it's no big deal, she'll be fine."

"She's not fine. I told you that something like this could happen."

"It's not my fault Candace decided to pull some stunt," he says defensively.

"That's what happens when you don't want to spend time with your daughter and foist her onto someone else-"

He cuts me off. "Just because I refuse to cater to her-"

"Your daughter wants reassurance. She needs to know you love her and that you will continue to love her after this baby is born. Instead, she's at the bottom of your list and she knows it. Frankly, I don't blame her for wanting to leave."

"It's just Sherry is not feeling well."

"Sherry's pregnant, she's not dying. Rachel needs you too. Why can't you apologize, fix it." *Please fix it!* I think to myself.

"Maybe it's better if you come and get her. When do you think you can be here?"

No!

I close my eyes. I am not surprised by his willingness to dump her back on me but I am stunned by how much I do not want to go. My conflicted feelings do not prevent me from doing what is right. I tell Rand I will make some phone calls and get back to him.

It is much later when I slip quietly into Mack's house and then his bed, molding myself to each of his sleep movements. His heart pulses against my cheek. My head rises and falls with each breath. I want each and every second to stretch out but the bedside alarm clock ticks away time quickly, the necessity to wake him growing. I hesitate, scared no words will come, or the wrong words might spill out.

I am leaving but I don't want to go. I want to see you again.

I haven't left and already I can feel a void, a dull vacant ache inside me. It is the height of stupidity to be missing Mack while still in his arms so I run my hands over his body. He rests so deeply it takes persuasion to pull him out of sleep. I skim my fingers along his stomach, between his thighs. He stirs under my hand, lengthening and hardening. I reach for a condom from the nightstand. It is not until I sheath and straddle him that his eyes open. Not fully awake, his hands manage to find my hips. Our mouths meet, our bodies mesh. I feel a tightening in my throat as it dries out. Maybe the moisture has been transferred to my eyes. They are swelling with tears. I try to keep them trapped beneath my eyelids, away from his view. He wants my gaze, he wants my eyes locked. They remain closed long after the kiss ends. It is the only time that we have come together and I don't peak before or with him. Wrapping me tight in his arms, he rolls our bodies. He reaches and switches on the bedside light.

"You're leaving." I hear the accusation in his voice. The truth is out but I still can't meet his eyes.

"I have to get Rachel and take her home."

Swearing softly, he leaves the bed. Returning from the bathroom a few minutes later, he asks, "There's no other way?"

"I'll be on a flight this afternoon. I should be in Calgary tomorrow evening."

"When will I see you again, Skylar?" I turn away from him and swipe at the tears that fall. I reach for my clothes, sorting through the heap on the floor by his bed, trying not to feel his eyes bore into my back. "Are you going to answer me?" I flinch at his angry raised voice.

"I don't know what to say. I have to go. My daughter needs me."

He runs a hand through his hair, and begins pacing. "Go to her. I understand. What I don't understand is why you think it has to end here?"

"Because it is what we agreed. Be reasonable, Mack. We don't even live in the same country."

"That's what airplanes are for."

"I'm a single parent, Mack. I make just a little over forty five thousand dollars a year. I drive a piece of shit car. I live in a little two-bedroom apartment, in a not-so-great apartment building. I can't afford to fly back and forth to see you."

"We have something here."

His pacing is making me dizzy. I stand in front of him and place my hand on his chest. "We have something. Here. I'm leaving. I won't be here."

"So that's it, huh? I had fun. Have a nice fucking life, Mack? That's what you are saying, right?" He runs his fingers through his hair again.

"It's not like that!"

"Prove it."

I groan in frustration. "We had an agreement!"

"No, you tried to make an agreement. I saw an opportunity to change your mind."

He lied. Right from the start, Mack never intended to just let me walk away. His eyes have lost their anger, and instead there is only a softly posed question. "I know you feel something. Something inside me says I shouldn't let you go. I've never felt that before. I am asking you to give us a chance. There has to be some way..."

"Rachel won't accept me having a relationship right now. And I won't let you hang in the background of my life for the next five years while I finish raising her. Please understand."

"No. I won't make it easy." His jaw clenches as he stares me down, watching for weakness, a betrayal of my body to tell him I don't mean what I am saying but for the first time around him, I am able to bring my body under control. Several more moments pass before I speak. When I do finally respond, my voice is firm.

"She's my priority, Mack. I want you. I love her." I don't want to be this person who has to throw his feelings back in his face. I see his old wounds reopen; once more he has picked the wrong woman. His mouth opens to continue the argument. No words come out. His shoulders drop. I feel sick, but I don't withdraw my declaration.

"I'll drive you to the airport."

I want to leave believing I am the only one hurting. I am not. Seeing his hurt makes this too difficult. I'm running out of strength.

"It was hard enough to do this once. Let me go now. I have to pack. I'll leave a note for Lexie explaining what happened."

He nods. "Call me when you get home. Let me know everything is all right, that she's okay and you're okay. Don't walk out of my life leaving me not knowing." And then he is kissing me. His mouth is hard on mine, his hands tangle in my hair, holding me firmly in place. "Call me?" he asks.

I kiss him back fiercely, feeling, for the last time, my body's quick response. I don't want to look back and regret missing the opportunity to kiss him one last time. Quivering, I mold myself against him, pressing into his body, unable to get close enough. All I can think about is how good he feels under my fingers, against my body.

His mouth lifts slightly. Against my lips, he whispers, "Please, Skylar."

"Yes." The word sighs out of my lips. I want one more kiss, one more touch, one more time with Mack.

He breaks the kiss. He steps back. With space between us, my mind clears. I understand in that moment what I have agreed to. Triumphantly, he is able to let me go, not because it is time but because until I make the promised phone call, it isn't really over between us.

Chapter 20

I expected to return from Eleuthera refreshed and excited to see my daughter; instead I arrive at the Calgary International airport feeling cheated. Braced to face my daughter and ex-husband, I also struggle with a desire to unleash my unhappiness on someone. They are not waiting when I disembark. I collect my bags from the luggage carousel and scan the throng of people for their familiar faces. After a few moments, a gap in the crowd opens. I glimpse Rachel shuffling slowly with a purse clutched tightly to her chest. Her gaze is fixed on the ground. Rand sees me. His narrow shoulders lift slightly with relief. Throwing an arm around Rachel's shoulders, he points me out to her. She shrugs his touch off. I'm not sure if it is anger or defeat that allows his hand to fall away. I am too far away to discern.

I draw closer. Their anxious expressions are focused on me; their expectations are tangible. A hot flare of anger almost stops me. I'm tired of their tension. I'm tired of being the solution to their crises. Pressing forward, I envelope my daughter in a hug. She clings tightly for a second. I smooth back her soft brown hair, searching her face, measuring her pain. Her feelings are as obvious as a mountain. I see relief and pain. She wishes her father wanted her. He is the one who is missing out, I want to tell her. I settle for nuzzling her cheek in greeting, missing the days when my kisses could dispel her pain.

"Did you find Candace?" I ask.

"I sent her home on an earlier flight. I told her she ruined your trip with her little escapade."

"She ruined my trip? She ruined my trip?" I repeat the question out of incredulity. His willingness to blame everything on thirteen-year-old Candace is typical yet still infuriating. "She is not the one who asked me to come back. She's a kid, Rand. They make stupid decisions, hence the need for supervision." I wanted to try and keep this civil but I am too raw, too tender. I can't keep my feelings from bubbling to the surface. He tenses. Our animosity electrifies the air.

"I am going to the bathroom so you can swear all you want at him." Rachel's announcement drains the fight out of me. My daughter should not be leaving so we can argue. Even if she walks away, she will not be removed from our hostility. Venting my anger will not change anything. If I can't go back to Eleuthera, I can settle for taking my daughter home.

"Come on. Let me have it." Rand's sneer does not have the desired effect.

At one time, his opinion mattered; now I am completely disinterested in him except for how he treats Rachel. It's a relief to feel the last of my personal bitterness fade. I won't miss it. After he neatly cut himself out of my world, it was a hard struggle to piece together a life from the unwanted pieces he left behind. For a time, it seemed there was not enough to build a future on; now I can't imagine why I ever felt that way. I can't even remember what attracted me to him in the first place.

His smile never reaches the four corners of his face, and there is no mischief or teasing light to his eyes. His clean-cut, slick, urban style does not measure up against Mack's raw, earthy appeal. There is no comparison. Admittedly, I am more partial to Mack because he left me with a restored sexuality and faith in my ability to keep a man's attention.

"We both know that you are chomping at the bit to give me a lecture. You can't resist rubbing my nose in a screw up."

"I am done, Rand. I am done fighting with you and making excuses for you. Most of all, I am done fixing things with her for you."

"I do the best I can. Just because I don't devote every bloody waking moment to her doesn't make me a bad father. I'll work out my issues with Rachel on my own without your know-it-all-school-counselor advice."

"Then why the hell did I just fly hundreds of miles? You are full of it. This is not rocket science! All she wants is you! You better figure out how to start giving her what she needs because I am this close to dragging your ass back to court and getting the pitiful amount of time you see your daughter reduced even further. If I could, I would have your parental rights terminated! I am so tired of picking up the pieces of her heart every time you break it. You don't deserve her."

"And you can't imagine the costs involved in going back to court. We both know you can't afford it."

"I'll beg, borrow, or steal the money if I have to, whatever it takes. That's the difference between you and me, Rand. My daughter comes first. I'll starve before I let you keep hurting her. I'll get a third fucking job. I'll borrow from Lexie."

"You'd have to drag Rachel into it? We both know you wouldn't," he taunts.

"I've done my best to protect her, Rand, but the more I shelter her, the more you damage her. This time you've crossed that line. I know it, you know it, but more importantly, she knows it. It stops today. I have spent the last four years documenting all the visits you have cancelled. I have notes from every incident in which Rachel came home to me in tears. I will use every shitty thing you've done to her and I will bury you. Lexie offered me the money. I'll take every cent she'll give me and I will win."

His smug arrogance fades and he begins to get defensive. "That's what it's all about, isn't it, you beating me?"

It takes everything I have not to scream in frustration.

"It's not about you! It's not about me! It's about Rachel! Tell me that you don't see the hurt in her eyes. Don't you notice how little she calls you, how seldom she even tries to invite you to her events. She doesn't hang on your every word anymore. Don't you miss that?" I plead with him to hear me, to understand. "Rand, I know that you made the best choice when you left. I'll admit that I didn't like it. It hurt like hell for a long time, but I am over it and I really, truly, wish you and Sherry the best. I am happy you have a baby on the way. But please, don't forget you have another child who needs you."

His gaze drops. "She doesn't need me for anything. She has never needed me for anything. You made sure of that." Rand's chin lifts as he tries to resume the battle, but I ignore the barb.

"She needs you more than ever now. The next few years are crucial. You set the tone for how she'll let men treat her. If she does not feel valued by you, the most important man in her life, she'll get knocked up by the first guy that tells her she's cute, like I did. She needs you. "

"Aw fuck, Skylar, I don't even know where to start." He casts a helpless look at me. "You always knew the right thing to do, the best thing to say. When we were together, you were the buffer. Now there is her and me. Sherry is clueless."

"All she needs is you. Make some time for her. Sometimes she can come across as sullen but if you look past that, you'll see she is feeling rejected. Mostly she is scared once the baby comes, you won't need or want her. She is excited to have a sibling, she really is. Don't let her be displaced. Include her." I grasp for an idea, a starting suggestion for him. "Maybe you could take her shopping for the baby?"

"I can do that. Do you think she'd like to do that?"

"I don't know but you've got to try. I believe it will be easier if she knows that she's not in competition with the baby and losing. She's coming back. Please think about what I said? And call me if she is giving you grief. We are in this together," I whisper as Rachel approaches. I hold my hand out. Instead of shaking the offered limb, he gives me a quick hug. Our shocked expressions inspire a sheepish shrug from him.

"Say goodbye to your dad so he can go," I direct my daughter.

Rachel doesn't move. Warily, she shifts her eyes back and forth between us, unused to the two of us on good terms, facing her together.

"I know I was mad at you for calling your mom, but I want you to know I am not mad anymore. I should have spent more time with you, Rachel. I'm sorry," Rand says and I smile at him encouragingly. Rachel looks at the ground. He hugs her. It's a stiff and awkward embrace. Rachel pulls back, brushing defiantly at a tear.

"Maybe next time..." he begins. I shake my head, warning him with a look that now is not the time for empty promises. "Let's try again in a few weeks? I do want to see you again on your next visit." I see regret in his eyes for the first time. If it is genuine then there is hope for the two of them. For Rachel's sake, I hope he tries. To me he says, "Here are your keys. Your car is parked outside. Rachel can show you where we left it. I'll catch a taxi home."

Rachel and I watch him walk away. This time she is the only one bothered by his leaving. When he is gone, she erupts with deep sobs. "I'm sorry, Mom. I ruined your holiday," she apologizes, losing the control she fought to retain in front of her father.

"It's okay!" I lie as I gather her in my arms. "Don't give it another thought. I missed you so much."

"I missed you too," Rachel chokes out. "All we were doing was fighting and arguing. The harder I tried to get Daddy to spend time with me, the more he and Sherry fought. She always won. I just don't understand, Mom, why doesn't he want me?" Rachel asks, breaking into a new round of tears.

I take her by the cheeks. My thumbs wipe her tears; my eyes beg her to believe me.

"He wants you. Your dad loves you. Unfortunately, he isn't showing it the way you want him to. I know that hurts. Sometimes we adults get so caught up in our stuff, we don't see what we are doing to the people around us. I talked to him, and I think he gets it this time. I let him know he is very close to losing what's left of the relationship you have. It scared him. It really did. He wants to try harder and when he does, Rachel, you have to be willing to meet him halfway. You have to recognize when he is trying and give him a chance."

"What if he does the same thing as usual?"

"I know your dad truly loves you." I grope for his side of the story. "He fell in love with you the day you were born and that kind of love doesn't ever go away. Sherry isn't having an easy pregnancy. Your dad isn't doing a good job managing both the girls in his life. I think he is holding out hope that once the baby comes, Sherry won't need him so much."

"What do you think?" Rachel doubtfully wipes the tears from her eyes.

"If he doesn't try harder, you will have to decide what you want me to do. I can try and get his visitation reduced. That is a last resort only; hopefully it won't come to that. If you both work hard things will get better. Besides, in a few months you will have a baby brother or sister who you will love so much, you won't have time for your dad. You'll be too busy cuddling him or her."

Rachel gives me a halfhearted smile. From there, it is easy to move on to the business of getting home. Rachel leads me and my luggage to the car. For the first part of our drive home, we share the details of our time apart. Rachel omits the parts that will reopen the wounds for her, and I omit any details of Mack. I tell her about the cottage, the ocean, my painting and even about Michael and Tracina. She tells me about her visit with Rand's parents and the rides she enjoyed at the Stampede. It is after midnight before we are finally home and in our beds.

Exhaustion threatens. Before I can give in to it, I have a promise to keep. Everything should be finished, done, ended. A swift clean cut, amputating the connection between us would have been best. As it stands, I have butchered the process of leaving with a knife too dull to cut. I dial Mack's number.

He answers on the first ring, his voice heavy with sleep. "Sky, babe, is that you?" Hearing his voice makes me feel full and empty all at once.

"We made it home, Mack." My voice comes out hardly louder than a whisper.

"How is Rachel?"

"Better now."

"How did it go with Rand? Was it ugly?"

"I'm wrung out but it could have been worse. I think I got through to him. God, I hope I got through to him because Rachel can't take much more of what he's dishing out." My exhausted yawn muffles the last word.

"Thank you for calling. I really didn't think you would. I'd have gone nuts wondering how you were doing."

"It means a lot to me that you care."

"I do care," he says.

I want to tell him I care too, and that I will never forget him, but it wouldn't be fair to express either of those sentiments. I close my eyes against threatening tears, hoping he can't hear how close I am to losing it. I press the heel of my hand to my forehead. I don't want the connection with him to end.

"I have to let you go," I manage to say finally.

"Don't say goodbye, say goodnight."

"Mack..."

"Not tonight, Skylar. This isn't goodbye, not yet."

"How can it not be? I am home. I am home." I am not sure who I am trying harder to convince, me or him.

"Please, babe."

In the morning, I will blame my lack of willpower on fatigue.

"Goodnight, Mack," I whisper.

Chapter 21

I feel like a foot crammed into a shoe a half size too small. It is as if, while I was gone, someone came and stole ten square feet off each room of my apartment. I miss Eleuthera's ever changing views. The closest thing to natural beauty I have here is a patch of green grass outside my window.

The inside of my apartment is no better. At some point my walls were white but over the years they have darkened to cream. Any darker and they will match the beige carpet. Last year I asked for a repaint. The management company turned down my request. It's been a while since I washed them. A good scrubbing might help but a part of me thinks the effort would be wasted, not unlike trying to cover a bullet wound with a Band-Aid.

The dry summer heat holds me firmly in bed. It sucks the moisture from my skin and the energy from my muscles. Eleuthera was hot, but the air moved. The humidity lubricated my movements. The Alberta heat is stifling. If I want to survive, I should get out of bed and go buy an air conditioner. Our suitcases need to be unpacked. I have laundry to wash. My fridge is empty. I can't make toast, or even cereal. I could open a can of soup, but the idea of eating hot chicken noodle on a hot morning… I'm not interested. I begin a mental list of everything I need to do but quickly realize there is too much to possibly remember. I get up and write the chores down. I found a reason to get myself out of bed and now I can put one foot in front of the other until this day passes. I'm back home, back to making it through the day, back to doing what must be done.

The phone rings.

"What the hell happened?" My sister barks loudly in my ear.

I hold the phone away from my head. When I am certain she is done blasting, I speak into the receiver. "Didn't you get my letter?"

"Sure. Rachel and Rand had a meltdown. So what? Why didn't you tell them to deal with it?"

"I tried but it was a bloody mess. Rand didn't want her and Rachel knew it. She was destroyed. I had to come home."

"That's a matter of opinion. I talked to Mack and got a very clear picture. I'll be back in a few days. We'll talk then." My sister hangs up the phone, leaving me to wonder about her discussion with Mack.

"Was that Aunt Lexie?" Rachel asks, emerging from her bedroom. "I wanted to talk to her."

"No you don't. She knows I left because of you and your dad. She is furious."

Rachel's forehead furrows slightly at the thought. "You should have stayed."

"I didn't realize that was an option." The sarcastic reply rolls out of my mouth. I can tell my daughter is uncertain how to respond. "We make choices and we live with the consequences. She'll get over it. C'mon. We've got lots to do. Get dressed. We'll have to go out for breakfast, and then we need to get some groceries. I want to get our laundry done so we need to unpack."

"Can I call Amanda?"

"No. The two of you will start to make plans. I have some things that I want your help with first." I sound bitchy but there's no way around my mood. Nothing short of flying back to Eleuthera will have an impact. All I can do is bury myself in my old priorities and hope that with time, I will re-adjust to the simple routines of my life.

After a quick fast-food breakfast, we hit our local grocery store and restock the fridge and cupboards. I start the laundry and realize that I need to reorganize my closet and dressers to fit my new clothes. This leads to a purge of enormous proportions. I decide since my bedroom is already a mess, I might as well wash walls and windows. If I am going to do my bedroom walls and windows, I might as well do the rest of the apartment. Rachel would rather watch TV but I ignore her protests and make it clear that she will have no social life until we accomplish my goals. It takes days but eventually every nook and cranny is washed, reorganized and divested of clutter. The apartment hasn't grown any bigger, but it's clean. Over bowls of chili and rice, I tell Rachel she can do supper dishes and then she is free.

"I still have to go through my old paintings and see if there is anything good enough to add to the gallery website." From my tiny dungeon of a storage room, I unearth several finished paintings. Some of them go back ten years, a few are even older. The old paintings are scattered around my living room waiting to be photographed and placed back into the storage room on the newly installed shelves I purchased. Assorted painting paraphernalia also waits to be returned to storage. "But that can wait until tomorrow. I am tired." I yawn and stretch, groaning as my stiff muscles protest. "I think I am going to drop into my bed and sleep for the next two days."

"What should I do?" Rachel follows me down the hallway to the bathroom.

"I don't have a clue but I am sure you will figure something out."

"Would you like some time to paint?" she asks. "You have a week before you start back at the group home, right? I think you should paint."

"That would be wonderful but if I do that, you'll be stuck sitting around, watching TV. You'll get enough of that once I am back at the group home. I figured we'd come up with a few things to keep us busy." I unsnap my jeans and slide them down my hips. A shower is going to feel wonderful on my aching muscles.

"Amanda was hoping I could go to summer camp with her. If I go, you could have a whole week to yourself."

I stop mid shimmy, my hands hanging onto the jeans I was going to kick off.

"You're kidding me, right? We've only been home a few days and already you want to leave?" With the next thought, I get a sick feeling in my stomach. "Is this part of the reason I had to fly back here? So help me God, Rachel, if you created that fight with your dad just because you were bored and wanted to go to camp with Amanda..."

"No, Mom. I wouldn't do that to you. Honest." Her eyes widen at the accusation. "Amanda just told me about camp today. I talked to her when you went to the store to get the shelves. Karen saw we were back and wondered if I would want to go. She even called the camp and asked if they have room. I never knew about it until today. Honest."

I want to be convinced but I also want a reason to be angry. It hurt to leave Eleuthera and it bothers me that she is unaware of my pain. This small, bitter part of me isn't willing to let my anger go.

"If I ever find out that you lied to me about this, I will strip your world, Rachel. Do you understand me?" She shakes her head rapidly. Her wide grey eyes beg me to believe her. "I know it's a harsh thing to accuse you of doing, but what am I supposed to believe? I dropped everything for you! I gave up my vacation to come and get you and you just want to be gone!" Having given a voice to my anger, I can feel it swell.

"I'm sorry, Mom. I don't have to go. I'll stay home with you." She backs up.

Now guilt begins to war with anger. At the root of both emotions is loneliness. I miss Mack and I was counting on Rachel to get me through this time. She is my focal point, my only weapon to hold misery at bay. I make my way to the kitchen table and crumple on a chair. Rachel stands where I left her, unsure about moving or speaking. I hate seeing her frozen by my anger. I don't want her to leave but if she stays, I will make her miserable. I am feeling more resentment than I can contain.

"I'll call Karen and make arrangements for you to go."

Rachel is gracious enough not to show any pleasure. For the rest of the evening and all of the next morning, we barely talk. I call Karen and I call the camp. They have room for Rachel. The camp is at a lake, two hours north of Edmonton. There is no need for both families to make the trip, so I offer to make the drive because I need to pay Rachel's fees and fill out some forms. Karen has already completed these tasks by mail.

It's a long drive. Rachel is subdued and Amanda gives up trying to coax her into talking. Still smoldering, I have no desire to play act and don't even bother to play the radio for their benefit. Bored, they fall asleep. When I finally turn off the highway and onto a gravel road, Amanda wakes. She nudges Rachel and the two of them watch out the window for the first glimpse of water. I brace myself, expecting the sight of sand and water to make me feel even worse but the need to shore up my defenses is unnecessary. The water is dark and murky; the sand is brown and not a fine pink powder. We park in front of the camp office. The musty lake smell fills my nostrils and does not spark any memories. Relieved, I head into the camp office. Then we haul the girl's belongings to the bunkhouse. Finally, I say goodbye. The drive back to Edmonton is long and miserable even though the sun is shining.

I reach home. My living room needs to be emptied of paintings and art supplies and it takes hours to put everything onto the new shelves. Eventually there are only my old paintings to sort. The largest is an abstract I attempted while going to university. The smallest is an eight by eight inch painting of Rachel as a baby. There are several landscapes. I photograph them and send them in an e-mail to Tracina and Michael for their examination.

With a full afternoon ahead of me, I decide to try painting. I haul my easel and paints to the apartment courtyard. I've painted in this space dozens of times and usually never have a problem finding something to capture on canvas but not even Mrs. Carlson's balcony overflowing with potted blooming flowers sparks my interest. I want to be back in Mack's bedroom painting him or on the beach painting waves while he putters nearby. The wooden weight of the brush in my hand and the bare canvas mock me. I give up. I have always painted with my heart as much as my hands and my eyes and right now, my heart just isn't up to the task. I take everything back inside. Without Rachel as a distraction, my island withdrawal will only become more acute. I call the group home and offer to go back to work early.

Chapter 22

There are fifteen messages on my voice mail. All are from Lexie. She's back from Eleuthera and from the quantity and quality of the messages she has left, I surmise she wants to chew a piece of my ass off. Her last message threatens bodily harm if I don't call her at home as soon as I get in. I dial her number.

Unfortunately, she answers. "Finally got up the courage to call me back?"

I keep my voice light. I can't avoid the coming argument but maybe she'll make small talk first. "I went to work at the group home. For the last few days, I haven't been home other than to sleep."

"I'll be over in a bit," she says. It takes a few seconds for me to realize she has hung up. There is no way I can put off her visit.

Of all the crappy luck.

I take a quick shower and fall asleep on my couch waiting for her to arrive. An incessant pounding wakes me from my doze. A large paper bag smelling suspiciously of our favorite Chinese takeout is cradled in my sister's hands. A plastic bag is looped over her wrist. It clinks as she passes by me. Dropping her packages on the table, Lexie returns to my kitchen, pulling plates and wine glasses out of my cupboards. "You can run but you can't hide. Not forever. You are so lucky I had a few days to cool off before I got home. When I got back to the cottage and got your note, I was pissed!" She rummages through my silverware drawer for cutlery. "So, where is the damsel in distress?"

"Summer camp."

"Let me get this straight. You blew me off for a daughter who couldn't be bothered to stick around?"

"I did not blow you off. You buggered off with Cal, remember. I couldn't get a hold of you and I had no way of knowing when you'd be back. I wasn't sure you would even return before we were scheduled to leave."

"I left to give you time with Mack. For the first time in over four years, you were having sex with a man and enjoying his company. I wanted to make sure I stayed the hell out of your way. Where's your cork screw thingy?"

"In the back of the drawer." She digs around, coming up with the implement before burying it into the cork. She sloshes burgundy wine into a glass and thrusts it into my hand.

I set the glass down. "I'm sorry. I did what I had to do."

"No, you did what they wanted you to do. Was she bleeding, was she injured? Did Rand hit her, abuse her? Or did she just want her mommy?"

Through clenched teeth, I warn my sister. "Leave Rachel out of this."

"I kind of have to, seeing as how she is not here, getting the kick in the ass she deserves. You should've forced them to work it out. Instead you had to race back and stick your nose into it."

"I did try and Rand told me to come and get her. You know what he is like. When has he ever done right by her?"

Lexie opens the bag of food. The tart vapors of the pineapple sauce waft up to my nose. My mouth immediately fills with saliva and my stomach starts to beg for the golden chicken balls which accompany the sauce. If I am going to have the argument, I might as well eat her food. I take the tinfoil dish she passes and begin spooning rice onto my plate.

"I bet it felt great, swooping in and showing Rand up. Not to mention it got you the hell away from Mack. No doubt it was getting pretty serious between the two of you. I saw him before I left. Want to know how he was doing?"

My spoonful of rice hangs in midair for a second. Lexie smiles. I return to filling my plate, wishing I wasn't quite so transparent.

"It doesn't matter."

"Keep saying the words, Sis, and someday maybe we'll both believe them. I only want to rub a little salt in the wound. Now that I have, I'm actually going to tell you something guaranteed to make you feel better. We have something to celebrate." She reaches down and pulls a long white envelope out of her purse. "Tracina dropped this off for you. It's a check for your seascape." Lexie plops a huge chicken ball into her mouth. Her cheeks bulge as she chews and manages to swallow the whole thing.

I open the envelope, gasping at the size of the check.

"Who would pay two thousand dollars for a painting?"

"She didn't say. But congratulations." Lexie raises her glass of wine. "To the beginning of a new career." She tops up my untouched glass.

"One painting sold is not a career."

"You just don't want to get your hopes up. Get that sour look off your face. It's time to do a little bit of celebrating. Since Rachel isn't here, why don't we head out on the prowl? Isn't there a little bar just down the block?"

"I'm tired."

"Suck it up. I'm the injured party here. You dumped me to come home. If I can get over being angry, you can put a smile on and drink some damn wine. Unless… Oh. I get it. This sour mood is about Mack, isn't it?"

"No, it's not. I just worked several days in a row and I have an early morning shift. I was looking forward to a nice relaxing evening."

"You are a terrible liar, Skylar. If it helps, I will tell you Mack looked just as miserable as you. We can stay in. I have plenty of wine. I'll keep you company while you wallow in your misery over Mack."

Lexie leaves when both bottles of wine are empty. I helped her drink more of the wine than I intended and now I wish I had convinced her to stay. I'm in no shape to be alone. The wine has sharpened my loneliness. It is weakening my resolve and clouding my judgment. My knees tremble as I walk to the phone, sitting on the end table next to my couch. My fingers punch in a number I only dialed once but memorized instantly.

Mack answers after a few rings. I close my eyes as his husky drawl fills my ear. I say nothing and wait for his voice again. "Skylar, I know it's you," he says finally.

I curse the inventor of call display. "I'm sorry, I shouldn't have called." Cringing, I intend on hanging up.

"No, don't hang up." He rushes the words out. "You called for a reason. Talk to me, tell me why you called."

"Stupidity. Loneliness. Take your pick. Lexie and I drank two bottles of wine and I am sorry. Drunk calling is not the sign of a mature woman. I'll let you go."

"Don't hang up." His softly whispered request stops me. "How are you doing?"

"I've been better."

"Me too. I'm no closer to getting you out of my mind than I was the day you left."

"It hasn't been easy for me either, Mack."

He huffs in disbelief.

"Did I not just take the first opportunity to call you, even though I knew it would only make me feel worse? I am in the middle of one huge pity party over leaving Eleuthera. I regret it already. Crazy, huh?"

"Your only regret is leaving the island early?"

I want to blame what I say next on the lingering effects of the wine, but the words go through my mind and I make a conscious choice to speak them. "I regret leaving you. I thought it would be easier than this. I honestly thought I could come home and plunge back into my life like none of it ever happened. I can't. I'm not the same. I miss you. I have no business, no right to tell you this after the way I left you but I do miss you."

There is a lengthy pause during which I expect him to hang up. His voice is soft, huskier, his accent deeper. "I miss you too, darlin'. I'm still mad as heck with you for leaving."

"You should be. I am mad at me too. I screwed up. I didn't realize I was racing home to be with a daughter who'd rather be at summer camp."

"Rachel's not home?"

"Nope. I dropped her off a few days back. I'm sorry, Mack. I made a mistake. I should have stayed. I wish I could have those days back with you."

"When is she back?"

"Sunday morning."

"I might be able to be there by Wednesday afternoon."

"No," I whisper. It's not a refusal but a 'no' of disbelief. He hears the difference.

"Try me."

"After the way I left things..."

"Yeah, I know. I'm a glutton for punishment, a real masochist. What can I say, Skylar? I'm only attracted to women who don't want me."

"I want you, Mack. Leaving had nothing to do with you and everything to do with my daughter and my life here. I left because I thought I had to. I'm pretty sure it was the stupidest decision I made in my life. I am sorry."

"Give me your address."

"That is a bad idea." I waver. I was never going to do this. I can't do this. I can't invite him here. It will change everything. What a terrifying and exhilarating thought.

"Give me your address," he repeats.

I should end the call and let him go but after having more, I don't want to live with less. I don't want to wait for the years to pass before I can live my life. I give Mack my information.

"I'll be there as soon as I can," he promises.

I drop the phone back into its cradle, uncertain if I have made the worst or best decision of my life. On Eleuthera, I was alive and hopeful. I haven't felt anything but horrible since I returned. I know the life I have here is not enough; Rachel is not enough.

Chapter 23

Twenty four hours later, I open the door to find Mack leaning casually against the door frame. His mouth is curved into a wide grin and his arms open when I throw myself at him. I swear he smells of saltwater and sand when I bury my face into his neck. My fingers reach to stroke his lips. He nips my fingers playfully, causing my stomach to loop as if I am in a speeding car, flying over short sharp hills.

Did I really think I could give up someone whose smile has the power to suck the breath out of me? What woman in her right mind would give up this man, with his sun-whitened curls and golden green eyes? I tremble, as much from his mouth on mine as from fear of what I nearly lost. Mack kisses me with such hunger I forget we are standing in the hallway of my apartment, in plain view of anyone walking by. His mouth loves mine. It does not lift as he pushes me back into my apartment, kicking the door closed behind us.

"I missed you too." He speaks the words against my mouth. "I hope you don't mind if we skip the tour. There is only one room I want to see." A backpack falls from his shoulder to the floor.

In my bedroom, I quickly tug his wrappings away. Mack takes a slower approach, reacquainting himself with every inch of my exposed flesh. I let him bare me to his eyes before bringing him to my bed. My thighs straddle his hips; his mouth is hot on my breast. Our reconnection shatters all delusions that I could find this again with someone else or that I could settle for anything less. Wrapped in Mack's arms, I descend into the first solid, satisfying chunk of sleep I've had since leaving the island.

* * *

I am slicing bananas into a fruit salad the next morning, when Mack emerges from my bedroom, wearing only his jeans. His arms encircle my waist. He drops a kiss on my neck.

"Where do you keep your glasses?" he asks. I point him in the right direction. He fills a glass and drinks thirstily. "Your apartment is bloody hot."

"You grew up in Texas, you live in the Bahamas, and you are whining about Alberta heat?"

"Want some help?"

"I'm almost done but you can grab the orange juice out of the fridge."

The juice jug and two glasses are set on the table. Mack sits. His eyes follow my movements around the narrow kitchen. I dig utensils out of the drawer and then take a plate of toast and the bowl of fruit salad to the table. A thick blue potholder protects my hand as I lift the lid from a pan filled with hot scrambled eggs and bacon.

As he scoops eggs on to his plate, he asks, "So I was wondering exactly how much time do I have before you kick me out of your life again?"

The question stops me briefly, but it is not unexpected. I empty a serving spoon full of eggs on to my plate. Then I take a drink of orange juice, buying myself a few moments while I struggle to formulate a response. The silence grows awkward before I finally answer.

"I haven't thought ahead, Mack. I have no answer. I don't know how this could possibly work and yet I can't bear to say goodbye again."

"This became more than a fling the second I left the island, Skylar. You better get used to the idea." Mack picks up his fork. "I didn't fly all this way for a screw and another goodbye."

"What do you see happening, what do you want?"

He clasps my hand across the table. "I want to see you again. I want to be here with you and I want you to come and be with me. I want to know that I am the only man in your bed. I want you to be the only woman in my bed."

I close my eyes and let a shudder roll through me. I want a future with him beyond today and he has surpassed my wildest expectations by throwing in commitment and exclusivity.

"I want you in my life, Mack. I'm just not sure how to have you, and not hurt Rachel."

"We take it slow until you are ready to bring her into this."

"You make it sound so simple but it isn't. We live a continent apart and doing this without Rachel being involved pretty much restricts us to every second weekend when she is with her father and I am supposed to be working at my weekend job. Can you handle that?"

"If you consider giving up your weekend job? Don't go getting all huffy. Think about it from my perspective. I will not fly here for crumbs of your time, for a couple of quick fucks in between your jobs."

"Every second weekend sounds like crumbs of time to me. And we may not even have that much. I sure don't believe you'll be able to fly here every single second weekend. And I won't be able to afford to fly to Eleuthera either, especially without the second job. I don't see how this is going to work." My chin wobbles before I let out a frustrated sigh.

"Skylar, look at me. We have distance and your concern for your daughter working against us. If you add a lack of time to this equation, we are dead before we begin. I'm not saying it won't be tough at times but tough is not impossible. We will talk this out until it makes sense and we make it work." His confidence makes me hopeful. "I won't put the burden of flying on you. I'll handle that. You have to meet me halfway."

"My job at the group home has been a saving grace. It's helped me pay for new tires, Christmas presents, and every emergency that pops up. But you're right. I don't want you flying all this way to sit around while I work. Between my counseling job and Rachel's child support, I can get by."

"Are you sure, because I don't want to add stress,"

"No, I can do it."

"As long as you are willing to try, that is all I ask. If we need to reevaluate down the road, we will. Flexibility will be required by both of us."

"And patience. Especially you. Can you really handle being with someone who puts her daughter first? How is that going to feel two or three months down the road? You deserve someone who can give you their full attention, who is not conflicted. I don't understand why you would even consider this?"

His eyes brighten; mischief dances his mouth into a smile. "A man will go to almost any lengths for good sex, darlin'."

I roll my eyes.

"I'm teasing! Seriously, when you aren't being all insecure, you blow my mind. Aside from my physical and sexual attraction to you, I respect you. I can tell by your protective instincts, you are a wonderful mother. I appreciate your work ethic and I admire your strong values even when they create friction between us. I think it is refreshing to spend time with someone who can take pleasure in the simplest things such as a nice meal, a quiet evening, a beautiful sunset. You are easily pleased."

"Thanks, I think."

"It is a compliment. You are a woman who knows what she wants and is happy when she gets it. I like that you are open minded to new experiences. You have your own interests and let me do my own thing. No diva tendencies. You love the island. We fit. There's never been a moment when I was bored or I wanted to be somewhere else. That's rare, Skylar. Laughing, arguing, playing, or talking; it's all interesting when I do it with you. And every time you open yourself up to me a little more, I feel like I have been entrusted with a rare gift." His thumb strokes the back of my hand. "Is this relationship going to be inconvenient? Is it going to cost me money? Yes. But the alternative is to never see you again. I tried that and I didn't like it."

"I didn't like not seeing you either. I guess I can't believe you would be willing to travel all this way, and put up with all my limitations."

"I am willing. I can be patient."

"I hope so. It's important for me to be sure we fit off the island, before you meet Rachel. Plus, Rand and Sherry are having a baby. I don't want to add you to the mix too close to that event. Rachel will need time to adjust to that change as well."

"That's fair. How much time are we talking about? When's the baby due?"

"Beginning of January. If everything goes well, maybe you could meet Rachel in February? March…maybe, at the latest?" I add when I see him frown. "We may not even last that long. Have you thought of that? Two months from now, you might be sick of flying to see me," I say, only half joking.

"Not going to happen." He dismisses my fears, not because they are of no consequence but because he refuses to entertain them. Mack doesn't get caught up in playing the what-if game. "I'll admit I am nervous about meeting your daughter. If it doesn't go well, that will be difficult to overcome. I'm in no hurry. We can wait."

"Thank you."

"I've got some news which changes things slightly. I'm going back to work in the States. After you left, I called Max and Sam and told them to line up some work. They've found a little project in Houston. I'm meeting with my brothers at the beginning of September. If I like the look of it, I'll be back in Texas fulltime at the end of September. I'll close up the house in Eleuthera and be closer. I've checked and a direct flight from Edmonton to Houston is a little over four hours."

"That is wonderful. Rachel will be going to see her dad when she comes back from camp and Lexie might be taking her to the island for a week before school starts. I might have a couple of weeks to spend with you in August, if you're not busy."

"I won't be."

"It won't be like this forever, Mack. I promise."

"No, it won't. I think we have a good start on this compromise and negotiating thing. What do you think? I know I am going to be telling everyone I have a girlfriend in Canada. Are you sure you want a boyfriend?"

I push my chair back from the table; my feet bring me to him. I sit on his lap and wrap my arms around his neck. Looking him directly in the eyes, I lower my lips to his. His mouth is warm, firm. I lick his bottom lip lightly. His mouth opens slightly and he expels a small breath. I stroke my way into his mouth until his tongue meets mine in a quick light greeting. I open my lips wider, nudging his mouth open a little more. My tongue dances out to find his again. My hands tighten in his hair and I wiggle a little in his lap. I put everything I can into the kiss.

"I want you. Nothing more. Just you."

The heavy discussions have come to an end. Now, as it was on the island, I can focus on being with him. And when he leaves, I'll be looking forward to the next time I am in his arms. What a comforting thought. He's coming back, of this there is no question. He will be back in my home and in my bed again. He has made it clear that how long he will keep coming depends on how hard I am willing to work to keep him. Rachel may not be ready for him but I have a few ideas on how I can help her along.

Chapter 24

Rand's slow response to the light chime of his doorbell has me wondering if I made a three hour drive for nothing. My palms are sweaty and I feel like there are a hundred little fingers trying to press their way out of my stomach. I give Rachel's shoulders a reassuring squeeze, but she won't look at me. She is upset with me for forcing this meeting.

Not since before the divorce have we all met without lawyers being present. After how we left things at the airport, I hoped Rand would be agreeable to this meeting but it took some persuading. I had to promise I was not going to upset Sherry. If our discussion deteriorates, I also promised to leave immediately. It was an easy promise to make. If Mack and I are going to have any hope of a future together, I need to get Rachel and Rand's relationship straightened out. It is my hope that once Rachel has stability and security in all her closest relationships, she is less likely to feel threatened by the introduction of Mack.

Rand answers the door. Rachel steps in first, struggling with her suitcase. She is spending the week here, provided we can get through this meeting. Mack is waiting for me in a hotel room in Edmonton.

This is the first time I've been inside Rand and Sherry's house. Divorce and remarriage haven't hurt him a bit; he's got a beautiful home. If I wasn't so intent on improving the relationship between Rand and myself, I'd consider hauling him back to court. A few pictures of this place and any judge would be convinced Rand could afford more child support than I am currently receiving.

"I'll let Sherry know you're here." Rand leaves us to wait in the formal dining room. Custom window treatments frame a large window and a chandelier light fixture floats above a contemporary oak table. I glance around and immediately find it hard to believe people actually live in this space. Every surface, nook, and cranny is immaculate. The only thing out of place is me, with my travel rumpled slacks and blouse. *I should have worn cashmere and pearls. Oh that's right, I don't own either of those,* I think and immediately give myself a mental kick for the slip into bitchiness. I am supposed to be on good behavior. Rachel carelessly drops her suitcase by the table.

"Be careful. These floors are hardwood. You'll scratch them," I hiss.

"Whatever. Like you really care about their floors?"

It's been one snide comment after another since she returned from camp. My eyes snap towards her, daring her to continue. She lapses into silence after a quick sideways glance in my direction. Slouching into the nearest chair, she crosses her arms over her chest and stretches her legs out. She better change her attitude. I've had my fill of teenage angst. Patience worn thin, I've warned her that her trip with Lexie to Eleuthera is on the line.

Rand rejoins us and escorts Sherry to a chair before seating himself at the head of the table. I choose an open chair between Rand and Rachel.

"You are looking well." I begin by complimenting Sherry. Accepting my compliment, she inclines her head and takes Rand's hand. I suspect the gesture is more for reassurance than to assert a possessive claim. Presenting a united front, their gazes lock on each other before finally meeting mine. The first time I met Sherry in person, I was thrown off guard by her innocent appearance. With a halo of soft blond curls and big blue eyes, she doesn't look like the home wrecking type. Over time, I've found her to be a little immature and used to being indulged. It has always amazed me that she could look me in the eye after sleeping with my husband. Now I feel a little in her debt. Thanks to her, I am free of Rand and that freedom brought me Mack.

For the last several days, I had planned out how I would start this conversation but I realize nothing I came up with seems right. I intended on approaching this situation like I would any family counseling session but I am not at work. I can't avoid the fact that I am not a detached, impartial mediator in this situation. I've got ownership in this mess.

After a deep breath, I begin. "The last visit didn't go very well, but before we get to that, I want to start by making some apologies. Rachel, I want to tell you that I am sorry because somewhere along the way, you have come to believe that in order to show your love and loyalty to me, you have to remain hostile to your dad. Rand, the way you and Sherry's relationship began, allowed me to feel, more than a little, morally superior and definitely justified in my anger. I've held on to this anger so long it's become almost habitual. You hurt me. But that was years ago and I need to get over it." I pause to refill my lungs, because I raced through the sentences, spewing everything out before I chickened out. Neither Rand nor Sherry has softened at all in response to my words. They are still waiting for the proverbial ax to fall. "I'm serious. I need to get over it and that requires nothing from either of you. I know there was no real malice behind your actions. Neither of you ever deliberately wanted to hurt me. That was just an unfortunate side effect." It feels good to say the words, but it feels better to know they are true.

"Just like that, you're over it?" Rachel's laugh oozes skepticism.

"Yes. Yes I am. And if I can get over it, so can you."

"Why is that the adult answer to everything. 'Get over it!' You might be ready to forgive them but I'm not!"

"You really hate me." Sherry's words are barely a whisper; her tiny teeth chew at her bottom lip.

"Of course I do! My dad would still be at home if it wasn't for you!"

"Please let me finish, Rachel. The way your dad left us was wrong. But everyone makes mistakes. Would you like your mistakes held over your head for years on end? How long are we going to stay angry? I'm done. I will not hold on to my anger for another minute. Rand and Sherry don't need or require my forgiveness and I am not here to dole it out." I pause momentarily, making sure Rachel is really listening before I continue. "When I got pregnant with you, in the middle of going to college, many people thought it was a terrible mistake and that keeping you would ruin my life and my future. Deciding to keep you made things a little more difficult but you were, you are, the best thing that has ever happened to me."

"And to me," Rand joins in. "Keeping and raising you was never a mistake."

"Exactly, but us getting married so young was a mistake. Over time, it became clear you were the only thing holding us together and that was never supposed to be your job. We regret hurting you, and failing to keep our marriage together but everything happens for a reason. If your dad hadn't met and married Sherry, you would not have this baby brother or sister on the way. I don't want to diminish what we put you through, but you need to remember you never really lost your father."

"You moved away! You didn't even ask me if I wanted to go with you!" Rachel hurls the accusation at Rand. Sherry winces, but Rand sits silently.

I tug her hands and her attention back to me. "I never gave your dad a choice."

"But did he even ask?"

"He wouldn't. He couldn't ask for you when he left, not because he didn't want you but because he had hurt me so much, he didn't want to make it worse by taking you away. That was a very kind thing for him to do. I knew your dad wanted you too, but I was so mad, I was certain he didn't deserve you. I never gave him the option; I never allowed the discussion. There was no way I could consider you living with him, especially if it meant, I could not see you every day." My thumbs brush away the tears stacking up under her eyes. My eyes are burning. Tears threaten to cloud my vision. I avoid blinking.

Hesitantly, Rachel turns to her dad. "Is that true? If you could have, would you have taken me with you?"

"Yes, Rachel." Rand's voice cracks. "I wanted you. Not fighting for you, packing up, and moving away were not the best ways of showing it. I wish I had not done those things because now it makes it hard for you to believe me but I always wanted you. I want you now. I would love to have you live with me but I could not ask you to. Not just for your mom's sake; I didn't want you to have to choose."

Rachel sits a little straighter in her seat. As she absorbs what we have told her, I can see her lighten, her anger diminishing. Able to look back at the past with new eyes, she looks at her father and smiles. His eyes shine back at her. I cover my mouth and my tears fall.

"Skylar, I know you are probably feeling like you should be all noble here and make the offer..." Rand suggests.

I nod my head as I scrub at the tears on my cheeks. As fast as I wipe them, they return. A solid wave of guilt takes my breath away and the rush of fear that follows takes my voice away. "I can't..." A sob stumbles out, dragging more behind it.

Rachel's lip quivers. "Dad, I feel better knowing that you do want me, but I don't think I want to move here."

I want to squeeze her tight and bind her to me but instead I bury my face in my hands, hiding my immense relief. My daughter pats my back.

"I think we all could use some tissues," Sherry gets up from the table. "I'll be right back." Her cheeks are just as tear streaked as mine. She returns with a box in hand and passes me a liberal stack.

Rand stands and hugs our daughter tightly. "I'm not going to lie, Rachel. It hurts but I understand. I love you and I promise, from now on, I will do my best to make you feel welcome and wanted here with us. I don't want you to ever doubt again how important you are to me."

* * *

Later that night in Mack's hotel room, I recount the day's events for him. I am able to keep from crying because nothing seems as bad when he holds me. "I was certain I would lose her."

"But in the end everything turned out okay?"

My fingers stroke his chest while I answer. "There is no end. Issues will continue to crop up but I could feel a change. Rand and Sherry have work to do with Rachel and I have to stay out of it, unless I can help. I've invited Sherry to call me anytime she is having a problem. My daughter has been warned that I will not accept her treating Sherry with anything less than respect. Sherry admitted that she is very insecure about Rachel and I, and the past we share with Rand. She said she will try to be less demanding of

Rand's time when Rachel is with them. A great many bad feelings were laid to rest. To show my sincerity, and as a gesture of good will, I bought a gift for the baby. It was presented with an offer. Sometime in the future, when the baby is old enough, if they feel comfortable, I asked if Rachel and I could have her little brother or sister for a visit so they can have a weekend away.

"That is a big gesture."

"Oh shut up." I give him a quick pinch. "I hear your sarcasm. I'll have you know, I really meant the offer and, surprisingly I think they will actually take me up on it."

"If you can baby-sit for your ex-husband and the woman he left you for so they can have a wild weekend of sex, I guess you are really over him."

"Did you have doubts?" When he doesn't answer, I reach for the ticklish spot on his hip. "Come on, did you really think I was still carrying a torch for my ex-husband?"

"Woman, stop! Before you get hurt." Mack rolls away but I follow, digging my fingers alongside his bare hip bone. "Okay, that's it. You asked for it!" The warning comes the second before I am pinned beneath him. He holds my wrists tightly above my head.

"Let go of me," I order.

"Not a chance."

"Lachlan, I'll only tell you this once, so you better listen. You will always be stronger than me. I, on the other hand, will always be meaner. Let go of me and we'll declare it a tie. Otherwise you are taking a risk that I'll get free and show you how incredibly vulnerable you are naked."

He loses his patronizing smirk. "You wouldn't dare."

"Is that a risk you are willing to take?"

His eyes disappear into a squint. He slowly releases me. The brief wrestling match is over. "Seeing you all feisty turns me on. Maybe next time I'll choose to see how mean you are."

"It's your body," I growl, biting his shoulder playfully.

Chapter 25

I am falling in love with Lachlan Mackenzie. A night of casual sex has grown to something more. I had strong feelings for him when I left the island. Nurtured by his constancy, his commitment, my feelings deepen. Every second Friday, he comes back to me, becoming a permanent reliable fixture.

Time apart is not the great obstacle I imagined it would be. Mack and I have the first whole week of August together while Rachel is with Rand and Sherry. He returns to Eleuthera. While he closes up his house, I have a week with my daughter. Lexie follows through on her promise and whisks Rachel away for ten days on the island. Very happy to hear Mack is back in my life, she also offers up a spare bedroom at her place. Mack accepts her offer, to my relief. Too often I find myself calculating the costs of his visit. Removing hotel rooms from the equation eases my guilt. I hate that he can't stay with me. Amanda and her family would be sure to notice him coming and going and make mention of him to Rachel.

After the long weekend in September, I start back to work at the high school and Mack returns to Houston to work with his brothers. It isn't the low cost housing project he hoped for but it is a small project which gets him back into work mode.

Leading a double life should be terribly complicated but with hard work, we make it work. The weeks pass and we settle into a comfortable groove. When Rachel is home, Mack and I sneak in daily phone calls to remain connected. When she is gone, he is always with me. The months pass and not even once has he called to cancel a weekend. My fears shrink as a future with him grows more probable than possible. I stop holding my breath.

Everything is going so well in fact, I am caught off guard by our first serious fight. The unexpected ripple, after months of calm, happens as we are enjoying a longer than usual weekend together. The November Remembrance Day holiday has fallen on a Monday. As a special treat, Mack has rented a hotel room with a Jacuzzi tub. Our champagne glasses are nearly empty. I am overheated to the point of sleepiness. My skin is flushed pink.

It was a tough week. Admittedly, I am beginning to rely on these weekends with Mack to get me through. It is nice to have someone to share my troubles with, to not feel so alone when I am struggling. My caseload at the school is full and I am overwhelmed by new responsibilities Krakow has given me.

"I think you should just quit," Mack suggests, immersed in water and bubbles. He lazily soaps my feet and legs.

"Wasn't that your solution back when I was working two jobs?"

"Yeah, and I think the same solution would apply here. You quit this nasty job and we'll have all the time in the world together." He gives me an exaggerated leer and begins to run the soapy sponge higher up on my thigh.

"What good would it be for me to be sitting at home all day when you are working in Houston?"

"If you quit your job, I'd be here so fast it would make your head spin. Sam doesn't need me. He could handle the work by himself. Think of all the fun we could have with no work to tie up our time."

"As flattering as that is, I'm not quitting my job to stay home and have sex all day with you. That would not pay the bills." Feigning indignity, I ask, "You'd reduce me from my position as your girlfriend to that of a paid prostitute?" I throw the sopping sponge at him. It lands with a wet smack on his chest.

"Okay, bad idea, but I if things go the way I think they might, I could use a secretary. Think you want to give up your stressful job for a stress free, secretarial position at a new Edmonton based startup construction company?"

"Are you serious?"

"Very serious. Alberta is booming. I've done some preliminary checking around and there is interest in services I can perform, and the money I can bring with me to invest. I put in bids for several low cost housing developments in Edmonton, Calgary, and Fort McMurray. I got news today, that my bid for Calgary was accepted." A bubble-covered toe brushes my breast.

"Oh Mack, that is so exciting! Are you happy?"

"Yes lovely lady I am. So happy in fact, I think it is time to kick things up a notch."

"If we have any more sex, people are going to mistake us for conjoined twins."

"No. I mean it is time for us to take the next step. I want you to meet my family."

"Yeah, right." I laugh. Immediately I realize he is serious. Feeling stupid, I watch him stand and step out of the tub. The drop in water level exposes me to the cooler room air. Mack grabs a nearby towel, and rubs bubbles and water from his body. "I'm sorry. I didn't realize the teasing had stopped."

He shrugs off my apology. "Thanksgiving is in a few weeks. My mom asked me to bring you."

Rather than answer, I ask, "Your mom knows about me?"

"I have no need to keep our relationship a secret, Skylar. Everyone who is important to me knows about you. They are anxious to meet you. I am anxious for you to meet them. Thanksgiving is a chance for us all to be together and do it right."

"Canadian's don't share the same date for the holiday," I stall. "I have to work."

"Take some time off."

"Rachel has school."

"Couldn't you arrange for Karen or Lexie to watch her?"

"I've taken advantage of every opportunity for us to be together. I don't want to get into the habit of dumping her on other people just to be with you."

"Just to be with me...?" He releases a sardonic chuckle and leaves the bathroom.

Shit! That came out wrong. I scurry out of the tub in pursuit.

"Mack, please! Being with you is important, but I can't make her disappear. I can't even imagine how I could explain a trip to Houston. In case of an emergency, people have to be able to get in touch with me. Quite frankly I've lied enough recently."

"Then maybe you should tell her the truth?"

My heart hammers in my chest as I realize his vast patience is disappearing. Is it this one refusal that sapped it, or has it been trickling away all along?

"You are not being fair, Mack." I drop the words softly between us.

"I have kept my end and then some. I have flown back and forth and hung out in Lexie's spare bedroom and in hotel rooms waiting for you to come to me. I have never asked for more time than you have been able to give…"

"Until now."

"For Christ's sake, Skylar, we've been dating for five months. We are supposed to be trying to see if we have something to build on but there is nothing normal about this relationship! Do you know how often I catch myself with the phone in my hand and then I have to hang up after realizing I can't call in case Rachel answers?"

"I warned you that this would not work, that you would not be satisfied." Sadly I acknowledge I cannot blame him if it's not enough. I have had my own moments when I've needed and wanted him and felt the same frustration.

"I'm not even close to being done with us, but I am pissed! The first time I ask something of you, you flat out refuse. You haven't even tried. That's not right!"

I am scared I can't give him what he needs to stay. I close my eyes and turn, but he doesn't allow it.

"Don't do that! Don't turn away from me. I've done everything I can think of to show how serious I am about you. It's your turn. This is something I need from you. I need an answer." Mack's eyes are devoid of all expression. A muscle twitches in his jaw; it's the only sign of how tensely he is waiting.

"You're right. It's not too much to ask. I'll do my best to make it happen."

Relief and a smile spread across his face. "I know you will, babe," he says, kissing me.

I return his kiss but for the rest of the weekend I fear what will happen if I can't meet his demand. Mack offers no reassurance he will be here if I fail. I'm too scared to ask.

* * *

Mack's flight back to Houston is not until the following morning so I leave him at his hotel. I have my usual drive to Red Deer to pick up Rachel. I've checked in with my sister and she is booked solid for work. After all her time off this summer, she has no more holidays. I am left to decide between asking Karen or Rand and Sherry. My neighbors would be the easiest choice since Rachel would not have to miss school but there is something about leaving my daughter with friends while I leave the country which does not sit right with me. Rand and Rachel are waiting for me when I pull into the parking lot of the huge truck stop. I roll down my window. It's time to have another awkward conversation with my ex-husband.

"Do you have time for a coffee? Rachel can give my car a wash while we chat."

"Sure," Rand answers as Rachel throws her things in the back seat and jumps in beside me. I start my car, pull into the carwash and park in an empty bay.

Curious she asks, "What's up now?"

"Nothing. I just want to talk with your dad and see how things are going."

"You can ask me."

"That would only be getting one side of the story." I reach out and tap her nose. "Here's my wallet, there is plenty of change. Make sure you do a good job. Come get me when you are done."

Rand is waiting inside the coffee shop, having claimed a booth overlooking the parking lot. I slide into the orange vinyl seat across from him, anxiously wondering how he'll take my request.

"Did you guys have a good weekend?"

"Don't beat around the bush. I can tell something is bothering you. Out with it."

"I need a really big favor. Could we skip her next visit and make it for the last weekend of the month instead? I'm going to Houston. I'm not sure of the exact dates yet but Rachel will miss a couple days of school."

"I don't see why not. Is this a girl's getaway with Lexie or is it work related?"

"Actually it's neither. It's personal. I'm seeing someone and he wants me to spend the American Thanksgiving with him and his family."

Rand's brows lift straight up in surprise. "You're dating?"

"It's complicated, sort of a long distance thing."

"Please tell me it isn't one of those crazy internet relationships." He groans. "Skylar, you are way too smart for that. I know you took the divorce hard but if you get out a bit, you'll meet someone. Do you know how many guys on these sites are losers or married? This is not a good idea. I won't let you go."

"You no longer have the privilege of allowing or denying me anything. At the risk of starting a fight, I have to say that I can't believe you think that I am desperate and stupid. You really don't know me at all." I shake my head. "I didn't meet him over the internet. I met him this summer when I went to the Bahamas. He owns the house next to Lexie's."

"Really? It's been going on for a while, then." Rand leans forward. "Why the secrecy? I'm okay with you dating, Skylar."

Like I need your permission, you philanderer, I think to myself. "Rachel doesn't know. I'd appreciate it if you didn't tell her. Until Mack and I know where we are headed, I won't involve her."

"Gonna show me up, huh? Show me the way I should have done it?"

"If we were still fighting, I might respond to that little jab with one of my own. I might be tempted to tell you that this has nothing to do with you and everything to do with putting my child's needs ahead of my own. I might be bitchy enough to accuse you of being incapable of understanding such a novel idea. I might say all these things but I won't. I'm going to try and be the bigger person here."

He smirks, enjoying my discomfort. "Where does he live, Houston or the Bahamas?"

"Both."

"And you only see each other on the weekends when Rachel's with me?"

"Rand, I am really trying to be civil. I remember you telling me it was none of my business when I tried to play twenty questions with you about Sherry. She was 'instant mommy' to Rachel, regardless of my wishes. Rachel has not met him. Until she does, he is none of your business."

"I don't know if I can support this, Skylar. I may not be able to grant you permission but I can decide whether or not I will take Rachel. I am not sure she should be missing school so you can run around with your 'boy toy.'"

"You are such a hypocrite! I can't believe you would dare sit in judgment of me. I really thought you wanted to work together with me but the truth is you are only interested in controlling me. Don't you have your hands full with Sherry? I guess not. Forget I asked!"

I storm out of the coffee shop and track Rachel down in the foggy wash bay.

"Let's go!"

"I haven't done the wax."

"Screw the wax! I'm done!"

She drops the pressure wand into the holder. "What's the matter? What happened?"

"This has nothing to do with you. Get in the car."

"Everything has something to do with me," she asserts. Her forehead is wrinkled with worry.

I suck in a deep breath. "Rachel, your dad and I are new to getting along. There are going to be bumps. We pushed each other's buttons but it'll be okay."

I'm still mad when we arrive home, but I put it aside, focusing on our Sunday evening routine. I'm gathering another week's laundry when the phone rings. My call display shows Rand's number. I grab the cordless phone and a basket of laundry and head out of my apartment, down the hallway to the laundry room.

"Hello," I snap into the receiver.

"Hi, Skylar? It's Sherry. I heard about the argument and I wanted to call and tell you Rand was completely unreasonable. May I take Rachel for you on that weekend?"

"What does Rand think about this?"

"He is coming to the conclusion that it is a very good idea. He owes you a huge apology. Right, Rand?" I hear him grumble in the background. "I mean, what issue could a married man possibly have with his ex-wife spending a weekend with her boyfriend? Unless he's jealous. Are you jealous, Rand?"

"I am worried you are going to pack my daughter off to the States and I'll be reduced to seeing her once a year," Rand snarls into the phone.

"I've told Mack no matter what happens in the future, I will not move Rachel away. I'd need your permission because there isn't a court who would grant me permission to move her out of the country against your wishes."

"I guess we'll see," he says and I hear more muffled background noise.

"Hi Skylar. I'm back. Now that we got that cleared up, are you going to bring Rachel? I'd love to have her. She can help me finish getting the baby's room ready. "

"Thank you, Sherry, for both the offer and helping us get sorted out. I don't want to create problems between you and Rand."

"Don't worry about us. Enjoy your weekend, and I won't say a word to Rachel. Now I have a favor to ask of you. Can this be the last visit she has with us until after the baby comes? It will be a good explanation for the longer visit. It's getting close to the end for me and I want Rand close by. Of course as soon as the baby comes, we expect her to come be with us."

"You don't need to explain. Thanks so much, Sherry." I drop the phone into my full laundry basket. I have good news for Mack. I can meet his family.

Chapter 26

The day before my trip to Houston, Rachel gives me a fright. With so much to do before my trip, I have put her to work folding a basketful of laundry while I peel potatoes for supper. She knows nothing about my trip, and believes she is going to her father's for an extra-long visit before the baby comes.

"Oh, I forgot to tell you, when you were checking the laundry a few minutes ago, some guy with an accent called."

Mack's Texas drawl pops into my head. My grip on the knife tightens reflexively as my heart leaps in my chest. He would only call if it were an emergency. Has something happened to him? Rapid-fire thoughts race through my mind. Rachel is setting the table for dinner and does not notice my sudden agitation. I force all emotion from my face and voice before asking if a message was left.

"He said, 'Would you be a good lassie and tell your mom to give me a call back.' Why would he call me Lassie? That's a dog's name."

Relief weakens my knees. "Oh. Michael." I laugh. "He's Scottish. Lassie means girl. I'll give him a call after supper. He is the gallery owner I told you about. It is too bad you didn't get to meet him and Tracina when you went to Eleuthera with your Aunt Lexie. It's not every day you meet two people who have been married for thirty years and are still in love. I think you'd like them."

"Old and in love? I hope they aren't like all over each other? That'd be gross." Rachel's lips tighten into a grimace as she erupts into a full body wriggle.

"Someday I'm going to remind you of those words." I run cold water over the peeled potatoes, rinsing the dirt left by my fingers. I cube the starchy vegetables into a small, stainless steel pot.

"You used to seem kind of old and tired. Now you smile more. You're always painting and you don't complain about my sports. I thought when school started, you'd go back to being tired but you haven't. I'm glad you quit the group home."

"I don't miss the graveyard shifts. You should know quitting that job isn't the only reason I am happier."

I turn away to fill the pot with hot tap water. Mack's face pops into my head and I have to hide a small, secret smile. My heart picks up speed again. This time it is pounding because instead of fearing I have been found out, I want to reveal my secret. I want to tell her about Mack and begin the process of bringing him into both of our lives.

"Eleuthera changed me, Rachel. I had some time to think about how I want to spend the rest of my life. I realized it is important to spend time taking care of myself and doing things that make me happy, like painting. Meeting Tracina and Michael also had a big impact on me. After spending time with them, I realized how lonely I have been. I want to be happy with someone."

Rachel doesn't answer right away. She chews a little on her bottom lip. "I thought we were all we needed?" she says finally.

For her, change and pain are intertwined. I have no desire to hurt my daughter but I want my future with a sharp impatience. I push on cautiously. "I'd like a bigger family. I want more children. I would like someone to grow old with." My honesty surprises me but I am more stunned when the admission does not relieve the built-up pressure trapped inside me. My longing for a life with Mack only intensifies.

"You have always said that we are all the family we will ever need."

"I was wrong. We've always needed and wanted more than each other. Your dad, Sherry, and Lexie are important to you. So are Amanda and your other friends. Different relationships make us happy in very different ways." I wonder if she can hear the plea in my voice. The words fall from my lips apologetically, begging to be understood. "I love being your mom but I want, I need more for myself."

I hate how defensive I sound. I hate how defensively she reacts. Crouching a little smaller on her chair, shrinking into herself, Rachel begins to chew a thumbnail. I don't remember at what age nail biting replaced her childhood habit of thumb sucking. All I know is at some point I stopped cajoling her to get her thumb out of her mouth and started telling her to quit chewing her nails.

"What else do you want to change?" she asks finally.

I don't consider lying. "I want to know if you'd be okay with me dating."

"You said you wouldn't date until I moved out."

"Minds change," I counter.

"And promises get broken," she says accusingly.

My daughter can't remember to do her homework without me breathing down her neck but she can remember a comment I made almost five years ago. A gust of frustration is forced out of my nostrils. I feel my hands brace themselves on the top of my hips.

"I was an angry, hurt, bitter woman when I made that promise. I did not believe I would ever want another man in my life ever again. I did not imagine how lonely I would be, how deeply I would regret those words. I was trying to make you feel better," I explain. *I certainly never saw the possibility of Mack.*

Rachel bends her leg, lifts her foot and rests her heel on her chair. A finger begins to draw circles on her bent knee. "It worked. I didn't want to have to share you like I had to share Dad. I didn't want to be left out."

I want to praise her for her honesty. I want to shake her because she has entwined her openness with equal measures of pouting, manipulation, and self-pity. I tuck the loose strands of my hair behind an ear. I clasp my fingers and bring my knuckles to my lips. I close my eyes and gather my next argument.

"Did you ever think you would get along with Sherry? You came back from the last visit telling me what a good time you had with her. I know the two of you started out rocky but it wouldn't have to be that way. I would do things differently. I'd never show up married one day and expect you to accept a stranger as a parent. I would talk to you and prepare you and give you time to adjust and get to know the person first."

"And I still would never accept him. You can get married, you can get divorced. I get no say. You can have fifteen kids and completely change my whole life. I get no say. It's not fair!"

"I am talking to you right now. I am not shoving something on you. I am getting your opinion and trying to help you feel good about a decision I want to make for myself. I don't think it is fair for me to have to wait. I'll be almost forty when you go to college. I could miss out on having more children. Are you really so selfish? Would you really make that decision for me? Do you really think I will let you?"

"You always say you'd be out of a job if people would stop putting themselves ahead of their children. When you are a parent, you give up the right to be selfish." Rachel corners me with my own lecture. She lashes me with my own words, stings me with my old judgments.

"When you love someone, Rachel, really love someone, you want them to be happy. That is love. I can't believe my own daughter does not want my happiness. I can't believe if the right person was to come along right now, someone who loved me and treated me well, you would expect me to let them go."

"I like things the way they are. I won't let some strange guy move in here and boss me around or have to put up with him pretending to be nice to me when you are around. Besides, you are always telling me that the right guy will wait. Right? If he loves you, won't he wait?" Once again, my daughter retrieves my words from her memory and with expert skill, she twists them around until she has me feeling like a hypocrite. I have been out argued, out manipulated and out maneuvered by a thirteen year old.

She knows. I've said too much. Stubbornly she chooses to cling to the charade. I let her. The choice does not come without cost. A thin wedge of resentment slides between us. For a second, I want to use that wedge to pry myself some space. I want to breathe freely again, just for myself. Motherhood is suddenly too heavy a mantle. Guilt and obligation follow on the heels of this sensation. My daughter may be selfish but she is just a kid. I'm a mother. It's my job, not hers, to be selfless.

"I love you, Rachel. You will always come first."

She smiles and walks into my arms, accepting my words as reassurance. She does not realize that I spoke the words to myself. I needed a reminder.

I started this conversation hoping I could bring Mack further into my life. The tight grip I had on my future with him weakens; I feel him slide a bit through my fingers. I tighten my hold and shove the panicky feeling away. Right now, Rachel is adamantly opposed to me dating but this evening is the first time I've broached the topic with her. She is bound to be difficult at first. At least I have an idea of her fears. Over the next few months, I can combat them. I'll prove to her that, in spite of my relationship with Mack, I can be a secure and stable fixture in her life. When she finally learns about him, the months between now and then will be proof his presence in my life is no threat to her.

I'll try again in a few months. There is plenty of time to work this out. Nothing has changed. I repeat these reassurances to myself until they become a mantra. I prematurely gave up Mack once before. I won't make the same mistake twice. *Nothing has changed.* I'll put in my full work day tomorrow, drive Rachel to Red Deer, and get on a plane to see Mack.

Chapter 27

My stomach rolls and I reflexively swallow a gag as the teacher in front of me lifts the sleeve of Lisa Morgan's sweatshirt. Covered with open, oozing cuts, a multitude of dried scabs, and raised welts, her arms look like something dragged off the set of a horror movie. *So much for coasting my way through the day*, I think to myself.

Lisa's tiny slashed arms are so similar to Rachel's, I find myself searching for breath. The mother in me wants to cringe, but the professional in me takes over. Lisa and I have been through this before. Unfortunately, I've already "helped" her. She isn't supposed to be in my tiny windowless office, worse off than before.

I rise from behind the comfortable barrier of my desk. She is not bleeding. None of the cuts are dangerously deep. I note dingy, gray remnants of previously worn adhesive bandages. I'd bet my weekend with Mack, the only medical treatment Lisa has received for these cuts has been self-administered. Standing at her teacher's side, Lisa's eyes are downcast.

"Why on earth would her mother send her to school in this condition? It's obvious she needs medical attention. Something serious is going on with this kid."

No shit, Sherlock. What was your first clue? I can't keep the sarcasm out of my thoughts, even though the look I give the teacher shows only professional concern. *What the hell happened? She was supposed to be getting therapy.* I hate boomerang cases, but they come with the job. Some files refuse to stay closed.

The teacher continues. "I've tried talking to her, but she won't answer me. Maybe you can get somewhere with her!" Expressions of concern and frustration alternate across his features. He is overwhelmed. No problem. Dealing with cut up kids is my job.

"Have you tried contacting her mother?"

"I did. There was no answer. Can I leave her with you? My class is without supervision. Mr. Krakow said to take her to the hospital."

For once, I'm in agreement with my boss. "Of course. Go on. I've got her from here."

Turning to Lisa, I motion for her to sit in a chair. I sit in its twin, next to her, rather than retreating behind my desk. Self-consciously, Lisa pulls down her sleeves, concealing her arms protectively with the baggy sweatshirt. The shirt is too large for her; the cuffs hang inches past her hands. She drops into the chair and hunches forward. Her long, stringy, unwashed hair curtains her face.

"Sorry about that; I mean, us talking like you weren't even in the room," I say. "Jeez, Lisa! Your arms, well…you have to see a doctor. If I can't reach your mom, then I will take you myself." I'm talking to a wall. She doesn't even twitch. "At the end of last year, you were supposed to begin seeing Dr. Conner." I watch for any movements that may signal a willingness to talk. "When did you start cutting again? Did you even stop?" Still no answer. "Okay. I get the message you don't want to talk. I'll call your mom."

"I don't want you to talk to my mom. I just want to go home." The burst of agitation is a signal for me to tread carefully. I have to be able to get her to my car if I can't reach her mom. I don't want to spook her into running. "I'm sorry but that is not an option. You can't be alone. You are hurting yourself and I am very worried about you." I fish her file out of the nearby filing cabinet, not trusting her to give the phone number to me. No one answers so I leave a message, explaining that if I do not get a phone call in the next few minutes, I will take Lisa to the hospital.

"You can't help me, Skylar. You made everything worse!" Lisa stands.

My hand clasps her arm and she flinches. "Please, Lisa, don't go." My fingers cup her chin and I lift her face. A single tear escapes to roll down her cheek, but her eyes are dead, blank. "My God! What's happened to you?" Slowly I loosen my reactive grip and gently take both her hands in mine. Her fingers flex and she seems poised to bolt. "Tell me. You know me, Lisa. Let me try to fix it. Please?" I whisper my request. Several moments pass.

"I can't go home. Don't bother calling my mom. You'll have to call my social worker. Her name is Susan Jacobs. Call her," Lisa says, and then pulls her hands from mine, and vacantly stares off at the wall, reciting a phone number from memory. "Tell her Harvey is back."

A receptionist puts me through.

"Susan speaking."

"Hi, Susan, this is Skylar Shay. I am a school counselor who worked with Lisa Morgan last year. She's in my office right now. She has sliced her arms up and needs medical attention. She told me to call you, and to tell you that Harvey is back." The social worker lets out several loud expletives. She eventually asks me if Lisa will let me take her to the hospital.

"I don't know."

"Let me talk to her."

"She wants to talk to you."

I hand the phone to Lisa. She takes it, listening for several long minutes before eventually saying, "I'll go with her." She passes back the phone.

"Take her to the Royal Alexandra Hospital. I'll meet you there. She'll go with you."

I hang up the phone. Lisa rises and follows me. I let the school secretary know I am leaving for the hospital. Lisa doesn't speak. She huddles into the passenger's seat of my car until we reach the hospital. It's a slow afternoon and we are quickly ushered to an examination bed. I cajole Lisa into lifting her sleeves for the young male doctor to examine, as I explain who I am and my reasons for bringing in Lisa. He asks Lisa to put on a gown, explaining that he feels it will be easier for the nurses to clean and bandage her arms, and because he wants to check the rest of her body for other cuts.

"No!" She leaps off the examination bed. As if in tune, the doctor and I both block her exit. "He's not fucking touching me, Skylar!" she shrieks.

"I don't have to touch you, Lisa, but I do need to see your back, your stomach, and your legs to make sure that you don't have any other cuts," the doctor explains calmly.

"I don't."

"I need to see for myself," he persists.

"I'll stay with you. I promise you I won't leave," I reassure.

Lisa begins sobbing uncontrollably, burying her face in her sleeve-covered hands. I shoot the doctor a silent message with my eyes. He disappears behind the curtain.

"Here, let me help." I delicately lift up her thick sweatshirt. Her shoulders, chest, and stomach are slashed as badly as her arms. I pick up a white hospital gown, holding it so she can slide her arms into the sleeves. I tie the gown closed. She unsnaps her jeans and slips them down over her hips. I pull back the sheets and she slides beneath them. I fold her clothing into a neat pile and pass her a fistful of tissues. From outside the blue curtain, the doctor asks to rejoin us. He is accompanied by a nurse. I hold Lisa's hand as the nurse and doctor examine the various slashes crisscrossing her body. Lisa stares vacantly at the ceiling.

"I don't see any that need stitches. A few could use some cream and bandages. Others are showing signs of infection. We'll get you started on some antibiotics. While the nurse fixes you up, I am going to have a talk with your counselor." Lisa does not acknowledge his words.

I untangle my hand from hers to follow the doctor to the nurse's station. Before disappearing, he tells me she'll be examined by the on-call psychiatrist. As I am about to return to Lisa's side, I am joined by a thin, frazzled looking woman.

"Skylar Shay?" she asks. I nod as she approaches. She doesn't shake my hand but motions for me to follow her. "I need a smoke. Come outside with me and I'll fill you in." I've met friendlier drill sergeants but I put my instant dislike aside and follow her across the street to the hospital parking lot. She lights up a cigarette, inhaling deeply.

"Can't smoke anywhere, anymore." The tall brunette gives me a quick onceover. "I should tell you it's none of your business and to go on home, confidentiality and all that, but you are the counselor who referred her to Dr. Conner, right?" I nod my head. "Last summer, Lisa disclosed to him that her mom's boyfriend Harvey was sexually abusing her. Dr. Conner called the police, and us. Harvey was arrested but is out on bail until he goes to trial. Heather didn't believe Lisa at first and we had to remove her from the home. After doing some work with Heather, Lisa was returned. Heather promised Harvey was out of her life for good. If Harvey spent the night, if he raped Lisa again, Heather's going to jail."

The pieces fall into place. "All that time I spent with her, and I never even suspected it. I know sexual abuse and self-mutilation often go hand in hand. Why didn't I ask her?" I feel sick.

"Don't beat yourself up. It's Heather who should be feeling like crap. She said she would protect her daughter. She had me convinced she'd do right by Lisa. Within weeks of getting her back, she's blown it. Can you imagine picking a man over your kid? What kind of mother chooses a rapist over her own daughter? Some people don't deserve to be parents." She grinds the cigarette under a thick black heel. "I've got Lisa from here. Thanks for bringing her in. She won't be going back to school. Say your goodbyes."

Chapter 28

On the smooth flight to Houston, my emotions are turbulent. I don't eat, I can't sleep. I must be radiating miserable vibes because my seatmate for the flight doesn't even attempt to strike up a conversation with me. All I get from him is a single request for me to move so he can go to the bathroom. It's just as well. A sympathetic glance could unravel my composure.

I shouldn't be on this plane.

"Some people don't deserve to be parents." Susan Jacobs was talking about Heather Morgan, but I can't stop aiming the judgment at myself. I want to believe I am a more perceptive and protective parent than that woman. Our situations are different. But as I sit on a plane, flying to be with my lover, knowing my daughter would be hurt by my actions, I can only see the similarities between myself and Lisa's mother.

Up until yesterday, I believed Mack would be as good for Rachel as he has been for me. My sense of security, my faith in Mack, has been rocked. With every fiber of my being, I know Mack is no rapist or child molester. I have not seen a single action or behavior of his which gives me pause or concern. I'm just as certain Heather Morgan did not know Harvey was going to rape her daughter before she moved him into her home. Unfortunately, trial and error is the only way I'll know for sure. No matter how wonderful or loving he may be, any man in my life will disrupt her sense of security, her emotional stability, and her connection to me. Like Heather, I want to pretend this is not the case. I want my relationship almost at any cost.

My admission makes me ill. I feel I am an even worse parent than Heather because even knowing what I do, I will get off the plane, put on a smile and make like the last two days haven't happened. Round and around my thoughts whirl. My stomach refuses to stop turning, my nerves are completely revved up. My doubt and self-loathing override the anxious feelings I have about meeting Mack's family. It's not the most auspicious beginning to a visit.

* * *

Brenham calls itself a city. Hardly anyone traveling through would call it anything but a large town. From the signage posted around the town, I can tell God, history, and sports are what matter most to its residents. High school athletes are celebrated as hometown heroes. In addition to a large civil war museum, there is a proliferation of churches. The downtown Brenham district has dozens of shops, none more than a few stories high. One sign boasts of the area's picturesque spring profusion of wildflowers but it's the end of November and the season has long passed. Surrounded on all sides by rolling hills, Brenham has not grown beyond its agricultural roots.

After only a few minutes of driving through Mack's home town, I know him better. He may have moved away but I can see the town's imprint on him. As we drive through the streets, pedestrians and drivers lift their hands to wave. Maybe they recognize Mack at the wheel of the truck; more likely they are simply being friendly. I now know why he makes connections with people so easily. It was here he developed the attitude that neighbors are not strangers; they are lifelong friends. An evening walk is more about the visiting than the exercise. In his old neighborhood, there is an abundance of well-used verandas. Front porch swings and comfortable chairs abound. The town speaks of a people living at a relaxed pace and loving to be outdoors. Brenham makes sense of Mack's attachment to Eleuthera. The island is littered with Caribbean versions of his home town.

When I left Edmonton this morning, we were buried under several inches of snow, firmly in the grasp of winter. Brenham's version of winter will not arrive until January, when the coldest temperatures rarely approach freezing. This afternoon, it is a balmy twenty-two degrees Celsius. Mack parks his truck. Towering oaks and elms shade a house from the late day sun. There are several vehicles parked in the long driveway and on the street front. As we walk up the sidewalk, we can hear the laughter and voices from inside.

"Are you ready for this?" Mack asks as we stand, suitcases in hand, outside the door to his mother's home. The white house with blue trim is two stories high and has been so lovingly maintained that I find it hard to believe the stately historical home was built before the turn of the century, and has been in the Mackenzie family for four generations. "They are going to love you. Relax. It's going to be fun."

I paste on a big smile and nod. We had two hours together in the car from the airport to his mother's doorstep. Several times I wanted to tell him that we needed to talk but I couldn't. I don't want to ruin this weekend for him. *There is plenty of time to work this out. Nothing has changed.* I remind myself of my mantra and force my doubts and concerns up on a shelf. We can bring them down and dust them off at some later point. For now, I want to keep the smile on his face.

Without bothering to knock, Mack opens the door.

"Uncle Mack!" a young, fair-skinned child squeals. A tiny body topped with a wild mass of chocolate ringlets bounds toward us and leaps straight into Mack's arms. He lifts the child high and he is rewarded with feminine shrieks and giggles. He sets the girl down as an older boy arrives for a toss in the air.

"Did we get any bigger?" They both ask, almost in unison.

"Bethany, I almost banged your head on the ceiling you've grown so much and Cory, I bet you put on a whole five pounds. I thought I was lifting a rock."

The children giggle.

"How's school?" He scowls in an unconvincing impression of strictness. "Still getting straight A's?"

They nod.

"Good." He kneels down, opens his suitcase, pulls out two presents and hands one to each of them. "Here you go. By the way, this is Skylar. Cory and Bethany belong to Max and his wife, Sable. They are the only ankle biters in the family, except for their older brother, David."

"Uncle Mack, I am not that small. I grew two inches this year!" Cory protests.

"David is with the grownups in the dining room. Is she your girlfriend, Uncle Mack?" Twin dimples appear in Bethany's cheeks, similar to Mack's. I can also see a resemblance to him in her mischievous grin. "Are you in love? Are you going to get married? Cause if you are, can I be the flower girl? Marci Anne, my best friend, got to be a flower girl this summer at her cousin's wedding and she got a beautiful new dress and she got to go to the hair dresser and have her hair all done in curls! She said it was so much fun. She showed me pictures. She looked so beautiful. I want to look just like she did! " Mack grins and shakes his head at the sheer volume of questions his niece unleashes. He is saved from answering as we are joined by a woman who resembles the two children.

"Bethany, let them come in. Young lady, you need to watch your questions. Some things are none of your business! Both of you may open your presents and then come join us in the dining room. Hi, I'm Sable. You must be Skylar." A tall brunette greets me with a wide smile and a welcoming hug. Her medium length, thick brown hair is pulled back into a pony tail and she is makeup free. In a simple sweater and jeans, she is the quintessential soccer mom; athletic, energetic and pretty. "They are here!" she calls over her shoulder.

"It's about time! Mack, we need you." A male voice booms out from the next room. The Texas accent is the same as Mack's but the voice is deeper, louder. "We are getting our asses kicked in here!"

"Leave your bag. We might as well meet everyone first." Mack suggests, giving me a gentle nudge forward. I follow Sable past the kitchen into a large dining room. Gathered around the table is Mack's family.

He greets them by asking, "What are we playing?"

"Lachlan Malcolm Mackenzie, where are your manners! You have a guest to introduce." Mack's mother rises from her chair, astounding me with her resemblance to her son. She has the same tawny coloring and golden green eyes. She also passed her golden curls on to Mack but hers are carefully styled and largely streaked with grey. Mother and son also share the same smile lines, but hers are deeper.

"Sorry, Mom. This is Skylar, Skylar this is my mother, Kay." Mack gives her a kiss. She pats his face before turning to me.

"It is very nice to meet you, Skylar." She takes both of my hands in hers and squeezes them before tugging me forward, taking over the next introduction. "This is Albert, my husband." In the roomful of big men, Albert is lost. He isn't even as tall as Kay. He nods his silver head in a brief greeting and sits back down.

Mack continues with the introductions. "You met Sable already. She is married to my oldest brother, the loud mouth in the corner, Maxwell. Call him anything but Max at your own risk. Next to him is his son David. I picked up a new video game for you," Mack tells the teenager. "It's in my suitcase, go on and grab it. This is Sam, and his wife Diane. She's not smuggling a beach ball, she's just very pregnant. Right here are Aidan and his fiancée Carol. Finally, there is the youngest and ugliest of us all, Ethan. Poor guy is too hideous to have a girlfriend." I laugh at his final remark because Ethan could be a younger twin to Mack. He stands and steps forward as if to hug me but Mack raises his hand. "Yeah I don't think so. Sit back down," he growls. Everyone snickers.

The Mackenzie men are all very good looking. All five are roughly the same height and size, except for Max who is slightly thicker around the middle than his younger siblings. Max, Sam and Aiden must favor their deceased father. They have blue eyes and dark brown hair.

"All I can say is that it's a relief to put a face to the name. All day long, all I hear is Skylar this, and Skylar that. Skylar, Skylar, SKYLAR!" Sam sings loudly. I feel my face flame.

"Boys, behave!" Kay admonishes. "I'm afraid I didn't beat them nearly enough."

"He is getting what he deserves. The first time I brought Sable home, they made my life hell. Mack was the worst! He spent the whole weekend campaigning against me, telling her she could do better. And I do prefer to be called Max." Half rising from his seat, Max shakes my hand.

Sam takes it from him as soon as he lets it go. "And you might as well call me Sam."

"I gave you all good names. Why you boys changed them is beyond me. Maxwell, Max, Samuel, Sam, Lachlan, Mack; it's just too confusing." Kay shakes her head with irritation.

"Maxwell? Seriously, Mom! You didn't think that would give me grief? You might as well have called me Wentworth, or Chandler!" I can't help but erupt in laughter at his burst of indignation. "How do you look at a newborn baby and decide he looks like a Maxwell, or a Lachlan for that matter? It was hormones, right? Pay attention, Diane. Let sanity prevail and have Sam pick your names now otherwise my poor niece or nephew could end up being called Gertrude or Copernicus!"

"What they name their baby is none of your business! You may have just denigrated one of the names they like." Kay's finger wags seriously but her eyes are crinkling into a smile.

Sam chokes on his drink. "She doesn't get any better with age. No, Mom. None of those names are in the running."

"Whatever. Lachlan, put your bags in your old bedroom. Skylar, what can I get for you? The men are having either Scotch or beer. The ladies are having tea or Diane's special slush. I'll warn you it packs a punch."

"The slush please," I answer.

"Did that son of mine feed you? We are going to have snacks in a bit but if you are hungry, I can bring them out early?"

"We stopped for dinner, Ma. Come on, Skylar, I'll show you our room. It's too early to leave you alone with the hyenas."

We pick up our bags and Mack leads me up a spiral staircase to a bedroom. I am disappointed to find no traces of him left in the room. The patchwork quilt, the furniture and the window coverings are feminine and homey. Mack tugs me to him and falls back on the bed, dragging me with me. He kisses me deeply.

"What if someone comes?" I attempt to wriggle away from him, blushing as I gaze over my shoulder at the open door. His hands cradle my hips, holding me snugly.

"Then they are going to see me kiss you. We are not going to have much alone time over the next few days. I'm grabbing my thrills when I can. Thank God we don't have to sleep in separate rooms. Max and Sable had to when they were still in college."

"Would your mom prefer that?"

"Naw. Back then, Aiden and Ethan were still at home and the rule about opposite sex sleepovers was in full effect. The rule went out the window when Ethan caught Albert sleeping over." The memory causes a chuckle. "We should get back. I should warn you. The teasing is going to get worse. You haven't seen anything yet. It's going to be a baptism by fire."

Mack's prediction proves to be true. I don't remember when I have blushed so much in my life. At first, most of the teasing and stories are about the brothers and their childhood exploits. Eventually, someone asks how Mack and I met and he launches into a description of my fight with Devon at the Fish Fry.

Kay gasps, covering her mouth. "She broke his nose?"

"And she kicked him, between the legs!" Mack informs the group proudly. "She's tougher than she looks. Cross her at your own risk."

I decide I want to crawl under the table. "Ugh! Mack!" I groan, hiding my face.

"You hold your head high, girl, and don't be ashamed of being able to take care of yourself. Lord knows, a woman in this family has to be tough." The pat on the knee and the wink from Kay allows me to drop my hands.

"I figured Canadians to be pacifists?" Aiden says.

"And I thought an American hockey player would be tougher," I retort.

"Nice one. You go, girl!" Sable says, offering up a palm for a high five.

"She may be good in a fight but let's see how tough she really is. I think it's time to introduce Skylar to our version of charades," Max challenges. "To the living room!"

I stand but Sable stops me. "No, Skylar, you are with us. It's men against the women so we'll stay here and make up the charades for the men."

"Sable, grab the paper and pens," Kay orders before she turns to me. "We have to whisper because we don't want the men overhearing us. We cannot lose. The losers do the dishes tomorrow."

"I made us lose the last one," Carol admits sheepishly. "It was the Fourth of July family dinner and the men cooked. They are kitchen tornadoes. I don't think there was a single dish unused. Even with the dishwasher, we were doing dishes for hours!"

"It's time for a little payback." Sable rubs her hands together with a cackle.

At first, the game is competitive but easy enough to include the children. But after an hour, Cory and Bethany are put to bed in an upstairs room and David is excused to play his new video game. From that point, the game changes. I blush as the women delight in making up the nastiest charades possible. Ladylike Kay, loosened up by several glasses of slush, comes up with some of the more raunchy suggestions.

"If we are this bad, I can only imagine what the men are coming up with." I gulp and look wide-eyed at Sable.

"Ah, they have nothing on us. Let me get you some more slush. Remember, you are up first. From here on in, you cannot pass a charade."

It does not matter how ridiculous or lewd the charade, everyone gives it their best attempt. I have moments when, after reading my selection, I want to die of embarrassment, but the enthusiastic cheering of my team and the taunts from the men keep me from backing down. By the end of the game, the women emerge victorious and there are no boundaries left. My face hurts and my sides ache. My mascara has long been wiped away with tears of hilarity. I have been teased and taunted. I have been supported and praised. These are people who treat laughter and teasing as an art form. Nothing is meant to sting or wound.

"I hate to be the party pooper but I am getting tired." Diane rubs her back. "If I laugh one more time, I think I'll go into early labor."

"Can you still give us a ride home?" Max asks her.

"Seeing as how I am the only sober person, I think I better."

"I'll help you haul Beth and Cory out to the car. Sable, you can sit up front with Diane," Sam says, following Max to the bedroom.

Kay stands. "It seems a shame for you all to go home only to have to come back in the morning, but there really isn't room since I got rid of the bunk beds. Lachlan requested an early dinner because he and Skylar are leaving for Houston tomorrow evening, so dinner will be at one." Hugs goodbye, and promises to see each other in the morning are exchanged. I find myself struggling to keep my eyes open. It has been a very long day, with most of it spent on a roller coaster of emotions. The evening of laughter and drinks has left me exhausted.

"Mack, take her to bed," Kay orders, after catching me trying to hide my third yawn in a few short minutes.

"I'm fine. Let me catch my second wind. I'd love a chance to just sit and visit before going to bed."

"Nonsense, girl! Off to bed with you, there will be time enough for that in the morning. You can barely keep your eyes open. Tomorrow will be just as crazy as today."

Chapter 29

"Good morning. Can I pour you a cup of coffee?" Kay is up to her elbows in a turkey when I join her and Albert in the kitchen the next morning. Mack wasn't willing to get out of bed. Long after I fell asleep, he was up with Aiden and Carol. I suspect it has more to do with how much Scotch he drank and not the lack of sleep. I had enough of Diane's slush to give me a slight headache and a sharp craving for a glass of ice water.

"You're busy. I'll just help myself, if you don't mind."

"Not at all. Coffee cups are in the cupboard above the sink. I'll make some breakfast just as soon as I get this turkey in the oven."

"I can fix myself some toast or a bowl of cereal."

"Thank you, sweetheart. Southern hospitality be damned, I got to get this turkey in the oven if dinner is going to be on the table on time. I overslept. There is bread in the bread box, and plenty of fruit waiting in the fridge."

"Perfect. Let me grab a bite to eat and I'll pitch in and give you a hand." Finding what I need, I am soon munching on a slice of toast and sipping a cup of coffee. While Albert holds, Kay stuffs the turkey until it is near bursting. Water is added to the roaster. Albert wrangles the heavy roasting pan into the oven.

"Thanks, Bertie. Now you can enjoy your newspaper on the front porch swing."

"Love, you promised." Albert's usual silence is broken by a gravelly warning. His silver peaked eyebrows almost touch as he stares at Kay. Her look of innocence is ruined by the sudden rise of red to her cheeks.

"What? I was just going to make conversation."

"No, you were going to start an inquisition. Mack asked you not to."

"I don't mind your curiosity. I am seeing your son. I am sure you have questions about me." I try to sound agreeable even as my stomach quivers.

"Mack mentioned that he didn't want me probing because the two of you have some complications to straighten out."

"She's been chomping at the bit to find out what he meant ever since." Albert's lips purse. He has an expressive face. He may not always verbally contribute to the conversation but what he is thinking is written across his features for anyone to see.

"Yes, I am terrible. A mind left to imagine the worst often does just that. I am sorry, Skylar. I really won't pry. Please don't tell Lachlan."

"Jeez, he makes it sound like I am hiding some horrible secret, like I'm married..."

"You're not?"

"No." I chuckle as she sags in relief. "But I am divorced. The complication he mentioned is my 13-year-old daughter."

"Oh. Well. Where is she? Why didn't you bring her? We'd love to meet her."

I can't help but think my daughter would love it here. This afternoon a family football game is planned and she would be right in the thick of it. If only she showed some sign she was open to the possibility.

"Yeah, well, that's the complicated part. Rachel doesn't know I am dating Mack."

"That's complicated all right," Albert comments.

"My ex-husband and his new wife are expecting a baby in January. I want to give my daughter time to adjust to the new addition before I spring more change on her."

"That is sensible. Give her some time to wrap her head around the idea. On the other hand, time may not make her come around. All five boys were up in arms when I started dating Albert. I wouldn't say they threw tantrums, but they didn't make it easy."

"I taught them all in high school, and they hated me," Albert explains.

"What they hated was me being with anyone but their father. They would have been happy to have me grow old and alone until I died, a grieving widow to the end."

I have to ask. "If they hadn't come around, what would you have done?"

"That, my dear, was never an option. I knew what I wanted and I never let the possibility of failure enter the equation. I don't believe there is a problem between people that can't be fixed. It just takes work. After I lost my husband and was left with five boys on my own to raise, everyone was certain I would never make it, that we would never recover. We not only recovered, we thrived. Not at first, and it didn't happen without time and pain. Sometimes you just have to have faith. I had faith my boys would come around."

"A little creativity doesn't hurt either." Albert grins.

"I wasn't raised to be a fool. They tried their little emotional blackmail games on me but I was smarter than that. When the boys tried to insist on me giving Bertie up, I offered to, but only on the condition that one of them would move back home with me and live with me until I died. I didn't have a single taker. Now you'd never know they had a problem with Bertie."

"You are a wise woman, Kay, but I don't think that will work in my case. Rachel is still young enough that she can't envision a life away from me."

"Where there is a will, there is a way. Believe in that. That is the best advice I can give you. That, and love is always worth the trouble. Now, we have many things to get done, but first, as a proud mother, it is my sacred duty to show you the family photo albums. No trip home to meet the family would be complete without a peek at your boyfriend's naked baby pictures. Quick, before Lachlan wakes up and wrecks my fun."

Mack misses my stroll down memory lane with his mother but Carol wakes up in time to join us. Carol and I sit on either side of Kay and examine the history of the men who brought us here.

"You know the one thing that strikes me as odd is how you've raised so many boys to be so close? Where is the sibling rivalry?" Carol questions.

"If your children grow up knowing that you truly love each and every one of them equally, then they are free to love each other, even if they are very different people. Max is a bit of a workaholic and Samuel couldn't care less about money and success. He's a family man. Lachlan is my wanderer. But I wasn't surprised when they went into business together. They like each other. Even when they don't see eye to eye, they work well together because they all bring different assets to the table. Maybe someday Aiden will join them, maybe not. He is full of ideas and politics."

Carol nods in agreement. To me, she says, "We both got jobs working for the Houston Public Defender's Office."

"My son the lawyer. I always enjoy saying those words. I'd hoped one of them might become a doctor, but they all go weak at the sight of blood."

"Has Ethan found a teaching position yet?" I ask.

"He's put off teaching to go back to school. He is getting a doctorate in environmental science. We call him the tree hugger," she whispers to us conspiratorially. "Uh-oh, I think I hear movements upstairs. Girls, help me get these photo albums put away."

Carol and I are at the sink peeling white potatoes and sweet potatoes when Mack, Ethan, and Aiden come downstairs at the same time.

"You boys look a little green around the edges," Albert comments, looking up from his newspaper at the dining room table. No one answers him. They come straight for the kitchen. Mack drops a kiss on my neck and gives my waist a quick squeeze before reaching up past me for three coffee cups. Aiden, with the coffee pot in hand, ready to pour, also gives Carol a morning kiss. Kay's spacious kitchen has just shrunk with the addition of her three large sons.

Ethan opens the fridge and barks at his mother. "No breakfast, Ma?"

"Didn't know when you would drag your sorry butts out of bed. It's almost eleven. I'm not making anything this close to our big meal."

"I'll go grab us some burgers," he says, closing the door.

"We definitely need something to soak up the alcohol," Mack agrees.

"No-you-will-not! Get out of my fridge! Go sit down. I'll bring you some toast and fruit salad. There is nothing open today, everything is closed."

"I figured those four pies you boys put away last night before you went to bed would have soaked up the alcohol nicely." Albert barely gets the words out before Kay shrieks. All three men cover their ears and flinch identically.

"My pies! You boys didn't!" Kay tears off into the adjoining pantry. They are wearing similarly guilty expressions when she comes back in cursing in a most un-southern-woman-like way. "My pumpkin and apple pies are gone. I knew I should have sent you to bed when I went. What in the world possessed you? Well, I don't care. You boys will replace those pies if I have to stand over you with my old wooden spoon."

Sam apologizes, approaching his mother with his hands up. "Sorry, Mom. We were starving. The stores are closed. What can we do? It's not like we can go buy more."

"The only thing that is saving you three from infanticide is my well-stocked pantry. Instead of playing football or watching football, you three will be baking pies. I'm sure there is canned filling in the pantry, and plenty of apples in the cold room."

"Great idea, moron." Aiden growls at Mack. "What's the worst that could happen?' you said. It's bad enough we are stuck making pies, but Max and Sam will be here any second. What do you think they are going to be doing while we bake pies?"

Ethan groans. "They will want to supervise."

Not long later we are in fact joined by the rest of the Mackenzie's. Albert and David watch football in the living room. Diane plays a game with Cory and Bethany at the dining room table. Everyone else crowds into the kitchen. Carol and I finish peeling potatoes and put them on to boil as Sable and Kay fix two different salads.

The three male bakers monopolize the kitchen island in order to meet their challenge as Sam and Max berate them to move faster. Fascinated, I watch Mack make pie crust from scratch while his brothers whip up two different fillings. Six pies are ready for baking in a little over an hour. It isn't fast enough to allow for a pre-dinner football game. The TV is turned off, the table is set. Everyone is sitting at the table or at the nearby kitchen island when Kay clinks her glass.

Max stands. Everyone falls silent.

"It is more than twenty-two years since Dad passed. The loss of a loved one, the pain of enduring an empty space at the family table, teaches you what is really important.

How lucky we are to be swelling this room with our numbers. How fortunate that we are adding chairs and expanding our table to make room for new loved ones." Max pauses. He smiles as his eyes fall to the pregnant swell of Diane's stomach. Sam kisses his wife's cheek. Max inclines his head towards Carol. Then all eyes are on me. Mack squeezes my hand. Sable pats my arm. I feel my face redden as I am included in the family welcome. Max continues. "Of all the things one might have, this family is what I am most grateful for. Nothing else comes close." Dinner napkins dab at eyes and male throats are cleared with discrete coughs. The oldest Mackenzie raises his glass in a salute. "Now, let's eat."

Glasses clink, conversation erupts, and food is passed around. I rest my head just for a second on Mack's shoulder and for a brief moment, allow myself to soak in the sensation of being included in a large family. I left Edmonton feeling this trip was a wrong choice. I was questioning my whole relationship with Mack, but I have seldom felt anything as right as this picture-perfect family moment.

Chapter 30

After dinner there is talk of starting a game of football in the backyard. Full stomachs prevail and the television version wins out. I am seated at the island watching Mack as he finishes drying the last pan. Everyone else has made their way to the living room. He snaps the dish towel smartly before hanging it on a rack. Crooking his finger, he beckons. I slide off the stool and make my way round to him. His white denim shirt is as soft as flannel. Underneath the material, Mack is an oven, throwing his body heat carelessly my way. He rests his hands low on my hips and I wonder if I will always feel a sharp thrill at his touch.

"Do you want to watch the game?" His chin lifts in the direction of the next room. "Or can I talk you into taking a walk? I'd like to show you around the neighborhood."

"A walk would be wonderful."

Tugging me to the front entrance, Mack grabs our coats from the front closet. "We're going for a walk," he announces. "Max, call Bill." Heads whip in our direction.

Max is off the couch in a split second. "Seriously? I'm on it. Give him a few minutes to get there ahead of you."

"Can I come?" Bethany asks.

"Nope, you can play a game of cards with me," Carol redirects.

Ethan imitates his niece. "Can I come?" He unsuccessfully dodges a cuff to the back of the head from Aiden.

"No. We are going to haul you out to the backyard and hang a licking on you," Sam threatens.

Out the door and down the sidewalk, Mack propels me until I make him stop. "What was that all about?"

"I have a special destination in mind."

The cryptic response has me curious but I don't push. The mid-afternoon sun feels great on my face. After the huge meal, it feels good to walk. With my hand tucked tight in Mack's, we stroll along the sidewalk. He tells me stories about the people and the homes we pass by.

"I think this would have been a great place to grow up."

"It was. My brothers and I know every inch of this town. I learned to ride my first bike on this sidewalk. Down that way was my best friend's house. On the negative side, there was always someone watching and willing to let our parents know if we had been up to no good. Often trouble beat us home. We'd walk in the door to find Mom or Dad waiting with that look in their eye. Here we are."

He stops and lets me get my bearings. 'Here' turns out to be Firemen's Park.

"This whole town is special to me, Skylar, but this place means as much to me as the house I grew up in. One of my earliest memories is of my dad pushing me on the swings. We played in those diamonds." He points to the nearby baseball field and small stadium. We continue walking.

"I thought you boys played football."

"We played everything. Ma said that sports were the only thing that kept her from killing us. Ah, there's Bill." An elderly man waves as we turn in his direction. He waits for us to catch up to him.

"Been a long time, young buck. Another one bites the dust I see." The words roll off his tongue as he pumps Mack's hand. "She's already to go. Just shut her down and lock up when you are done." He hands Mack a thick set of keys. "You pass these on to Maxwell later. He offered to drop the keys by later on tonight."

"Thanks, Bill. I appreciate it. Skylar, this old coot is a longtime friend of the family."

"You Mackenzie boys sure can pick out a pretty filly." Bill winks as he shakes my hand. We continue walking; our pace slows to accommodate Bill's shorter, unhurried strides. We stop at the front door of a large octagonal building. Although there are numerous windows interrupting the wood and stone façade, I can't see inside. A sign tells me that we are about to visit an antique carousel.

"I appreciate you bringing me the keys. I hope it wasn't a bad time."

"I was in the middle of a pre-dinner nap. I'll catch up on my sleep later when the ol' stomach is full of turkey." He pats his rounded belly with appreciation. "I got here as fast as I could. Never been one to stand in the way of tradition."

"It means a lot to me. We won't keep you. If Margaret has to hold the meal and anything gets cold, she'll skin me alive. Take care and pass on a hello," Mack finishes.

"It was nice meeting you," I add. Bill tips his cowboy hat before shuffling off towards a late model pickup truck in the nearby parking lot.

"And here I thought you were walking me to the local make-out spot." I follow Mack through the door with my hands hooked into his back pockets.

"I would not mind swinging by my old parking spot by the lake." He stops suddenly and I bump into him. He reaches out and turns on a light switch. Then he pulls my hands out of his pockets. "You are a terrible distraction," he says and disappears through a nearby doorway.

"What a beautiful carousel!" I say as the music starts and it begins to turn. I feel the urge to look around for little girls in ruffles and ringlets.

"My family and this carousel have a long history." Taking my hand, Mack brings me closer to stand in front of the twirling, multicolored wooden horses. We are facing the carousel; his chin rests on my shoulder. "It fell off a passing train and into a farmer's field in 1932. The town bought it from the farmer, and set it up for the country fair that year. My granddad was operating the carousel when he first saw my grandma. He said that as she passed by, he took one look and fell in love. A week later, he proposed to her on this carousel and she accepted. It was moved to here shortly after. My dad grew up riding the carousel. My folks were high school sweethearts. The year they graduated, they volunteered to help run the carousel for Maifest, a big festival we have every year. At the end of the festival, alone on this carousel, my dad proposed to my mom. Max proposed to Sable here, Sam to Diane and Aiden to Carol. Now it's my turn."

He unclasps his hands from mine and turns me around. Dropping to one knee, Mack reaches into his coat pocket and withdraws a small, black velvet box. Nestled inside is a sparkling diamond solitaire.

I can't breathe. Dumbfounded and shocked, my mouth falls open.

"I considered doing this on the beach in Eleuthera, but I felt like I needed the good luck this carousel has brought to my family." His hand is shaking and there is a matching quiver in his voice. His golden eyes hold me still. "Do you remember the night we met, the second we first looked at each other? I winked at you and you blushed. I haven't been the same since. You were so beautiful; I could not keep myself from watching you all night long. Lust and attraction drew me to you, but by our first kiss I knew there was more to it than that. You stole my heart, Skylar. It's been yours since that night."

His love is transparently displayed. It is there in his eyes. I never doubted the words when they came from his lips earlier, but to see the emotion shining in his eyes makes me tremble.

"When we first made love and I held you in my arms and we watched the sun come up, I knew I had stolen yours. I felt you give it to me. I knew in that moment, as I know in this moment, I want to be with you. I love you, Skylar. Will you marry me?" Tears blur my vision, distorting him and everything he holds out to me. I cover my mouth as a silent cry catches in my throat.

I did not expect this.

"Skylar, darlin'," he whispers, pulling me down into his arms, "talk to me. Nothing has changed. This is not an attempt to force your hand or speed things up. I needed to let you know I am serious about you and our future."

"Shh." I cover his lips with my fingers, as a sound finally emerges from my own quivering lips. "I love you. I want to spend the rest of my life with you. You are not rushing me, and it is not too soon for you to be asking me this. I want to wear this ring. I want to put it on my finger and wear it for the rest of my life."

"I hear a 'but' coming."

My fingers entwine with his. We hold the box together.

"I had a talk with Rachel. I didn't exactly tell her about us but she knows something is up. She made it very clear to me that she doesn't want... she is scared of-"

He cuts me off before I can finish. "Whatever it is, we can work through it."

"Mack, she doesn't want me dating, never mind getting engaged."

"She'll come around."

He argues with a blind certainty. I wish I had his faith but my memory holds that vision of her resolutely terminating the topic.

"I don't think she will. And part of me thinks she shouldn't. I'm scared to bring us all together. Mack, you consume me. When I am with you, I have a hard time remembering my own name. I'm terrified that I won't be the mother she needs when you enter into the picture. Rachel will notice and she will fight it. Never in my life has anything come before her, but you could. Six months with you and I'm torn between doing what's best for her and what is best for me. Six more months and I don't think I will care what she needs!"

He interrupts me. "I know you, Skylar, at your core you won't change."

"I already have. This week I had a situation at work-" Remembering Lisa's arms causes me to pause. "I found out a client, a young girl I worked with last year, was sexually abused by her mother's boyfriend. The girl ended up this week in my office with her arms slashed and hacked up. She did it to herself because her mother allowed the man back into their home this week, knowing he had sexually abused her daughter. I know this is an extreme example but it rocked me!" I stumble back until I feel the carousel behind me.

"Skylar, I would never hurt your daughter."

"I know, Mack. I trust you with all my heart. This incident didn't make me doubt you. I'm scared my daughter has more to fear from me." I sit. Mack rises from his knee. I take his hand, needing the connection to him. "Too many times, I have seen parents put their needs ahead of their children's needs. I never thought I could. Now, well, if

Rachel doesn't want me dating and I thrust you at her, isn't that what I am doing? Isn't that the plan? When parents choose their love interests over their kids, it has horrible consequences. Some of my clients have attempted suicide. Others escape into drugs or sex. I don't want my daughter to be one of these kids. But right now, knowing she stands between us, I understand what it means to resent your child. I want to put my own needs ahead of hers. And if I do, I am a worse parent than those I have judged because I'll do it knowing the consequences of that decision. Mack, I want nothing more than to tell you yes, to wear your ring, and make you mine. But how can I, knowing what I know? I don't want to hurt her, and I don't want to hurt you."

My composure fractures as I feel myself being splintered into two. I throw my arms around him and sob. He lets me cry. He rocks me in his arms, holding me close. Then he brushes my hair back and cradles my face gently in his hands. His thumbs brush away my tears.

"It's okay. We'll be okay. We knew it wasn't going to be easy. When it is time, I will win Rachel over. Give me some credit. Give her some. Once she knows she has nothing to fear from me, we'll get along fine. Okay? Have some faith."

"That is all I have, faith and hope, because the obstacles seem tremendous and they don't appear to be lessening. When we are apart, I don't see how this can possibly work. And when we are together, I can't envision the rest of my life without you."

"Maybe we need to have less space between us? I am flying back with you tomorrow. I want to begin the process of moving to Edmonton. We will be rid of the strain of being separated. It's not the solution to every problem we have. There will be others and we will deal with them as they emerge until we find a way to make things work. Nothing is impossible if we keep working at it, if we believe we will end up where we want to be."

Mack kisses me softly. "I believe. I love you. I will spend the rest of my life with you. It is for sure. I believe it enough to slip this ring on your finger, and to tell you I won't take it back. This ring is yours and you are mine." He slides the ring on my finger and I let him. "I am yours."

Doubt has no room in me. His love and commitment have chased it away. "And I am yours. I love you, Lachlan Malcolm Mackenzie."

The words are barely past my lips when he stands and lifts me from the ground. His mouth crushes mine and he spins us both around until I am dizzy. My feet finally hit the ground. Mack presses his forehead to mine so that we are eye to eye, nose to nose.

"I really needed to hear that," he says, before kissing me again.

The next morning, as Mack and I fly back to Edmonton, my ring sparkles up at me. I can't take my eyes off of it. I can't stop stroking it. I've been afraid that Mack and I are grasping at the clouds, reaching for something too elusive to last, but the presence of his ring on my finger gives me hope. I have a platinum and diamond proof of our love. He loves me. This incredible man loves me. I don't know what tomorrow will bring, but right now I am happy. The only part of the equation missing is Rachel.

I bring Mack's hand to my lips.

It exists. Happiness exists.

I have found it for myself.

Chapter 31

"Shit, it's cold!" Mack complains as we hurry across the airport parking lot.

"I'm afraid you haven't seen anything yet. This is mild, maybe minus twenty with no wind. You have to get a new coat if you expect to survive the winter," I tease. We fill my car's trunk with our suitcases and shiver while it warms up, blowing puffs of freezing breath until finally the temperature gauge moves and I can turn the heater on. "What is the plan? Are we going to Lexie's or are you getting a hotel?" I ask Mack before shifting my car into drive.

"I hadn't really thought that far ahead."

"Why don't we swing by my place first? I want to drop my suitcase off and get some fresh clothes. I don't have Rachel until Sunday afternoon, so wherever you decide to stay, I can be with you until then."

"Sounds good," Mack says.

We stop to pick up some lunch on the way to my apartment. My first inkling something may be wrong occurs when I insert my key into the deadbolt lock. It isn't locked. Neither is the lock on the door handle. The door swings open.

"That's weird." Puzzled, I examine the unlocked door. Mack steps past me.

"Let me check it out," he orders protectively.

I follow him, hearing that my apartment is not empty. The TV is on. Rachel emerges from the hallway. Mack stops and I run into his back. Shock knocks the air from my lungs. Time stops, leaving me stuck in the middle of this collision. Somehow, air makes its way into my lungs. The next moment arrives. Mack and Rachel are going to meet despite my efforts to delay.

"Rachel. You are home." It's the dumbest, most obvious conclusion I have ever reached in my life. Given the circumstances, I am grateful I can think, let alone speak. My words are shrill and breathless. The cheery tone I adopt is forced. I step around Mack. Rachel eyes us both. A frown pinches her brows together. Her full lips tighten into a straight, thin line.

"I've been home since last night. Grandpa brought me back because Sherry is having complications. She might lose the baby. I couldn't get a hold of you. There is no one at

Amanda's house so Auntie Lexie came and stayed with me. Where were you? Who is he?"

Lexie joins us in the entryway of my apartment, and I use her presence as an excuse to ignore Rachel for a moment. I need a second to try and formulate an answer.

"Lexie," I say. "Thanks for coming to her rescue. I must have left my cell phone shut off. I am sorry if you were worried."

"I wasn't worried. I knew where you were. See, I told you, Rachel, she is fine. You didn't have to panic. She's fine. She's home. Everything is okay. It's good to see you, Mack."

Rachel looks from Lexie to Mack and then back to me. "So, where were you?" she demands.

"I was with my friend Mack." I push Rachel a step forward so Mack and I can clear the doorway. I shut the door to avoid giving any passing neighbors a view of what is going to be an interesting discussion. "Rachel, this is a friend of mine, Mack. This is my daughter."

Mack nods and smiles. "It's nice to meet you, Rachel," he says.

Rachel refuses to acknowledge him or even look his way.

"I'm so sorry you were worried. That must have been awful for you to not be able to reach me. What's wrong with Sherry and the baby?"

Lexie answers. "She started having contractions. She is in the hospital and they are giving her meds to stall the labor and to get the baby's lungs ready. I talked to Rand this morning and so far the baby seems willing to wait a bit longer."

"Yeah, we had to rush Sherry to the hospital and she was in a lot of pain and everyone was so scared. And I couldn't get a hold of you!" Rachel butts in. "I was stuck at the hospital from Wednesday night until Thursday night when Gran and Grandpa came. When I realized Dad and Sherry were going to be at the hospital for a long time, I asked Grandpa to bring me home. I figured you would be home but you weren't. Gran and Grandpa waited with me for hours. At first I thought you were shopping but you never came home. I even phoned the group home in case you decided to go back and work there. No one knew where you were. I was finally able to get a hold of Aunt Lexie, and she said she'd stay with me until you came home."

"It was nice of your grandparents to drive you home. I'll have to call and thank them."

"Where the hell were you?"

Lexie's eyebrows rise at Rachel's choice of words but once again I ignore her tone. Rachel has a right to be angry and concerned. It is time to come clean.

"I went to Texas with Mack to meet his family."

I reach out a hand to give her a comforting apologetic pat. Too late, I see the ring sparkling. Lexie's eyes widen and she grabs my hand.

"Oh my God!" she squeals. "You guys got engaged!"

"Lexie..." I groan. I had planned to store the ring in my jewelry box. Now it is too late. This situation has just blown up from bad to worse.

"That's an engagement ring? From him?" Rachel accuses.

There is no denying what the huge sparkling diamond represents.

"Yes, Rachel. I took your mom to meet my family and asked her to marry me."

Lexie's smile increases with Mack's confirmation.

"Who asked you? I mean, seriously, who is this guy and why is he buying you an engagement ring, Mom?"

"Hey there, pipsqueak, watch the snarliness. Mack is a real great guy. You'll like him if you give him a chance. He's my neighbor on the island. That is where they met." My teeth grind together as my sister interjects herself into the proceedings.

"That's what you were trying to tell me before you left. You've been seeing this guy?"

"Yes."

"And now you're engaged?"

"Yes."

"When were you going to tell me? Before or after you got married?"

"Rach, honey. I know this is a shock and a surprise."

"You are just like dad. No wonder you guys are all buddy-buddy now. You are exactly the same."

"I know it seems that way. I am sorry. I shouldn't have hidden this from you. I was trying to protect you. I did not want to get you involved. It didn't make sense to introduce you to someone until I was serious."

"I don't believe you." She spews the words out as she steps up to me and yells in my face. "I'm not listening to anything you have to say. YOU'RE NOTHING BUT A FUCKING LIAR!" she screams, the last word coming out as a shriek.

The smack is so loud Lexie and Mack recoil. The sound reverberates throughout the room. Rachel's face crumbles into the same pain-filled expression she wore when Rand told her he was leaving. I see the palm print on her face and realize what I have done. I reach my hand out to her and she flinches. My stomach heaves.

"Apologize to your mother," Lexie demands.

"You can go to hell too!" Rachel whirls and heads to her bedroom. She slams the door so hard a picture falls off the wall. The glass shatters.

For several long moments, no one says anything. Lexie breaks the silence.

"I think she is pissed. I'm going to go and have a word with her on the proper way to close a door."

I watch my sister disappear into my daughter's room. It is anyone's guess as to what she is going to say but at this point, it could hardly be worse than what I just did. I let her go to Rachel, knowing it should be me. I take a step back until I feel the wall behind me. I slide down the wall, arms wrapped around my middle.

"Don't panic, Skylar. We can work this out." Mack kneels on the floor in front of me. His hand is stroking my hair, his fingers trying to lift my face. I won't lift my face. I can't look him in the eye.

"I've never hit her, Mack. Not once. Not ever."

"I believe you. She was pretty mouthy. If you hadn't, I think Lexie was going to. Your daughter has your temper. Okay. I can see you're not ready to inject a little humor into this situation. Sorry."

"She has never spoken to me like that before." Tears fall from my eyes and land on my lap.

"Skylar, look at me. She needs some time. We all just need some time," he says soothingly.

I hear the words and the worry in his voice. Horrified by what she said and at what I did, I can't respond. Her words, my response, they eclipse everything else, everyone else.

With all emotion drained from my voice, I finally say, "I don't think so."

"I'll be the best thing that ever happened to her."

"You have to go."

"I'm not leaving. This is it. This is our chance. Let's bring her out and work it out with her. Start talking with her."

"I hit her, Mack. I have never hit her. How do I talk about that?" I am stuck in that moment, watching her face change, seeing the shock and the pain of my slap as it registers on her face. "I told you. I warned you this would happen…"

"Don't do it, Skylar. Don't look for the end. This isn't the end."

"It can't be a beginning. Not like this. There is no way past this. This is too much. I can't fix this."

"We'll find a way. Don't push me out. Skylar, babe, I'll wait..." He cradles my face in his hands and forces me to look up. His eyes are as wounded and pain-filled as Rachel's.

"I can't live like this, pulled apart between the two of you. I can't do it to you and I won't do it to her. I love you, Mack. I love you both. But if you don't leave, I'll end up hating one of you. I know I will. I can't bear it to be her. I can't bear it to be either of you. Please, if you leave then I'll only hate myself."

He lets out a frustrated snarl and slams the floor with his fist. He stands and I can feel him stare down at me for several long minutes. Time freezes again, neither of us budges until he grabs me by the arms and lifts me up. "If you want me to leave then you have to tell me. Say the words, Skylar. Say it's over. Say you don't love me and you never want to see me again and I will walk out that door!"

The words are there, in my throat. They hang there, lodged. I can't get them out. I choke on them; I choke on every attempt to get them out. I cannot say what needs to be said. So I ask him to. With one single word, I beg him, I ask him to end what I cannot.

"Please?"

"Damn you, Skylar!" he says before he pulls me into his arms.

"Please, Mack. If you love me… please?"

I barely get the words out before his mouth tears at mine. Crushed in his arms, crying and holding him tightly, I kiss him one last time. Then I pull out of his arms. I slip the ring off my finger and place it in the palm of his hand.

He takes it; he closes his fist around it. He closes his eyes.

"Goodbye," he whispers.

I hold in my sobs until the door clicks softly behind him.

Mack is gone.

CHAPTER 32

Lexie emerges from Rachel's room much later, and finds me still sitting on the floor staring vacantly at the door.

"You let him go."

After several moments of me not answering, she steps over me on her way to the kitchen and returns with a glass. I take a swallow. The alcohol should sting and burn my esophagus but I am numb.

"I'm not sure which one of you I'm more disgusted with." She plants her hands on her hips. "Rachel needs to know you have the right to your own life, to be loved. If she can't see that then we raised one spoiled rotten little brat!" She raises her voice to make sure Rachel can hear.

"Go home, Lexie."

"It's all over but the crying, huh?"

"Leave, Lexie."

"Oh, I'm going, eventually. But not before you get a piece of my mind as well. I thought you finally understood you are entitled to happiness. I guess you are not done eating shit."

"I want you to go."

"Yeah I bet you do, 'cause you don't want to hear the truth. You let him go not because of her but because you are terrified one day he will wake up and realize you don't deserve him. Everyone leaves, right? Mom died, Dad picked booze over you, and Rand walked out on you for Sherry. Rachel will only love you if you jump through hoops for her. And even so she will leave you too one day. Isn't that what your distorted thinking has you believing? You are wrong. The only reason Mack left is because you are a coward, a victim, and one stupid woman." There is no sympathy, only disgust in her eyes. "You fucked up royally! This guy was never going to walk out on you, Skylar. He loves you. But you didn't love him enough to fight for him."

"Get the hell out of my house!"

"I will and when I leave, you can take comfort in the fact that your safe little world remains intact. You can play mom, work at a job you hate, and never ever have to wonder if it could be better. You gave it a pathetic little try and it didn't work out! Just what you figured, right?"

I throw the glass of alcohol against the wall and explode with it.

"GET THE FUCK OUT OF MY HOUSE, LEXIE!" I shriek at my sister.

She doesn't even flinch. "Is that the best you can do?" she asks as she slides her shoes on.

"Aunt Lexie?" Rachel asks, sticking her head out of the doorway. "Mom?"

"I'd love to stay and see how the two of you work this mess out, but you don't need me. You made your beds. Enjoy lying in them." My sister turns and walks out the door, leaving it open.

"Mom?" Rachel repeats.

I get up and shut the door. I walk past my daughter.

* * *

I don't ever want to wake. I don't want to get out of bed, I don't want to eat or drink. I just want to stay wrapped in exhaustion. I want oblivion, not the mess of my waking life. I want to cry. Most of all, I want to be alone.

I stay in my bed for the rest of the weekend, leaving only for the bathroom and for water. Each time my bedroom door opens, Rachel rushes to meet me, hoping that maybe this time I'll talk to her. I send her to Amanda's. I go back to bed and I stay there. When the tears stop, all that is left is rage. I am angry with my daughter, who is so selfish she doesn't care how much pain I am in as long as her world doesn't change. I hate my job and I hate my life. Most of all, I am angry with myself. I am angry at risking more of my heart than I could handle losing. I am angry for not fighting harder. My sister was right. I am a coward, a chicken and a truly stupid woman.

Mack isn't replaceable.

The truth of this realization is the source of my pain. I want him beside me, his breath on my cheek, and his hand on my hip. I want him watching me paint, inspiring me, supporting me, loving me more than anyone ever has before. I can't get past the loss and so I escape into sleep. I dream of him. When I am awake, I drown in the memories of every moment we shared.

Monday morning I tell Rachel to go to school and I call in sick. I do the same Tuesday and Wednesday. Thursday Krakow calls and demands that I show up to work or provide a doctor's note explaining my absence. I tell him to jump up my ass and then I hang up the phone. There are other jobs if I lose this one.

My depression frightens Rachel. She forgets her anger. She is like a whipped dog, cowed by my grief. She brings me water and food. I eat and drink after sending her away. I know I must reassure her that life will go on for me but I have nothing to give. I need every last ounce of strength to find that answer for myself. Just this once, I tell myself, I've got to put myself first. I go in to see my doctor and get a one-week medical leave and bury back into my bed. By the end of the week, when I show no sign of improvement, Rachel is panicked. She brings the phone into my room and gently nudges my shoulder.

"Aunt Lexie is on the phone," Rachel says. "Please talk to her. I am scared."

"I don't want to talk to her," I snap from my den of blankets and pillows.

"Please, Mom?" she begs. Eventually I take the phone. Relieved, Rachel backs out of the room.

"Lexie, leave me alone," I say when Rachel is gone.

"I didn't call, she called me. You haven't gone to work? She said you haven't moved from that bed since I left other than to go to the doctor?"

"I've used the bathroom."

"Your daughter needs you. You remember her, don't you? She is the same daughter that you will do anything for, right? So get off your ass and be a mother to her. She's all you need to be happy, right? So put a smile on your face and get happy!"

"Fuck you, Lexie," I say, hanging up. I just want to go back to sleep but I'll wet the bed if I don't get up. I drag myself to the bathroom. Rachel is waiting when I emerge.

"I didn't mean to make you and Aunt Lexie fight. I just wanted her to check on you and make sure you are all right. I am worried you are going to do something..."

"I'm heartbroken, not suicidal."

"Are you going to stay up?"

"Probably not."

"Are you going to be okay?"

"Yes, Rachel, I will be okay. But not today."

"Well, how long are you going to be like this?" she demands.

"As long as it takes!"

"What am I supposed to do? Just sit around here and feel sorry for you?"

"That would be a first."

"You're not the only one feeling bad!" Rachel storms into her own room and I hear the door slam.

She needs, she needs, she needs... But for once I ask myself, what about what I need? I throw her door open.

"Don't you ever talk to me that way and don't you ever slam a door in this house like that again!" She is stunned into silence. "What do you have to feel bad over, Rachel? You won. Don't you get it? You won! You broke my damn heart but that isn't enough. You still are not happy. You want me to act like it never happened! Right now, I need to deal with this hurt so that eventually I can get back to being your mother and pretending that I didn't give up the next best thing to you that ever happened to me. Maybe tomorrow or the next day I will be able to do that but right now I need to cry! And the fact that you are as selfish as to not see how much I'm hurting, makes me seriously think that I made the wrong choice. It makes me think I hurt myself and Mack for nothing!"

The look of anguish that crosses Rachel's face does not bring any guilt. Lexie is right. I've overindulged my daughter. She barely sees me as a person.

"Mom. Mom, I am sorry... I don't mean to be selfish..."

"Well, I need to be Rachel. To get through this, I need to be selfish."

I leave her room and head to the kitchen. I dial my sister's number.

"Lexie, can you come and get Rachel? I am not much of a mother to her right now. I can't be. She needs someone."

"She needs a kick in the ass."

"I gave her one."

"Good. I'll give her another one. I will come and get her, Skylar, but I am leaving for the island in a few days. You know it is Christmas next week."

"I can't even think about that right now."

"Then I will. She can come with me. In fact, you should come too. Come spend Christmas with me in Eleuthera. You'll snap out of this eventually and when you do, she'll need you."

"Probably but right now I need to be alone. Can you do it or do I have to call Rand?"

"We both know his plate is a little full right now. But I'm warning you, I won't be back until just before New Year's. I need a tan before the best pick-up night of the year."

"That's fine."

"So you will come down for Christmas?"

"I don't know." I am unwilling to promise anything.

"You will. You are having your little tantrum, and letting Rachel stew in her juices, but I know you. You'll pull it together and give her a Christmas. A few more days, that's all you get!"

"Okay. I'll get myself together. I'm sorry, Lexie. I never meant a damn thing I said."

"Well I did. You let him go and that really does make you stupid!"

"I know."

"I'll be there later to pick her up. What a bloody fucking mess!" I hear my sister say as she hangs up the phone. I find Rachel waiting in her room with big nervous eyes.

"Pack some things. Get your passport and the traveling forms that I got for you. You're going back to the island with Lexie. Pack enough for a few weeks."

"What about school?"

"I couldn't care less about school."

"Mom," she whispers, "I don't want to leave you. I love you."

Finally, an honest gesture of concern, I think. Her attempt to reach out inspires me to provide a bit of reassurance.

"I love you too. It may not seem like that right now but I do. I'll call the school and let them know you will not be there until after the Christmas break."

"Why don't you come with us? We'll visit your friends. Didn't you say that just being with them made you happy? Come with us and maybe you'll be happy again."

"Rachel, I was happy before because I was with Mack. Going to the island won't make me happy. It will be painful." Her face falls as she realizes her blunder. "Just go. Do as I ask. I'll be fine after a bit more time alone. When I am feeling better, you can come back or I'll try to come down. By Christmas, that's what I told Lexie."

I don't feel sad when Rachel leaves. I shower and burrow back into my bed. There I stay for the next two days. Lexie calls when they reach the island. Then Krakow calls, demanding I give him an explanation for my absence. I get out of my bed and change the sheets. I shower, dress, and eat. I comb my hair and then I go back to my family doctor before taking Krakow another note requesting an additional ten days of stress leave. I ask Krakow if he is going to accept it, or if I need to give him a resignation letter instead. He takes one look at me and says he'll see me in the new year.

I return home but don't go back to my bed. I'm sick of my prolonged grief. I am unable to escape into sleep so my bed is no longer a haven. I sit on the couch and watch TV. I open cans of soup and eat them without tasting them. I do the dishes. I vacuum. I scrub my bathroom. I go through the motions of living, glad I sent my daughter away so she doesn't see me struggle through the most mundane of tasks.

I try to paint. I sit in front of my easel, and all I see is Mack's face. I want to clutch on to my memories of him, capture them all before they fade. Soon I will not be able to remember his scent, and then I'll forget his touch. Eventually I will even forget his smile, his face, his eyes. The urge to paint him while I still remember every detail is strong. One day I'll wake up and he'll be gone. The pain will be gone. I leave my canvas blank.

It is snowing lightly and it is dark. With three days until Christmas, I acknowledge that I'm too depressed to get through that day alone. Mack is sure to be in Houston spending Christmas with his family. I am free to go to the island. My decision is something to move toward. I drag myself out to the mall and pick out gifts for Lexie, Rachel, Tracina and Michael.

I miss my daughter. My anger towards her has lifted. I don't know if I will ever forgive myself, or if she'll forgive me for hitting her. It's time to find out, to try to make a fresh start. This time, however, it will not be solely on her terms. I want peace with my daughter but not at the expense of myself. Guilt and duty will not direct our relationship. This lesson I've learned too late.

I call Lexie once I've arranged my flights to Eleuthera. She promises to meet me at the airport. I pack some clothes. I watch television and eat a dinner of oven heated French fries and fish sticks.

Chapter 33

"You look like shit but I am glad you came. At least you are up and moving." My sister's tight hug softens her words. I open the vehicle door, seeing no sign of my daughter.

"Where's Rachel?" I ask.

"She stayed at the cottage. She's hanging out on the beach... with Mack."

My world tilts.

"What did you do?"

"I gave your daughter a long hard kick in the ass once I got her alone. She needed it. I tried to talk to her the day that shit hit the fan but she was being as stubborn as you. When she got down here, she was ready to listen. You scared the hell out of her." Lexie pulls her shades from the top of her head down on to her small turned up nose. Shoulder checking, she puts the jeep into reverse.

"I told her she was being a brat. I reminded her of everything you have done for her from switching your degree, to working two jobs, to going without so she could have, and now giving up the man you love. After laying on the guilt nice and thick, I asked her to tell me what she does to show you her love. The little twerp couldn't think of a single thing. She had no right to make you choose. I pointed out how happy you were these past few months and explained it was solely because of Mack. She broke and asked me to call him."

"You had no right!"

"I had every right!" Lexie slams on the brakes and throws the jeep into park. Her hand pounds down hard on the steering wheel. "I've been a second parent and your backup every time Rand failed. I love you and your daughter more than anyone else in my life! Don't tell me I have no right!"

"This is going to make everything worse." My fingers massage my temples as I try not to get angry.

"The only one who can make things worse at this point is you, Skylar. Before you see them, there is something I need to say and you need to hear."

"I'm listening," I say.

"Sky, there have been times in my life when I get a feeling deep in my gut. When I get that feeling, I know I have to do something about it. The first time I felt it was when I realized Dad's drinking could separate us. I was seven years old and being questioned by a nice social worker, who was asking me about Dad. My gut told me to keep my mouth shut. After that I made sure we stayed the hell under everyone's radar. I was forced out of childhood. As hard as it was to grow up so early, I am glad I listened to my gut. It kept us together. I had the same gut feeling when I made the choice to be a doctor. No one thought I could do it and raise you. I ploughed ahead and proved them wrong."

"Okay so your gut is psychic. What does this have to do with me?"

"There have been times that I have disregarded my gut feeling; the result has never brought anything but pain. Mack is it for you; I feel it in my gut. Your life without him will never be the same. I don't think you'll ever get over him, and I don't think you'll ever forgive Rachel."

"Your gut should mind its own business, Lexie."

"Don't blow me off. Think about what I said. What do you have to lose? How could things get any worse?"

I digest her words all the way to the cottage. When we reach the familiar white house, I don't want to get out. I want to see my daughter but I can't bear to see Mack. I can't bring myself to hope again. Lexie gets out and walks around the vehicle. She opens the door and takes me by the hand.

"I was starting to heal. Do you know what this is going to do to me?" I ask, crumpling into tears.

She wipes tears from my cheeks and then kisses me. "Trust me, Skylar. Trust yourself. Trust them."

I follow her around the cottage and down the steps to the beach. Like a fist to the stomach, seeing Mack is painful. The pain outweighs the hope. My shoulders slump, but my eyes devour the sight of him.

"I didn't drag you here to tear the scabs off your wounds. I'm trying to help you. Skylar, don't you see this could work? Look at them out there on the beach. They are getting along. Rachel has spent several days with Mack. In spite of all that has happened, in spite of her resistance, they like each other. He is great with her. You have a chance. All of you have a chance."

I want to believe her.

"You need to do this. How is Rachel ever going to learn to fight and work for her own happiness if you don't teach her? You've made a career of putting yourself last and everyone first. Today that stops. Give up the martyrdom. The loves of your life are out on that beach waiting. They have something to say to you, Skylar."

I turn from Lexie and take a few tentative steps to the beach, watching my daughter and Mack. A bright white volleyball floats back and forth through the air between them. I don't see tension or discomfort in their play. They stop rallying. Rachel walks towards Mack. He takes the ball from her and tosses it lightly into the air above him, and then jumps, flawlessly pounding the ball into the sand. The ball hits, sending up a spray of sand. In a flash, Rachel is off after it. She captures it and brushes off the sand before replicating Mack's movements. Her hand misses the ball and she falls to the sand, laughing at her mistake. Mack grins, reaches down and tugs her to her feet. Rachel accepts his hand, bouncing to her feet, brushing sand from her bottom. They dissect what she did wrong. Rachel throws the ball up. This time, her hand connects and the ball is pounded into the sand.

Back home, Rachel didn't even want to acknowledge him, and now she seems comfortable with Mack. How strong could their connection be? Doubt flares within me. Could it possibly withstand the difficulty of blending our three lives together? I want to hope but with no road map to guide us, I don't know how to make this work.

I take a few more steps forward to retrieve my daughter. Rachel spots me and glances at Mack nervously. He pats her back before nudging her forward. She takes a deep breath and lopes toward me. I look past her advancing figure. Mack hasn't moved. Our eyes meet for no more than a second and then he turns and begins walking down the beach in the direction of his place. My daughter reaches me, puffing from exertion, her cheeks flushed. Sweat beads across her forehead.

"Don't be mad at Aunt Lexie for calling Mack and don't be mad because we didn't tell you about it. I am glad we did it. This is yours." Rachel pauses to pull my diamond ring off her finger. She holds it out to me. "I want you to marry Mack."

"It's not that easy, Rachel! You can't just give this to me and think that fixes everything. Look, your Aunt Lexie laid a guilt trip on you. That wasn't right and it wasn't fair."

Rachel drops to the sand. She holds the ring up in the sunlight watching the facets sparkle back at her. "I am glad she yelled at me. It made me want to meet Mack, to talk to him. I don't want you to choose me over him. Like you said at home, I won and you were miserable."

I sit on the sand beside my daughter and throw an arm around her. "I'm better, Rachel. I'm okay now. You don't have to do this."

"Yes, I do."

"Rachel…this situation is very complicated and your feeling guilty is a temporary thing. It won't last and once it fades, then what? You'll be stuck with a new step dad and a whole new set of problems."

"Yes, and they will be our problems to work on, not just yours." She picks up a handful of sand and lets it trickle to the ground beside her before repeating the movement over and over. "I have to do my share to make things work. Things are better with Dad and Sherry because I am trying. When we rushed Sherry to the hospital, she held my hand and said she was glad I was there for her. I talked to dad last night. I have a new baby brother."

"Congratulations! That's good news." I squeeze her shoulders. "And I'm glad that things are better with your dad and Sherry but this isn't the same situation. Rachel, you don't know Mack. Hanging out on an island together won't be the same as living together as a family."

"I know. Maybe we won't get along, then again maybe we will. I am sure it won't be all good, but it won't be all bad either. He makes you happy so he can't be all bad. Plus he likes to play sports. It's kind of nice to have someone who knows how to play sports and likes it. Especially since you and Dad don't. We have things in common. And he doesn't mind having me around. He truly doesn't. I can tell when someone is faking it. He isn't."

She pauses for a breath and earnestly continues with her arguments. "That's what worried me. Some guy faking to like me just to be with you. He and I want to try and be a family. You are not the only one who should have a say in this decision. Please, Mom. We wrote you a letter, all three of us. He has it. Go read it. Let him tell you what he has to say. He has some great ideas on how to make this work for all of us." She takes the ring off her finger and slides it on to my finger. Then she stands and walks to the cottage where Lexie is waiting.

The ring shines up at me from my finger. Mack is waiting. Rachel is all that has stood between us and now she has removed herself. All I have to do is find the courage to move forward. Lexie was right; as much as I love him, so much of me is fearful. I am scared to believe, I am scared to trust.

What if…? My inner voice warns. I shove aside my fear. *Yes. What if?*

Mack's hands are in his pockets and the ocean wind is ruffling his hair. He does not turn when I approach; he stands still, staring out over the blue water.

"You have quite the daughter, Skylar. I understand why you were so fierce about protecting her. She is like you, wanting to love and be open but so scared and certain of hurt. Not only is she smart but she is incredibly perceptive. She sizes people up very fast. Initially, she terrified me. I think it was best for us to get to know each other without you. She knows me as someone other than the guy in love with her mother. We've spent almost every day together and we like each other." He turns around and smiles. "I won her over," he announces proudly.

"You think so?" I brush the tears from my eyes and give him a small smile in return. "And how did you accomplish that?"

"By being honest and offering her a few bargains."

"You mean you bribed her?"

"I allayed her fears. I promised her there would be few changes."

"You two are dreaming. There will be changes..."

He interrupts me. "The changes Rachel was most worried about were being moved away from her friends, and her dad, the baby, and even Sherry. I told her we all might travel a bit, but home would be Edmonton. I promised we would buy a house in an area where she would not have to switch schools. I told her you would be able to quit your job and paint the days away in between having, God willing, a few more children.

"She doesn't want me taking you away from her. Once she realized I don't want to harm your relationship with her, she opened up about her fears. Mostly to Lexie but she did share some with me. Every question and fear she had, Lexie and I have tried to come up with solutions for. It went well and we both agreed I should ask you again if you will marry me. But before I do that, I want you to know that ring comes with strings attached. Before you answer, you should know what they are."

He pulls a folded up piece of paper from his back pocket. He smooths and hands it to me.

"Rachel typed this up," he explains.

> *"We, Lachlan Mackenzie, Skylar Shay, Rachel Shay and Aunt Lexie all agree that we want to be a family but before we can be a family, Mom and Mack need time to date and have a normal relationship so they will have a long engagement. Mack will not live with us until he and Mom are married.*
>
> *We don't know all the problems that may come up so in order for this to work we have to have help. We agree that Mom, Mack, and Rachel need to attend premarital family counseling before the marriage. If we have any problems, we agree to continue counseling after this period.*
>
> *Mack promises to not try to take over as a parent for Rachel. Mack understands that Rachel already has two parents and they are responsible for Rachel's rules and discipline. Mack's role is to be a source of support and help for Rachel.*

Rachel will always have a home with Mom and Mack wherever they live and in return Rachel agrees to treat both Mom and Mack with respect.

Mom needs to learn when to get involved and when to let Mack and Rachel work out issues on their own. She needs to take care of herself, and to stop thinking every problem is her responsibility to fix.

Lexie promises to spend more time with her family, to not meddle any more than necessary and to throw Skylar the best stagette bridal party ever! (Whatever that is)

We all promise to respect each other's relationships, and to work hard every day to get along. A family has to be committed to work. We all agree we are committed.

There are four lines for us each to sign on. Mack and Rachel have already filled in their signatures. Lexie's signature is also included.

"So what do you think?"

"I can't believe the three of you came up with this?"

"Skylar, love, that sounds a bit like an insult."

"No, I don't mean it like that at all. But premarital counseling? I am surprised."

"Lexie said doctors and counselors often won't ask for, or accept help, because they know it all. I think this is important if we are going to have a chance. Rachel needs someone on her side to support her if there are issues."

"What about the long engagement? And not living together before getting married?"

"Call me old fashioned, it was my idea. We have an example to set for Rachel. I can't go back to being boyfriend and girlfriend, but I don't think we are ready to get married today and all move in together. There has been nothing normal about our relationship, Skylar. We need time to adjust. Hell, I need time to get my head around being a step dad. But I want it. I want you. I want her."

Mack drops to one knee. He pulls a pen from his shirt pocket.

"I promise, Skylar, to love and honor both you and your daughter. I promise with my whole heart to go into this relationship with a willing heart. Quitting will never be an option. All I ask is you go into this with the same level of commitment. You have to trust that you are enough for me and you have to trust me when I say you are enough. You are all I want, all I need."

"I love you, Mack."

"But..."

"There is no but. Only fear. I failed once and I am so sure I can fail again. But being a coward has never got me anywhere. It's taking a risk that brought you to me. Give me that pen!" The last letter in my name is barely finished before he stands and I leap into his arms.

I kiss Mack's beautiful mouth. Beneath the sun, on the sand, with the ocean just feet away, I kiss the man I love with all the love I have, with every corner of my heart. I kiss him until we are both breathless and until Lexie and Rachel bowl us over into the sand.

Happiness exists. I have found it. I will never let it go.

* * *

I fell in love on this beach. It is a fantasy location, as beautiful and perfect as a daydream. The love I found here isn't a fantasy and it's not the perfect living happily-ever-after kind of love. It is better. I found real love, the kind which will exhaust all the counseling sessions we've agreed to and maybe a few more. It is the kind of love grown by work, tears, and compromise. It is a love that will make mistakes, and a love that will make apologies. It is a love that will last.

The End

Acknowledgements

It took an embarrassing number of years to get this book finished and published. Learning to write, pregnancy, childrearing, house building and just life in general, made this a very long process. The length of the process means that I now have so many people to thank.

The first and most important person I need to thank is my husband. Without your support, editing, hard work, encouragement, and belief in me I do not see how this could have been possible. My writerly tendencies would and could wax poetic for pages about you and all you have done but just let me say I love you, I appreciate you, and I cannot thank you enough for allowing me to try for my dreams. There is no better husband on this earth.

The second most important person I need to thank is Suzanne. Your friendship is a gift, but having a friend like you to accompany me on this journey, has been the greatest blessing. Thank you for holding my hand, putting up with the whining, insecurity, and writer's angst that has plagued me so often during this act of creation. I wish you as much success and inspiration as you can handle on your creative journey. Thank you so much, my friend, for all that you have done and will do. I could not have done this without you.

To my girls, Sara and Lyric, thank you so much for your love support and understanding. My writing sometimes took away from me being the best mom in the world, but I hope that chasing my dream will help you both feel confident to chase your own.

Mom, Dad, and Paulette thank you all so very much for not only your support but the hours of free babysitting you provided so I could write.

Through this process I have had many friends read, edit, support and encourage me. To my early supporters who read for me, or babysat so I could write, thank you all so very much Olga, Aunty Terry, Joleen, Anne, Geraldine, Doris, Miranda, Tamara, Marcy, Heather, Monique, Nicole, Deana, Keith, Gisele, Maggie, and a few more that I will be horrifyingly embarrassed to remember later.

I also would like to thank all the members of the Lakeland Writers Group for their friendship, encouragement, and support.

I would also like to thank Marlene @ First Editing.com. You polished my manuscript beautifully and your kind comments gave me the courage to take the next step.

And last but not least I would like to thank Tanya, my friend with the great photography skills. It's not everyone who has a photographer friend coincidently going to the Bahamas when shots for a book trailer are required. In addition to being a great friend, and an excellent photographer, you also have wonderful timing.